FAKING IT

Nigel Planer is one of Britain's best known comedians. His role as Neil in *The Young Ones* made him a household name. Since then he has appeared on *Saturday Night Live*, *French and Saunders*, *The Lenny Henry Show* etc. as well as writing and starring in *The Nicholas Craig Masterclass*. His book about fatherhood, *A Good Enough Dad*, sold nearly 20,000 hardback copies in the trade, and his first novel, *The Right Man*, was published in October 1998.

'Excellent, a sort of cross between Nick Hornby and Kingsley Amis if you can imagine such a thing . . . Nick Hornby and Tony Parsons cover similar ground but not, I think as deeply and honestly as Planer . . . For all its playfulness and comedy, *Faking It* deals with serious moral issues . . . Deserves to be a bestseller'
Lynn Barber, *Observer Magazine*

'The book's prevailing themes of people's hidden sides and the powerful attraction of opposites. Stereotypes are gleefully subverted . . . An intelligent comedy of contemporary manners'
Wendy Holden, *Daily Mail*

'Barry is a magnificent comic creation . . . Planer combines the novel's sustained humour with often tender insights into the confusion of men's emotions, but the comedy has the upper hand; Barry's night at the men's group is a perfectly paced comic scene balancing slapstick and wit'
Stephanie Merrit, *Observer*

Also by Nigel Planer

The Right Man
A Good Enough Dad
I, An Actor (with Christopher Douglas)

Faking It

Nigel Planer

ARROW

Published by Arrow Books in 2003

3 5 7 9 10 8 6 4 2

Copyright © Nigel Planer 2001

The right of Nigel Planer to be identified as the author of this work
has been asserted by him in accordance with the Copyright,
Designs and Patents Act, 1988

First published in 2001 by Hutchinson

Arrow Books
The Random House Group Limited
20 Vauxhall Bridge Road, London SW1V 2SA

Random House Australia (Pty) Limited
20 Alfred Street, Milsons Point, Sydney
New South Wales 2061, Australia

Random House New Zealand Limited
18 Poland Road, Glenfield
Auckland 10, New Zealand

Random House (Pty) Limited
Endulini, 5a Jubilee Road
Parktown 2193, South Africa

The Random House Group Limited Reg. No. 954009

www.randomhouse.co.uk

A CIP catalogue record for this book is available from the British Library

Papers used by Random House are natural, recyclable products made from wood
grown in sustainable forests. The manufacturing processes conform to the
environmental regulations of the country of origin.

Typeset by SX Composing DTP, Rayleigh, Essex
Printed and bound in Great Britain by
Bookmarque Ltd, Croydon, Surrey

ISBN 0 09 940986 0

ONE

'With a coarse pepper grinder? Inside her?'

'Not actually when the body was found, no, sir. She had
. . . inserted it below – if you'll pardon my frankness – and it
must have sort of popped out when she choked.'

'You mean it was twisted? Turned inside her, like someone
was grinding her ovaries? Oh my God!'

'No, sir, not exactly. It was the other end of the pepper
grinder which had been inserted prior to the demise. The
smooth end. The bulbous end, if you'll pardon me.'

'You mean she was using the knob end of a pepper shaker as
a dildo?'

'Not to put too fine a point on it, sir.'

'And that killed her?'

'Well, no, the evidence suggests there had been a significant
amount of substance abuse – cocaine, amphetamines – and she
appears also to have been suffering from acute alcohol poisoning.
The Ecstasy probably finished her off. We're waiting for the
blood and vomit test results to come through on the e-mail now,
but I'm afraid our computers have all gone on the blink. I must
advise you that we do now have a counselling link-up service
should you wish to make use of it. Or you can always ring us

if you feel you need help. Here's my card. My name's Chris, by the way, just ask for me or extension 7591. We also have a free "Coping with Loss in the Family" pack with useful phone numbers, advice and stickers to help you come to terms with it all. And I can only say again how sorry I am to have to be the bringer of this awful news; there can be very few things more difficult and upsetting than the death of a husband or wife.'

'She's not my wife. I mean, we didn't actually . . . she didn't want . . . I'm so sorry, I haven't offered you a cup of tea or anything . . .'

'That's quite all right sir, I had one before I came out. Maybe you need a couple of minutes to let it all sink in.'

'What was she doing in New York anyway? She was supposed to be in Chicago, at an opening.'

'Foul play is not suspected, sir, and has evidently been ruled out by the New York department.'

'It was in her hotel room? No one else . . . involved?'

'I believe not, sir. If and when you feel ready — and do take your time — we could make an appointment for you to go along and identify the body and sign the papers so we can pass it on to the undertaker of your choice. It's a terrible thought, I know, but we find most people feel better for doing it, sort of more complete. On the other hand, if you decide that is something which is definitely not for you, then perhaps you could suggest another relative — a sister, perhaps, or . . .'

'There's only her son, and he's at college in Manchester.'

'And how old is he?'

'Oh, er, twenty, nearly. And her ex-husband, of course, but he probably wouldn't even recognise her anyway. How long do I have?'

'In you own time, no rush. Sometime in the next couple of days?'

'Thank you, er, Chris.'

'Would you like me to put my arm around you, sir? You look in need of some support.'

'No. Thank you. I know you're only doing your job, but I'm not sure if it would make any difference. Sorry.'

There is a certain angle of sticking-out bottom, a slight arch in the female lower spine, which is not natural, nor particularly comfortable, but which is definitely one for the boys, or at any rate, one that will ensnare most men's lustful attention. It is not the tucked-under muscularity of the dancer, nor is it voluptuous, Rubenesque or thrusting. It is petite, tippy-toed, quaint and, coupled with a slight stiffening of the neck and shoulders, implies vulnerability and raunch at the same time. It can be seen on countless billboards advertising downmarket news-papers, is just enough of a stretch to lift a short skirt over the foothills of the buttocks, and the woman in Oliver's consulting room was doing it right now as she climbed on to the massage table. He was sure she was.

Did she realise that she was burning an image – another bloody image – on to the innocent blank page of his retina? Well, actually the same image as the usual one, really, the one that was projected on to the back wall of his mind roughly every seven seconds: waistline, panties, thighs, waistline, panties, thighs. Was she putting it on, this strange duck-like posture, or did she actually walk around like that? He'd soon find out.

Oliver preferred powder to oil and got his free from Hardicot Lewis. He'd been part of a market test scheme in 1998, and their 'MediLube 3' had come out way on top for low friction, smell and convenience of usage – especially in the Hardicot Lewis plastic plunger bottles. Sure, some osteopaths preferred aromatic oils, but not Oliver. If you wanted to drift off into an ethereal trance, then go to an aromatherapist. That's not to say he didn't believe in having the patient relaxed, but not so relaxed that you couldn't get a 'movement'. There had to be some resistance, however small, for a successful osteopathic 'stroke' to be properly beneficial, and the cracking noise made people understand what they were spending their money on. Not that Oliver was cynical about his chosen métier; in fact he was a co-founder of the holistic centre as far back as 1991, when you couldn't even get a so-called 'straight' doctor to return your phone calls. How times had changed. It was more that he believed osteopathy, acupuncture and certain aspects of nutrition – his three areas of expertise – should be accepted as part of mainstream medicine and not sidelined as 'alternative' along with reflexology, homoeopathy, rolfing, reiki, herbalism, black box and the Feldenkraus Heller technique. Even a state-registered physiotherapist was treated with more respect and had more universally recognised letters after her name – sorry, his or her name – than Oliver, who treated the whole person with better results than a mere physio, not to mention the fact that his training was longer. If you took cranio-sacral work into account, three years longer. Not long ago, a GP could be struck off for referring a patient to an osteopath. Now, with back pain clogging up the practices, it was common. Physiotherapy was, in Oliver's opinion, an ineffective, machine-orientated form of rehab. But the whole comparison was stupid really, because he got at least half of his patients from GP referrals nowadays, and anyway it was only letters after your name, wasn't it? It wasn't as if he came from a medical family and would ever be on the receiving end of any kind of paternalistic dis-approval. No approval *or* disapproval there. Nothing, in fact. And even if his partner had been the type to be impressed by qualifications, she was dead now, so it didn't matter.

The softly pornographic images in his mind were momentarily supplanted by the memory of his dead co-habitee, Andrea, laid out on the etherised slab at the police mortuary three days earlier. Her skin a waxy primrose, the dull gun-metal blue of her glazed eyes seeming to peek out from the three-quarters-closed lids. He snapped shut the door on this recent memory and returned his focus to the living woman reclining on the osteopathic table in his surgery.

'Let's see if we can straighten out this roving neck, shall we?' he said, running his spindly fingers delicately along T_2, T_3 and T_4. Her hair was dark and dank, her skin just a couple of degrees too warm. 'Oooh, my.' He came across a sizeable muscle knot at T_5 with both left and right facet joints jammed. That would account for the stiffness in her shoulders earlier, but not for the saucy bunny-hop on to his padded bench. There she lay in front of him, beneath him. Trusting yet slightly nervy – excited even – in her black thigh-rise knickers, which had a tantalising lace panel about three inches square just below her navel. Many men would pay money to be where Oliver was now, to see what he was seeing. But then they didn't have to look at all his other patients; restaurateurs in baggy boxer shorts, hump-backed secretaries with psoriasis, actors with their endless whining monologues about themselves, the old with incipient osteoporosis. No, this was one of the perks of the job. Very perky. Although Oliver would never use that word or words like it in public, or even in a small room, and was an expert at keeping such thoughts locked in a very far-away dungeon to which even he had to have permission – from himself – to use the key.

'Yow, yes, that hurts when you do that. Is it meant to?' She had been talking all along and Oliver had been responding, asking the occasional question to keep the atmosphere friendly, yet maintaining a certain formality. Although this one didn't need much to make her feel at ease as many patients did; she seemed happy to chat away, looking at the ceiling while he dug his fingers into her trapesii. So far he had heard how much her house had cost, by how much it had increased in value in the two years since she and her husband had bought it, that she took occasional work as an extra on film sets and once had a part with a spoken line in an episode of *Inspector Morse*, that they had no children as yet, intending to wait a few years until Peter – who worked as a broker for some company Oliver pretended to have heard of – became a partner, that he worked long hours to try and achieve this goal and that she had once met John Thaw in a bookshop and he'd asked her advice on Thai cooking, about which she knew absolutely nothing. Oliver let her nattering and minor indiscretions wash over him, making a casual mental note of one or two details to put in the box file later, in case she returned for a second visit. Even hairdressers do this. It's a simple one. Under B: Baldry, Sally. Children's names: none. Husband: Peter. Stresses: large mortgage in Clapham, new Almilmo kitchen, late delivery of. Likes: *Inspector Morse*, white-haired older men off the telly. On her subsequent visit he would be able to greet her with, 'So how's your dream kitchen coming along then?' This attention to personal detail would make the patient feel remembered, respected and hence relaxed – at home with you, good about herself, ready even to make you feel good about yourself. The best conditions in which to work. Elementary stuff.

Oliver gave good caring and was blessed with a thirteen-year-old's fresh good looks. Neither man enough to be handsome, nor sultry enough to be sexy. A face from a teen boy-band atop a thirty-five-year-old's lanky six-foot-four frame. The glasses helped as well, of course; reassuring frames from Dollond and Aitchison. People seemed happy to entrust him with the secrets in their lives.

'Let's have you on your right side then.' Might as well check out L4 and L5, lumbar jams often being the cause of difficulties higher up in the cervical spine. Important to establish whether Mrs Peter Baldry had an ascending or a descending problem. She rolled obediently on to her right side, taking care with the painful section of her neck and shoulders and talking all the while. He adjusted the green-vinyl-covered wedge cushion under her head.

'And if we could have your upper knee to chest and give me your lower arm . . . here.' By leaning over her and clasping her right forearm under his armpit, he was able to rotate her spine, opening all the facet joints enough to get his fingertips in and feel for any locked sections or trapped nerves. Standing with his back now to her upper body, this also afforded him an unspoilt view of the escarpment of her left buttock and thigh, a perfect rounded rise and gentler falling-away to her knee. She was not particularly long-legged, and the knees and ankles were quite thick and sturdy. A few small flecks of cellulite around the upper and outer thigh, nothing to worry about unduly, although no doubt she did.

And then, leaning further forward, Oliver noticed something he was not expecting, something he'd not seen before on a patient, something which he had not covered since Anatomy 2 at the osteopathic school in Baker Street. Across her left buttock was a peppering of red around a central stripe of purple edged with yellow. At the centre of this stripe, the tough skin of her seat had been broken in a few places and must have bled, although now it was lightly scabbed. The whole thing looked rather like a bad make-up job from a TV hospital soap. Oliver needed a second or two in which to register what he was looking at, and in that time she noticed the change in his touch.

'Oh that!' she said, and giggled. 'You've noticed my medals.'

Oliver blinked and was lost for words, caring ones or otherwise. He continued to investigate her lumbar vertebrae.

'Went a bit far, that one!' she continued, easily taking on this new subject matter like a train going over well-oiled points. 'I suppose I should have waited a bit for that to clear up before coming to see you, but my neck was giving me such agony. How embarrassing.' She giggled again, sounding extremely unembarrassed. 'Though not half as bad as if my husband ever saw it! I'd have a job explaining this one, wouldn't I? Still, it'll be gone in a few days and then he'll be able to get his oats again. I might even let him do it with the lights on. I've been telling him I've got a headache for a week now so he wouldn't get to see me in the nude.' Hearing herself say this, she burst into an unashamed loud cackle. She had a dirty laugh, Mrs Peter Baldry, thought Oliver.

'I just realised,' she said, 'I've been telling him I've got a headache all week, but I really have got a headache this time so I needn't have lied. That's why I came to see you, isn't it?'

Oliver wanted to say something, but his mouth had gone suddenly dry. He cleared his throat instead, making what he hoped was the kind of noise that told her he was easy going and non-disapproving, that she should feel free and relaxed enough to say whatever she might want. She needed no encouragement, however, and continued her light-hearted confession without pausing for breath or reflection. People are always keen to confide, reflected Oliver. It was one of the reasons he'd adopted this career path. Being the trusted custodian of the stories of others salved his sense of worthlessness, fulfilled a need in him. He knew that and had worked it through.

'I do it for a bit of extra money, which is nice, you

know. Always comes in handy, doesn't it? Can't wait around all my life for my husband to make his million and retire.' She gave a big laugh here, out of proportion to her commentary. 'But mostly I do it for the excitement. It's something a bit naughty, like living a bit close to the edge?'

Her buttock rested beneath Oliver on the slab, with the red bruising covering it like fine wet sand on a melon. He considered how it would feel to cup his palm over it, even to stroke it lightly. He cleared his throat again and asked her casually how she'd got it. He was finding this session difficult.

'I'm still only twenty-seven, you know, and Peter's always working up in town, and it can get a bit boring really. I've got to have something, you know, for me.' She had a friend who had asked her if she wanted to be spanked for cash, she'd said yes and found she enjoyed it, was exhilarated by it even. She'd built up a small client list.

'You get to meet all sorts of nice people – really interesting people – and they give you lunch too. I think it's good if you can have something a bit different in your life. Some of my "one-on-one" clients are, you know, top lawyers, doctors, important people. All ever so nice.'

Apart from her 'one-on-ones', she was a regular at 'The Paddle Club' on a Tuesday evening, where an evidently mixed age group of men gathered to role-play spanking two or three girls, who would be dressed, Mrs Baldry explained, as either nurses, schoolgirls or secretaries. Oliver found the clichés excruciating.

Oliver considered himself a feminist, although he understood that, being a man, he would never be entitled to call himself such. Although living with Andrea, who was seventeen years older than him, had, he felt, gone some way towards improving his credentials. He knew he would forever be condemned as an also-ran in the gender debate, by the very nature of his gender. He accepted that agreeing with the basic tenets of the Women's Movement – two thousand years of oppression, backlash conspiracy, men have to evolve, etc. – did not necessarily qualify him to have a voice. For instance, here he was, treating Mrs *Peter* Baldry, whose real name was Sally, for a stiff neck and a headache, and it turned out that she was being hideously exploited, beaten and abused, yet all he could think of asking her was whether she actually had sex with her clients or whether her activities were entirely restricted to the puerile spanking games she had described. Typical man. Sometimes his own prurience was a mantle of shame.

'Oh no, I don't do that,' she said, then added, 'Not yet. There hasn't been anyone I fancied.' She laughed again. 'And I've never done any videos or anything like that in case anyone found out. But I'd quite like to.'

Oliver tried to force away the images from the seedy screen of his imagination, to flush them out, and asked her, in a concerned tone of voice, if she wasn't ever afraid for her safety, if she had ever found herself in danger in any way. He feared the answer might be yes, and that he would yearn for details.

'There was one guy who was a bit domineering once, got a bit carried away in the scenario. And then afterwards it was "would you like a cup of tea dear?" He was about seventy-seven, though. I was very nervous the first time. But everyone I've met so far has been really kind.'

Oliver felt protective and almost paternal towards her. Obviously she could not see how she was being used by these men. She seemed, however, quite happy in her ignorance, and it would have been patronising of him, he felt, to push her on this.

'I'm not exactly what you'd call a submissive,' she continued, as if answering his unposed question, 'but I am definitely a bit that way inclined. I've always fantasised about being restrained and spanked, and if it's done properly, where's the harm?'

Where's the harm? His thoughts on gender had not spent years germinating, they had arrived suddenly one day, fully formed. It was like the road to Damascus, except it had happened on Kilburn High Street when he was a student. At 3.05 p.m. on 13 June 1988, Oliver had realised that his girlfriend of the time, Jude, had been right all along; in fact all the girlfriends he'd ever had. His life up until that point had been an infantile sack race to try and gratify what he had thought were his male needs, to notch up as many sleeping partners as possible, which in Oliver's case at that time was four or five, if you counted Helen Parsons. But suddenly these behaviours had seemed like mere insecurity and childishness. On that day, with a sudden and blistering certainty, Oliver knew the answer. What's wrong with the world is men. It's as simple as that. They can't express their feelings, they deny their feelings, they don't have any feelings, they leave the toilet seat up.

Every single thing that's wrong is down to men. War and famine and pollution, it's all men. They're the ones who build the rockets, who jangle change in their pockets. Their brains are strawberry shaped – and roughly that size too – and sit on the end of their penises, which probably explains why they don't even know how many t's there are in the word 'commitment'. And Oliver had certainly been no exception. He'd been unreliable, unfaithful, had had a one-night stand with whatever her name was. Well, two one-night stands if you counted hand relief. And many secret, intimate conversations with women friends while he was supposed to be with Jude or whichever girlfriend he was seeing at the time. Funny, but for some reason, intimate friendships with other women seemed to wind up girlfriends more than a genuine confessed drunken snog.

But that afternoon on Kilburn High Street, every-thing had changed. What had actually triggered this moment of blinding revelation was not Jude, but Tricia, another osteopathic student, who had, she claimed, been thrown out of her digs for refusing to have sex with her landlord. She was homeless, crying into her cup of tea and confiding in her trusted friend Oliver, the gentle giant. He caught himself calculating, in her moment of need, exactly how much sympathy would be required to maybe get his hands under her blouse and down the front of her knickers. He was just imagining what kind of knickers she might have on – those high-thighed white cotton ones, he hoped – when he thought, What am I doing? And then he thought, What have I been doing for the last eight years? What's it doing to me? To my psyche? To my bruised inner child, standing there with his winky permanently on stand-by?

From that day, Oliver resolved to change completely. He determined to transform himself, and to help others by transforming them as well. Not being the sort of man to hang about when an error had been uncovered and a new idea hatched, he had joined various men's groups in Camden, eventually starting his own group from home. They would discuss issues such as phallocentricity in the media, and the role of masculinity in physical medicine, and they met, ironically enough, on Tuesdays, just as Mrs Baldry's Paddle Club would be teeing off.

Of course, his relationship with Jude hadn't lasted long after that day – she found his new zeal rather too ostentatious and something of an embarrassment among her friends – so he'd been on his own all through qualifying until he met Andrea and moved in with her, here in Rylance Avenue, Clapham Common North Side.

It had been so much easier when Andrea was alive. Fantasies could remain fantasies; illicit, guilt-inducing and hence exciting. Andrea had been his superego, his conscience, his better side. She was real and did not approve. He could load all things forbidden on to her. Because of her he couldn't or shouldn't look at girlie mags. Because of her he didn't flirt, because of her he was trying to evolve from the Neanderthal and become a real man. Now he was joltingly free of all that and would have to be his own guardian angel. Now he didn't even know what newspaper he should read. Should it continue to be the *Guardian*, or could he now buy tabloid rubbish with impunity and ogle at the depravities of the awful world out there? How dare Andrea leave him to his own devices like this? He hated her for dying. He hated himself for thinking that way.

As Sally Baldry dressed, Oliver scrumpled and binned the hygiene paper and rolled out a new sheet over the bench, punching a hole through the top end for his next client's face to rest on. He always took care to have his back to his patients while they dressed or undressed. People were somehow more nervous in the act of taking clothes off or putting them back on than in the standing or sitting naked for examination or treatment. Once it's out it's out, I suppose, thought Oliver. The excitement is in the unknown or the forbidden, which explains the success of striptease and lap-dancing – the fuss is over shortly after the organs are actually exposed. Once the allure part is finished the clinical part begins. Oliver considered all of this, which did not mean he was actually visualising a stripteasing, lap-dancing Mrs Baldry as he washed his hands carefully in the medi-basin. Heavens no. Those kind of thoughts and projections were concealed well within the starch of his short-sleeved white HL topcoat and could be stored for use later.

'It may be a bit sore for twenty-four hours or so . . .' he said, immediatley aware of the possible double meaning.

'What are you talking about? I won't be able to sit down for at least a week,' said Mrs Baldry with a broad grin.

Oliver coughed. 'But after that the headache should go away. Make another appointment for about ten days' time?' Oliver was not above a little commerciality, his waiting list was not yet very long. 'Just to make sure.'

'Oh, you mean my neck!' She guffawed theatrically, milking her own joke. 'I thought you meant . . .' And she touched the top of his hand as she indicated her behind with her eyes. Her fingertips were giving off warmth; had he got the central heating too high?

Outside in the avenue it looked cold and was darkening early. Drizzle spattered against the double-glazing. A wet Border collie was chasing a ball-on-a-string on the common. Mrs Baldry was swinging her coat on, a tailored maroon tweed. The reflected light from its collar was making her cheeks glow pink, either that or her circulation was extremely overcranked. She had no right to be so hot when she'd been the one with her clothes off. Maybe the treatment had stimulated the blood flow more than was normal. Oliver felt cold, dry and inadequate alongside her. He pushed his spectacles back up his nose – something he had to do often since his height made him stoop – and escorted her towards the door.

'I tell you what,' she said. 'I'll give you my mobile number in case . . . you know . . . you ever feel like . . .' She fluttered her lashes at him momentarily before looking down to rummage in her bag for paper and a pen. Oliver stood frozen. To decline the number would be impolite, to tell her that he would never, ever feel like . . . whatever she was suggesting might hurt her feelings. And anyway it would be a lie. He had not spent all these years working on himself and his masculinity to allow himself a lie.

He imagined himself having total control over Mrs Baldry. Ordering her to bend over the osteopathic table. He imagined her soft compliance, her dedicated desire to please him. And then the memory of Andrea returned; the imperious sneer that death had painted on her face. He struggled with the mental image of Andrea in the hotel room in New York with a pepper grinder.

'Oh my God! You look like a ghost standing there. Like Frankenstein or something. You all right, lofty?' As she was writing the number, Mrs Baldry shook a strand of dark hair from her face, and continued.

'It's not just the men who enjoy it, you know. I find it quite bracing, actually. A lot of women feel a bit guilty about enjoying sex, especially if their feller is, how should I put it, a little indecisive? Maybe a bit too generous and understanding? And at the end of the day, when it comes to the bedroom all these women want to do is relieve themselves of any responsibilities and decision-making and just place themselves in the hands of a strong, dominant male.' She tore a page out of her Filofax and handed it to him. He took it and, swallowing, thanked her like a child. Then she dipped out of the room, clicking the door shut quite abruptly so that the extra plastic hangers on the hook clanked against it.

Oliver stood for a moment, holding the torn-off slip of orange Filofax paper. He imagined recounting these events to his male colleagues in the Tuesday group, and posited what their responses might be. Claude, their newest and youngest recruit, could be relied on to have a standard, laddish 'way-hey'-type reaction, but would probably nevertheless advise binning the number on the grounds that he would object to paying for sexual activity of any kind. John and Keith, both heavily involved in child-custody nightmares, would advise throwing the paper away on the grounds that this would leave more group time to discuss their own problems, and George, the only genuine psychotherapist among them, likewise but for more sanguine ideological reasons. Michael would agree with whatever George said, and Mark would still be away skiing. A unanimous consensus then – Oliver considered – to dispose of Mrs Baldry's mobile number. He felt his heart rate rise minutely and the tips of his ears went pink. Oliver had always had low blood pressure, and since he ran for at least four hours a week, his heart would normally beat at a slower pace than most, just as his long legs took one stride to other people's three. As he buzzed in his next patient he slipped the paper into the back pocket of his trousers, where it generated heat for the rest of the day.

For Oliver, walking home from work consisted of six paces across the hall into the open-plan kitchen, which was situated at the back of the house and overlooked the expansive garden, now sombre in a sort of pre-Christmas sepia. The rain had stopped, leaving the bare trees still and stagnant. No birds, no movement of any sort, even the earthworms must be comatose. It was only two thirty, but the absence of light out there hung off the wet branches like sleeping bats. There was none

filtering through the French windows of the conser-
vatory extension, so he turned on the fluorescents. Out
there across the lawn was the space he had set aside in
his mind for an all-timber 'homelodge' treatment cabin,
to be built with argon gas heat-retaining glass, vaulted
ceilings and maybe even a steam room/sauna. The
breakfast counter was still covered with the colour
brochures and price lists, now out of date. With Andrea
gone, this dream would obviously have to wait. He
pinned a note on the cork board reminding him to ring
a solicitor to ask about death duties. He had read of
people who had to sell the family home to pay death tax,
which would be a shame, he thought, when he was just
beginning to build up a client list here. He paused to
castigate himself for having such selfish thoughts.
Andrea was dead, for Christ's sake! That should be the
most upsetting thing, not tax, or losing your all-timber
homelodge cabin. He put on the Gel kettle for a ginseng
brew and stood gazing out of the window with his knees
against the radiator. Where did the squirrels sleep? In the
summer they darted all over this garden, burying food
for the winter. Sniffing around in their grey coats like
little insurance salesmen. But now there was no sign of
them. He envied them the hibernation thing. When it
all got too much, they could just curl into a ball and
disappear for a few months until it was happy hour
again.

He ought to feel sad about losing Andrea. He was sad,

but he couldn't connect that sadness with Andrea, with the feeling of her being gone. His mind was just a sink full of trivial detail: the homelodge, the solicitor, whether he would be able to keep the house, the squirrels or lack of them, Mrs Baldry's roughened buttocks. He scanned the branches of the sycamore from top to bottom to see if he could make out a sleeping squirrel, but there was none. I wonder if this is normal, he thought – in a bereavement – to feel nothing. He just felt cold. Except for his knees, which were scalding against the radiator. He made his herbal tea and sat on one of the Conran stools. Much too expensive these, he remembered saying when he and Andrea had bought them. That was early on, when they were still fucking on a regular basis and would not only bother to consult each other over things like the buying of stools for the kitchen, but Andrea actually put the time aside to come with him to the shop and have an opinion on the matter, rather than just signing a cheque in the evening. He couldn't remember which one of them had first lost sexual interest in the other, nor could he decide whether their difference in age had played a part in it. Most likely his fault. Most things were.

Oliver wondered whether this lack of passion in his mourning of Andrea was due to a lack of proper passion for her while she was still alive. A shiver rippled across his back; Andrea, no doubt, come from the grave to reprimand him for not being more openly emotional, not wailing like those Turkish women they'd seen on the TV after the earthquake. As a female ghost, she would have every right, of course, to haunt him. It was his inadequacy that had let their relationship freeze over, his denial of his own feminine side, his inability to enter into the intimacy required to make a partnership. It was no wonder she had had to seek solace elsewhere – in the arms of her artists, particularly the ethnic ones, who were, let's face it, more centred, more in touch with their spirit than Oliver could ever hope to be.

And then, to make his self-chastisement complete, the little orange slip of Filofax paper in his back pocket started to trouble him. Why hadn't he just thrown it away? He had no intention of ever ringing Mrs Baldry. He'd be struck off for a start if it ever came out. She was a patient, after all. But maybe she knew someone else of similar jocularity and warmth whom he could ring without breaking his healer's code of conduct? Someone from whom he could get sexual fulfilment with absolutely no involvement. Someone to whom he could give orders which would be obeyed. Nothing, no feelings, no relationship, just action. Uncomplicated. That part of his life dealt with, leaving him free to concentrate on mourning or work or the solicitor or selling the house or counting squirrels. Anything he chose. Anything was possible now Andrea was dead. That was the problem.

And what of Felix? How would he be reacting to his

mother's sudden and distasteful death? He had sounded typically unaffected on the phone, but even so, Oliver had decided to spare him the more unpleasant details. He had given Felix the train times from Manchester, but Felix had declined his offer to be picked up from the station. Oliver tried to imagine Felix wailing like the Turkish women. Worse, he thought, would be having to console Felix, having to put his arm around him, maybe even having to wail with him for a while. But the thought of Felix revealing anything of himself to Oliver was impossible to conceive. There had never been a discernible sign from Felix in all the time he had known him – which was getting on for eight years now – that Oliver was welcome in even the most mundane areas of the boy's psyche. Felix was a locked bottle of pills to Oliver, and he had given up trying to find the knack of opening the lid. He considered his future with Felix for a while and found it unimaginable. He was too young to be a father to him, too old to be a friend. With Andrea alive, increasingly it hadn't seemed to matter, since Felix would soon be qualified and presumably off their hands. It was most uncomfortable to have to contemplate the years ahead as including Felix but not Andrea. It felt almost unfair, but then perhaps he should try to see it as a karmic lesson, as George the therapist would no doubt encourage him to do. Shit, it was only Thursday and he'd have to wait for five days before he could talk to the guys in the Tuesday group about it all.

He felt an urgent need to see them. Maybe he could invite one or two of them to the funeral. No, they looked too weird, and it would break the last vestiges of the confidentiality which Oliver had been the keenest member of the group to maintain. It was a shame; he would really like someone to hold his hand over the next few days, especially when dealing with Felix.

He checked down the list of invitees to make sure that there was no one he had missed. Rebecca from the gallery, obviously, Andrea's best friend Janie, a few of her media chums, and then Barry, Andrea's ex-husband. Oliver shivered again in the certain knowledge that Andrea, wherever she was, would be vicious with rage at Barry's presence at her funeral. Over my dead body – he could hear her saying it, and for a moment he almost laughed. He knew she would be spitting, and he did consider excising the hated name, but Barry Fox, old BF, Bloody Fool, Bastard Fucker, Big Fart, whatever one chose to call him, was nevertheless the Biological Father, and somehow Oliver did not have the courage, nor the right, he felt, to exclude him.

TWO

The mornings were best for editing. You could wake up
– whenever that was, say eleven, eleven thirty – flop
straight over to the old WP, a gloriously outdated and
posture-ruining Toshiba laptop, print out whatever
drunken garbage you had spewed on to it the night
before while the kettle boiled for the first cup of instant,
then slump on the sofa with the sides of paper, the
caffeine and a Gauloise or three and try to work out
what the hell you'd been banging on about before
passing out. The intervening few hours of snoring in the
fart-sack afforded a kind of distance from yourself,
meant that you could see your work as if through
someone else's eyes. Indeed, some mornings there was
absolutely no recollection of what you'd written the
previous night. This made the morning editing session
challenging and hence pleasurable. Barry Fox had a low
boredom threshold and needed constant mental
stimulation.

After a morning's remarkably disciplined reorganising
of what had been sporadic thoughts into nuggets of wit
and virulent bile, he was usually ready for a spot of lunch

at Picasso's – outside if it was nice and look at the pretty girlies – otherwise sit right at the back with all the newspapers, including especially the fucking *Express*, of course, and scour the printed world for anything worth picking up on, for anyone worth picking on. Have a few more Gauloises, take a few notes, perhaps have a little bottle of house to bring some colour to the cheeks, maybe chat about the sixties with a couple of the fellow lunching dinosaurs, then slope back for a snooze before waking at five like a baby for its bottle.

Of course this routine held only for Mondays through to Thursdays. The bloody article thing had to be in, finished, faxed by four every stinking Thursday, although Barry knew that ten a.m. Friday would do, and was sometimes indeed preferable when the piece was contentious, say, and he wanted to give them less time to ask for changes, the gloating little fuckers. The pampered yuppified, superannuated CUNTS.

Fridays, Saturdays and Sundays were for what Barry liked to call 'other pursuits', but which would be more or less the same as the weekdays, hopefully with the addition of some female company. But between midday on a Monday and four p.m. on a Thursday, Barry Fox belonged to the newspaper, he was their man, much as he might rail against it and curse their cotton frocks. The POOFTERS.

It was Wednesday afternoon and still no one thousand words, nor even a rough theme – or 'thrust', as Barry liked to call it – which might suddenly crystallise on to the WP. He often wished for vinegar to brush across the invisible writing on the blank page of his mind. There, from behind the white-out of his subconscious, whole novels might slowly become visible, like a spy's secret messages. Essays which upheld a proposition with clarity and wit, until now sitting patiently behind the screen, would be exposed in spidery brown. A sequel to his one and only novel, *The Misandrists*, perhaps? But try as he did by daily dousing his brain with spirits, wine and beer, this magic writing never would appear, leaving him instead with that other property of vinegar, a pickle. Oh, he knew he'd come up with something for the bloody *Express*, he always did, but that didn't relieve him of the weekly anxiety, nor prevent the underarms, chest and back from sweating. There was a particular acrid aroma to a Wednesday-evening pre-dateline sweat.

He gulped down the last of the red and asked the lovely Teresa for the bill. He put his empty writer's notebook back in his jacket pocket, stretching the black elastic over its cover and slotting in the biro. Not to have an inkling even. Not even a dicky bird of an idea of an angle or a gag. Impatiently slamming a ten-pound note on the table for Teresa, he gathered up the newspapers – nothing in there at all today, dammit – and strode out on to the King's Road. Built like a barrel, Barry rarely felt the cold and went out in his jacket and shirt in all weathers, except for those occasions when he really couldn't be bothered and sauntered up the King's Road in dressing gown, pyjamas and trainers. This morning he had made a concession to the prevailing weather by wearing a scarf knotted and tucked behind his corduroy lapels. Oh God, it was going to be Christmas again. How awful. He could tell by the unusual amount of shoppers bagging the taxis. He'd covered the awfulness of Christmas too many times already, so no possibility of a piece there. And it was cold. Tucking his scarf down over his chest, he plodded eastwards towards Sloane Square in search of a taxi that would take him south.

There is a lot of hoo-ha about north of the river and south of the river in London. Jokes about people from Islington not being able to understand the road signs in Kennington, people from Tooting needing phrase books to order a drink in Hackney. The main premise being that, since the south is less well served by public transport and you have to cross a bridge to get to the centre of town, people in the north are somehow swankier, smarter, classier. Property prices are generally considered to be higher north of the river, though this is not necessarily the case, if you compare Acton, say, with Dulwich. The reality is that, like the line between right and wrong, between true and false, the Thames is very wiggly. Who would have thought, for instance, that you would be north of Knightsbridge in Waterloo, or south of Bermondsey in Fulham? That Barnes is on the same latitude as Battersea or that you would still be north of the river in Twickenham? How you see the world depends of course on where you are standing. Barry had pointed all this out in one of his early occasional pieces, and covered the north-south-of-the-river thing in countless articles, so that was out. However, if only people would understand that the line between good and bad is a wiggly one, the magnificent Andrea might still be alive now.

'Two people vow to stay, in love as one they say,' in the words of the Stevie Wonder lyric, mused Barry, as he wandered through the revolting happy couples with their large carrier bags, 'but all is fair in love.' He hummed the tune to himself, glossing over the next plaintive line: 'I should have never left your side.' Too painful, that one. He was passing York Barracks now: 'A writer takes his pen, to write the words again that all in love is fair.' Bloody songwriters have it easy, he thought. You write it once and it goes on and on earning you money. You don't have to think it up again each week only to have it devoured, chucked away and wrapped around the fish and bloody chips. And so long as it rhymes, people think it makes sense, and you've got the music to cover up any dodgy bits of writing, to wash people along with you. Beguiled again, a child again, I must get my bathroom retiled again thought Barry. Bloody songwriters.

Past the fashion shop with the large photos of young

girls in their pants in the window. Chelsea smelt, as usual, of perfume and chocolate mixed with diesel. American couples with designer bags emitted from every shop, the men wearing those long cape-shouldered loden coats in green. Any male but an American would feel like a patsy in such a garment, thought Barry, but somehow the Yanks think they look tough in them.

Engerland swings like a pendulum do. Bobbies on bicycles. . . are a thing of the past. Barry had never had this dateline problem before his separation from the magnificent Andrea. But since 1989, the annus acrimonious, the bloody woman kept hoovering up his thoughts and jumbling them around in a bin bag, mixing them in with FEELINGS. And he didn't even know if they were his feelings or hers. This malaise had not appeared immediately, but rather had crept up on him slowly, like cooking a Christmas turkey, and as the years mounted up, he had grown accustomed to suffering that little corner of panic in the tin can of his life, like Alan Bennett's famous last sardine. Bloody Alan, he was another TORMENTOR. Thousands of words a day, no doubt, the asexual little TWERP.

Since 1989 it had become increasingly effortful for Barry to remain shipshape, present and correct, even-keeled and twenty-twentied. And his liver had suffered a bit, of course; well, a lot, as a matter of fucked. He had had to develop a technique for stowing thoughts of

Andrea in the hold, where most days she stayed. But this bloody thing in New York, her dying and all that, had bloody got to him. He couldn't write a jot and it was her fault. He wished he were a songwriter or any bloody thing other than a columnist. Except an osteopath. At least he wasn't a frigging OSTEOPATH, for that he could be thankful.

Barry liked to refer to Oliver, when speaking to Andrea on the phone – which had not been often – as 'your homoeopath'. It suggested gay and psycho at the same time, whilst showing a delightful disdain for the man's profession, as if all the alternative therapists were cut from the same quilt, harbouring the same dodgy beliefs. There was no telling an osteopath from a herbalist; they were homogenous, generic and hence sad and unsexy. It also implied, Barry felt, that he was so uninterested in Oliver as to have forgotten what the man's job was. He was deluding himself with this last one, of course; calling your ex-wife's new and younger man names was a bit of a giveaway. Bloody little squirt with his homespun homilies. Nevertheless, the pinko masturbator had invited Barry to the funeral, and flowers would probably be appropriate. He stopped off at Tara's on the corner of Flood Street and Montpelier Walk.

Tara was paradoxical, a very pretty girl, yet with a lot of weather in her face. Also, her sound was different from her look; she combined the timbre and accent of a debutante with the clothes and physique of a con-

struction worker. Her readiness to chat meant th_
had many friends and acquaintances along the K_
Road. She worked the flower stall on Flood Street on
Tuesdays and Thursdays and the rest of the week she was
a conceptual artist. Conceiving art to be redundant in all
but its essence, she battled nevertheless with plastic and
steel and her own personal waste materials to produce
obsessive pieces of work which she would talk about
endlessly but show to no one until they were ready.
Until the people were ready, that is, not the works.

Barry was a bit in love with her, especially on a
Thursday at five after delivering his piece to the
newspaper. Sometimes he would buy a bouquet from
her because, despite her aggressive appearance – army
boots, overalls and spiked turquoise hair – she could
arrange flowers with more skill and aesthetic delicacy
than a geisha. And she always undercharged him. He
would dawdle by her stall, feeding her with Gauloises
while she talked of sex, the Turner Prize and the Tate,
explaining to him who was in this year, what was
happening in the world of modern 'so-called' art, why
the shadow of a suspended bird cage revolving on the
ceiling was rubbish whereas a perspex box filled with the
artist's used sticking plasters and hairs taken from Freud's
actual mattress was not.

He loved to watch her frozen hands as they tore off
ribbon to wind the stems, then quickly return to her
mouth and the cigarette. She was more of an addict than

Barry or anyone Barry had ever met. And Barry prided himself on being the only man he knew who could smoke in the shower. Just as well she worked out of doors, her quarters must smell like pub upholstery. He'd brought her a cappuccino with a lid from over the road. Most of the middle-aged men in the area did. She was fed and watered by the male population of Chelsea, who hung around her like worker bees around their maggoty queen. And yet Tara somehow stayed friendly with the women as well. Maybe there was more wisdom than Barry had credited her with in her sartorial choice. Any outer sign of cuteness and she'd have been out, a traitor to her gender.

'I shagged this beautiful, beautiful man last night. Young too,' she said, sucking in smoke with a quick whistling rush. 'God he was beautiful, and you know, really good at it. He went on and on, and was really young too, beautiful body, but. . .' She wasn't looking at Barry but at the bunch of flowers, deciding whether it would be more apt, funereally speaking, to retain the irises or replace them with freesia. 'I wouldn't want to see him again. I couldn't. It's such a shame.'

Barry knew not to ask why. She needed no egging on, this one. Lurid tales of her sexual exploits were part of the deal.

'I mean, he's into Outsider Art, for fuck's sake, which is crap.' She took another long drag on the Gauloise, as if it were a particularly welcome joint. 'I mean, I sort of knew about the Outsider Art bit before I went to bed with him, but I suppose I let the sheer lust of the moment blind me to it. It was only after we'd had all this amazing sex that I thought, Outsider Art? No, girl, can't do this.'

'Outsider Art. Isn't that the one that's done by untaught artists? Ethnics, aboriginals and nutters?' he asked, his opinion of 'Art Brut' and its aphrodisiac qualities coloured not a little by his own personal memories of a particular outsider who had shagged his late ex-wife in 1992.

'Sort of, yeah. It's become terribly trendy all of a sudden, and I hate that. And he was a dealer, so it would be really embarrassing to be seen with him in public. It would look like I was, you know, going out with him to sell my work or something. Which wouldn't be such a bad idea if he was a really important dealer like, you know, Samuel Park or something.'

Tara was an obsessive. She had only two subjects on which she could pass an opinion: her sex life and the art world as she saw it. Since most of the former happened in the latter, she seemed to have an almost blokeish one-track mind.

'You know, that Greek who tried to get into my pants last May? The one with the Audi? That was Samuel Park.' Barry couldn't actually remember this particular anecdote; there had been quite a few since then.

'Which one was he, remind me?'

'The one with the wife and kids and the jacuzzi that I had with him while she was in Stuttgart?'

'Oh that one. He was a bit old for you, I seem to remember.'

'And this one last night was so young. I mean, like twenty-two or something, and fucking gorgeous. Hispanic, from New York.'

'You are careful, Tara, aren't you?' said Barry, taking out a twenty for the flowers. 'Use a condom and all that bollocks, especially if he's from the Big Rotten Apple, you know? Dangerous place, as my old tart found out last week, God spank her soul.' This avuncular concern for Tara, playing on their age difference, made him feel a bit sexy. Well, it sometimes worked on women less savvy than her.

'Yeah, yeah,' she said dismissively, taking the money and handing him the wreath. 'But he was soooo cute. Here, look . . .' And, keeping the gifted Gauloise clamped between her lips, she reached into a back pocket and unfolded a gallery card. On the front was a colour print of a mad multicoloured drawing that looked to Barry as if it could have been done by a five-year-old, and on the back, just above the small print of e-mail address and land-line numbers, was a black-and-white photo of a healthy dark-haired American youth.

'Yes, he is good-looking, I'll give you that. But did he have real passion or were you just bonking?' Barry was shopping for details now and Tara knew it.

'Oh, just bonking. But real fucking bonking bonking, you know?' But Barry had been distracted by a name on the gallery card. Andrea Fox. For the Andrea Fox Gallery, contact 537 Houston and Second Avenue, NY 10023.

'That's my ex-wife,' he said flatly. 'So that's what the bloody hell she was doing in New York, the acquisitive old trout.'

'Oh yes, I meant to ask you about that, I thought it might be her. You said she had a gallery.'

'Well, hardly. She had a converted garage in Old Street last thing I knew, which she nepotistically fuelled with rubbish by people she met when she was dabbling in PR and flogged off to the unsuspecting bourgeoisie of North Kensington at exorbitant prices.'

'That's the art world for you, all nepotism,' said Tara, starting on her cappuccino now that it had had time to cool. 'So she had contacts in the East Village too; classy, that's where all the trendy New York galleries are. Smart woman.'

Barry scrabbled for the last Gauloise stuck in the back of the packet. An ageing but well-preserved television actor came by for some tulips. Barry stood to one side to let Tara serve him. He was riled now. His ex-wife had always been a smart woman, that wasn't the point.

No, the point was that if the magnificent Andrea Fox was the part-owner or whatever of the Andrea Fox Gallery in New York, which would seem a fair assumption to make since the magnificent and smart Andrea had been an ethnic art dealer of sorts, then how the flying fuck had she paid for it, and why until last month was she still coming to Barry – BF – Fox begging for funds whenever she felt in a suitably victimish mood, and how come she was still living in Clapham, and why was he, BF, still paying the mortgage on 137 Rylance Avenue, and who – for Christ's sake – was looking after his son, the horrible Felix, commonly known as Ozone – short for ozone deficiency, short for deficient human being who should be able to earn his own fucking living by now, snivelling little mummy's boy, should have gone to boarding school?? There were several fucking points, that was the point. And more pertinent than any of the above mentioned was the one re the title deeds of the property at 137 Rylance Avenue, as in whose fucking name was on them anyway, as in a large bite of what the Americans like to call real estate on the north side of Clapham Common bought in 1979 for monkey nuts, must be worth a fucking fortune now and wouldn't Mr Hopalong Cassidy, Seamus, Barry's bank manager, love to hear about all of this??? Not to mention his darling landlady, Sophie the Class Tart, and the small matter of seven and a half thousand owing????? Many question marks on the end, but not as many question marks as questions raised. Baz Fox – Bile and Fire – felt twitchy as blood circulated to places where it had not been in a decade.

★

However he tried, Barry could not imagine Andrea the magnificent, the person he knew, being with Oliver, having sex with Oliver, even talking with Oliver. What had she seen in him? Not her type, nor even her species. He conceded that the man was considerably younger than himself and therefore, feasibly, more physically fit, hence capable of sustaining a sexual encounter for a longer period of boredom. But why would she want to go those extra yards with someone so like a chilled herring? So obviously incapable of whispering dirty suggestions in her ear to make her laugh? So unfun? Maybe he possessed a member of impressive proportions, and despite all the literature to the contrary, that's the only thing a woman really wants. When Barry had questioned Andrea's new choice of partner she had said: 'He's kind.' But this seemed to Barry to be a piss-poor reason to bed the creep and invite him to live all over your house. 'Kind' doesn't do much in the underwear department. You can't yearn for 'kind'. You can't take teenage drugs and puke into the toilet together with 'kind'.

Despite the warmth of the taxi, Barry kept his scarf pulled up over his chin all the way down Royal Hospital Road, past the Chelsea Physic Garden, where medicinal plants have been studied since the sixteenth century, and on to the embankment at the Lister Hospital, where he'd once had an anal cyst removed. The taxi driver wittered on about which hours of the day were best if one wanted to avoid being gridlocked, concluding as they always did, that it was impossible to say these days. Then adding for good measure that Barry should be careful going south of the river in case he was kidnapped by the cannibal south Londoners, boiled in a pot and eaten. Highly amusing stuff. Barry had covered the subject of the endless rotational verbiage of the London taxi driver quite recently in one of his pieces, and was not of a mind today to have it out with one of them in person. Hence his scarf position. It had been rather foolish to criticise taxi drivers as a breed in the national press, considering the amount of his life Barry spent in the back of London cabs at their mercy so to speak. But sometimes one just had to publish and be stuck in Knightsbridge in the rain. Right now it was darkening and cold outside. The taxi heater was blowing hard and Barry was too warm.

Maybe young Oliver felt like doing it in the mornings. The thought suddenly struck Barry that a man who was kind, who got to bed early because he had to take in his first patient at eight o'clock in the morning and who once ran a half-marathon would probably feel like having sex in the mornings rather than in the middle of the night like he, Barry, did, or used to do, and that this would probably have suited Andrea rather well, the randy cow. He wondered why he had not worked this one out before. As wet as Oliver must be in every other respect, he was, most likely, an a.m. erection-holder, a lark in bed, a porn chorus, and as such no contest. Hats off to him in fact. These thoughts cheered Barry a little. At least he knew now that he could not even begin to compete with the man, that the game wasn't a game.

If only women realised all the shenanigans we normal chaps go through to get them in the mood of a night; the preparandum coitus, so to speak, he thought glumly: the tickets, the meals, the movies, the candles, the poetry, the literature, the language, the smiles, the breath freshener, the clean underpants, for God's sake, the bloody listening the endless listening – to her problems, her friends' problems, her mother's problems, matters medical, matters decorative, matters trivial, matters sartorial, biting one's lip in case one accidentally mentions anything interesting like politics, religion or cricket which might distract her from the job in hand, i.e. are we going to fucking do it together tonight or not? Barry was thrashing an imaginary little Oliver in his mind's eye now. The morning! Who wants the morning? I need a pee when I wake up, I don't know about you. The smell of both your breath, the oodles of regret about too much drink the night before, the headache, the itching, not an ounce of seductive lighting, children wanting to go to school, buses outside picking up pensioners. What the hell is sexy about the morning?

The taxi drew to a halt in the traffic on Chelsea

Bridge, and Barry gazed down into the dark khaki of the river.

So if somehow Andrea did feel like it in the morning – although on reflection, Barry found that incredible – what would she do about it? Stroke you gently with tulips? Tell you your boss just rang and said you could take the day off on full pay? No. Oh no. Straight for the crotch to grab your dangler, to see if it was in working order, to see if she could get a rise out of it. To see if you were functioning. No play, no romance, only gender. No plying with drinks now, no gazing into the eyes now. I'll tell you why she liked it in the morning, matey, because she knew you didn't, that's why. Because what turned her on was control, control of you, control of when, where and how you did it.

Half an hour away from his last drink, and it was unclear whether he was talking now to Oliver, to himself or to Andrea. He fumbled for a Gauloise and, ignoring the 'Thank you for not smoking' sign, fugged up the back of the cab.

Although he would have liked to have been able to say he had drawn a line in the sand and walked over it as far as Andrea was concerned, had moved on, had 'started over' as the damn Yankees are so fond of putting it, Barry had to admit to himself that she was bugging him today. How could she still have existed without him? How dared she? Annoyingly, he found himself, like some social worker, trying to remember what it was that had gone wrong between them, and reassuring himself that it was definitely her fault.

The way he saw it they had been in it together: love, sex, whatever you wanted to call it. Sex, mostly. Then suddenly, around the time of Felix's arrival, Andrea hadn't felt like it any more and he'd been left out in the cold, wanting her warmth, needing closeness still, feeling like he'd made a fool of himself by giving her so much already. Suddenly she didn't want him any more, only needed what he could provide. He had been high and dry every night, stretched out on the sheets with a bloody erection pulsing through his system, demanding satisfaction. And Andrea drifting off to sleep beside him, worse, wanting to snuggle her head into his shoulder, to rest her arm across his chest, her fingers gently lying on his then flat stomach, near but not near enough to his groin. Wanting him to float into slumber beside her. But not the real him. She wanted a him that didn't have that erection. She wanted a cuddle. Nothing wrong with a cuddle – afterwards. The memory made him shudder. Of lying there charged like a full battery, like a dog that needed a walk, like a horse that was ready to bolt. He could ask her for a hand job, and if lucky she might do that with mere diffidence rather than actual disdain. Either way he was shamed; either way what was shared was gone, turned into something he wanted and she might or might not give. It was at that time he had begun writing at night on the kitchen table, and it was from that genesis that *The Misandrists*, his only sustained piece of prose, had been born. Andrea had been scathing about the book and its title. 'There is no word for the opposite of misogynist,' she had shouted at him one night, 'because there is no such thing.' To prove her wrong he had had to refer her to *The Extended Oxford Companion to the English Language* – the one issued with a magnifying glass because the print was so small: *misandrist*, one who hates men.

He could remember when women were encouraged to do everything possible to please their man, to keep their man, to flatter their man – wear certain underwear, cook diligently, listen to his monologues, satisfy his needs. Nowadays the fucking reversal of this is complete, he thought; men are encouraged to sublimate their needs or rename them as dysfunctional, as 'ADDICTIONS', for crying out loud. For a woman to want to please her man now she would have to be very unfashionable and would keep very quiet about it lest she invite the ridicule of her sisters on daytime television.

Cramming his toad-like body and a large funeral wreath into a freezing call box, Barry dialled a number he had memorised from a 'House For Sale' board they had just driven by.

'Rutworth, Porritt and Littlejohn. Can I help you?'

'Yes, I rather suspect you can. I'm looking for a property in the Clapham area, four bedrooms, say, with a double downstairs reception, bit of a garden out the back sort of thing, you know?'

'And what sort of price would you be looking at, sir?'

'Well, I rather hoped you could help me there. Been out of the country for a few years, you see,' Barry lied. 'Was hoping to find something in the Rylance Avenue area – well, in Rylance Avenue in fact – and was wondering if I'd be able to afford it or whether I should just go and shoot myself right now sort of thing, you know?' As ever, the old public school accent was invaluable. Never mind the social upheavals of the sixties, the seventies or the eighties, people still made the assumption you were loaded when they heard those round vowels being squeezed through that square larynx.

'Well, sir, we don't actually have any properties actually in Rylance Avenue at present,' said the girl. From the sound of her voice he assumed it was a girl and not some old bat. If she could stereotype him then he could stereotype her back. 'They don't actually come up all that often, it being a very popular location, actually.'

'Yes, but if you did have one, how much would you be asking for it, hmm?' Barry was not terribly good at patience.

There was a short silence from the other end of the line. Barry was sweating a little. It was only a minor deception, but nevertheless bad for the blood pressure.

'Well, actually it's difficult to say. The market is

moving at the moment but only just, and we haven't actually had anything there for a few weeks.'

Oh Christ, don't start giving me your second-hand comments on interest rates and the national bloody debt, thought Barry, I just want to know how much, roughly, a four-bedroomed house in Rylance Avenue could be flogged for, because I may, just may, own one, or at least an arguably sizeable piece of one. Seven hundred and fifty thou? A mill? One point three? Just let me know how much I might be worth. When thinking of large sums of money, Barry became uncharacteristically optimistic.

'I could send you our mailing list, sir. What's the name?'

In the second's pause before replying, Barry zipped through any possible implications of his giving his actual name and address to the estate agent. Any way that news of this enquiry could reach solicitors of any description. He decided to risk it anyway.

'Fox . . . erm . . . Barry Fox, Flat C, Phoenix Mansions, Tite Street, Chelsea.' He could hear her typing it in. He hated being on anyone's hard disk.

'Excuse me for asking, but are you THE Barry Fox?'

Sort of a stupid question since he'd just told her and she'd just pegged it into the computer at Rutworth, Porritt and Littlejohn, but he knew what she meant.

'Yes I am, as a matter of fact,' he replied in his seductive, pleased-to-be-Barry-Fox voice. Which of course he wasn't really. He always thought he would have preferred to have been someone else. Oh well, the conversation had begun with a deception so it might as well continue in that vein. No matter which way he owned up to having a well-known name, he ended up sounding like a waggish cad, so he had given in to it long ago.

'I always used to read you. You made me laugh actually.'

'Used to?' queried Barry, cursing again the enforced move to a smaller-circulation newspaper in 1992. Bad year for Barry, that.

'Are you still doing it then?' she asked, innocent of innuendo.

'Oh yes, very much so,' he replied, trying to sound overtly sexual now. 'Doing it all the time. Whenever I get the opportunity, which at the moment happens to be every Saturday in the *Express*.'

'Actually, I always wanted to know, didn't you make a lot of enemies when you wrote that kind of stuff? Didn't people get really angry with you and take you to court and things like that?'

Her use of the past tense when talking of his career pricked him considerably, but he could ride that for now. They'd only just met, so to speak.

'Well, there have been a few narrow scrapes, yes, a few constricted corners, and I am the only person ever to have been sued for libel by *Private Eye* . . . actually.

They lost as it happens, but only on a technicality, so you know, one gets by. *Nescit vox missa reverti*; a word published cannot be recalled.'

He went into a corner newsagent's to replenish his Gauloises, only to discover that they didn't stock anything stronger than Marlboro. It was going to be a stressful day, and one without a wine worth speaking of, knowing the awful osteopath.

Barry had found that becoming unexpectedly well known at around the age he should have been embarking on his mid-life crisis had had an extraordinarily potent effect on the way he was perceived by women, and hence on his libido. Which in turn had had a deleterious effect on his bank balance and on his, until then, relatively settled home life with Andrea and their horrible child Felix. When presented with this kind of temptation, Barry had succumbed and then succumbed some more. To excuse or at least explain his change in sleeping patterns to Andrea, he had used an analogy that he hoped she would understand. 'Imagine a woman,' he had said at some point in 1986, 'at the overgenerous age of thirty-nine, suddenly growing a pair of curvaceous and full breasts with genuine upward-pointing nipples. This combined with sudden and effortless massive cellulite loss.' He had gone on to explain that this hypothetical woman would have to be a very strong and self-contained person, surely, with no interest at all in fucking, to remain unaffected by the onslaught of hitherto undreamt-of offers from the opposite sex. Andrea, and later her new life-partner, Oliver, found this interpretation of his activities distasteful, INCORRECT even, but the sudden interest from females of every shape, age and hue after the publication of the unwittingly controversial *The Misandrists* had taken him by the seat of his pants and whisked him, stunned and drunk, to a different place. Chelsea, to be precise, along with all the other ageing would-be roués. All this had left him cynical about the inner workings of women, who until then he had believed to be the fairer sex. Fair as in more just, if not always prettier.

In two chaotic years he became a curiosity, a bit of a spunky catch for a certain type of woman. A threat to all cosy bourgeois marriages including his own. The man you slept with if you really wanted to piss off your controlling husband, or were bored with your existence in Croydon or Swindon and fancied being introduced to all the photographers in town, or all the publishers in town, or all the advertisers in town. Whichever career or social circle you aspired to, Barry Fox had the invite to the do. He also had his press card. He would have been able to get you in anywhere, from a *Star Wars* premiere to a Tibetan refugee benefit, anywhere serving cheap white wine and satay. And being seen with him meant you were a bohemian, a bit daring, took drugs most likely.

This interest in him from predatory females had

waned in direct proportion to the declining success of his work. Barry's life as a stud after the sudden fame brought on by his book had been short-lived, as indeed had been his subsequent career in broadcasting, which ended as quickly as it had begun in 1991 when he used the word 'cunt' live on air to describe the ever-popular and wholesome Sir Cliff Richard. Which, while being an obvious mistake career-wise, had also marked the decline of his popularity with the ambulance-chasers, front-door scratchers and gold-diggers who had so recently been prepared to bed him. Never mind men treating women as sex objects, Barry had opined, when trying to wheedle his way back into Andrea's life, what about men being treated as success objects? That was a good one, he thought. He had made a note of it and included it in his column the following week.

Barry had long ago realised that his performance in bed was immaterial; most women just wanted a cuddle anyway. Neither was it particularly important for him to be young, sober or good-looking. Handy, that last exception, because Barry had certainly never thought of himself as physically attractive. He'd never played a sport, except cricket, and that was more for the lunches and the summer afternoons hanging about in whites. Not for him the new-fangled helmets and multi-coloured sponsorship outfits. In fact he had always been honest with himself about his lack of sexual magnetism. He had a round and hairy back, for goodness' sake! The epitome of turn-off according to most women's magazines. Nowadays he had a large and taut belly too, like the hull of an overloaded freight barge, and a neck like a tree trunk which had a straight line where he stopped shaving clearly visible above the collar of his shirt. He'd grown his hair long in 1971 and kept it that way ever since, although now it was grey and flattened like a crop circle at the crown. For occasions such as book launches he might tie it in a ponytail. No, as far as meeting and sleeping with women was concerned, there was – since his aforementioned scramble to some kind of notoriety – no need for Barry to be or look like anything other than what he was: an ex-public-school ex-hippy alcoholic. When it came to satisfaction, however, he was aware that he was among the I can't get no's and, after a few years, had given up trying. That ghastly nuisance love had been at best overrated, in Barry's opinion, and at worst a total rip-off. He recalled thinking that he was in love when he'd agreed to marry the magnificent Andrea, but that was before her having to have a bloody child and refusing to stroke his back any more. It seemed as if love was something he'd given to Andrea more than a decade ago and that she'd absconded with it and then gone and bloody DIED, the selfish harlot.

THREE

Andrea Fox, prefixed 'the magnificent' because of her equine physique and exceptional arrogance, wasn't expecting to die, and so her funeral was perhaps not arranged in quite the way she would have preferred had she written the script herself – something she would undoubtedly have liked to have had the chance to do. The opportunity of making a statement, of being different, even in death, would have been one she would have been appalled to miss. The desire to be special had been an overriding feature of her life, and was made tragic by her lack of any one talent to draw her forward. She would at least have had a troupe of African drummers at her sending-off. The speeches would have been mytho-poetic, the priest a Guatemalan shaman. What she got – through the cruel reality of her sudden death – was a couple of hymns, a bit of Bible and a shunt into the automatic incinerator of Wandsworth crematorium just off the A217. The wine wasn't even organic.

Her extravagant and much heralded interest in New Age concepts, alternative medicine and Aquarian conspiracy theories was partly genuine and partly opportunistic. She was renowned from Hampstead to the Groucho club as a woman who was into everything – crystals, black box, hara power, raja yoga, tantric sex. The short spell she'd had in therapy was with a Jungian and she'd come out of it with runic stones and mandalas. Her summer holidays were often spent up a mountain in Tuscany chanting with Tibetans, her Easter weekends at the Findhorn foundation. This tendency in her had been mostly latent during her marriage to Barry, which was fortunate for them both because he, like Kingsley Amis, was of the opinion that if there is one word to sum up what has gone wrong in England since the war, it is 'workshop'.

Whereas Andrea believed that the answer to millennial malaise was 'positive thinking', and she could get out of any difficult situation by telling her adversary they had a negative aura, Barry felt that her aspiration to relentless positivity was merely a way for the insecure but healthy to taunt the clinically depressed. If ever a couple had epitomised the cliché 'growing apart', it was Barry and Andrea Fox.

Where Felix got his extreme cleverness from had been a mystery to both Barry and Andrea, who, rightly or wrongly, each considered themselves fiercely intelligent in their own fields but had not the slightest scientific or mathematical ability between them. Barry felt at home with words, Andrea with feelings and images. Despite Andrea's desire for their son to go to a progressive and arty school where you went to lessons only if you felt like it, Felix had been a disappointment to her in demanding a traditional and academically stringent education. At the age of seventeen, he had passed his physics, chemistry and biology A levels with special commendations, and was now doing a degree in biotechnology at Manchester University. His thesis was to be on the freezing of embryos for transplants.

All freezing is a question of timing. Yes, you can just bung some fresh fish in the ice box and leave it there for three months, take it out, run it under the hot tap and cook it, but it won't taste fresh, might even have gone powdery, won't have the same texture, the same feel and flavour. Things all have their own freezing and defrosting times, but none but the most conscientious householder actually studies the manual, let alone obeys its instructions. Felix had freezing times memorised by the age of eleven. This principle applies even more strictly when freezing medical matter, like blood or tissue, for transplant. Each item has its own tolerance speed for temperature drop. Freeze or defrost faster or slower than this and you risk destroying cells. And this doesn't just mean that heart cells differ from kidney cells or whatever; it means that each individual cell has its own freezing speed. To coldstore successfully, the speed of each individual item's temperature change must be monitored by machines with cybernetic intelligence. That way they can find themselves at freezing point without, as it were, having realised how they got there. In fact, Felix was very much like that himself. He arrived at zero temperature at about the age of ten, a few months after his parents had separated, but this descent had been so gradual as to have been noticed neither by himself nor his teachers and guardians. Maintaining extremely good grades at school helped to keep everyone off his back. Getting consistent A's in all exams made it unlikely that any adult would have bothered to be concerned that Felix's veins now contained liquid nitrogen instead of blood, and that there was a block of dry ice where his heart should have been.

As Felix had developed into his late teens, though, there had been signs of this emotional cryology, had anyone wanted to read them. His complete lack of friends and his obsessive interest in cooling systems being the most obvious. At the age of eighteen he had devised a way of running a small household fridge without electricity by using the heat from an ordinary radiator as its element. This invention had won him the junior prize of the Society of Low Temperature Biology. He was a very bright boy with a nonexistent social life. It was not so much that he was crap with girls, more that he would have needed to thaw out before even attempting to communicate with them. Something that might have steamed up his calculations.

Any free time he had at university, in which others might drink lager or have promiscuous sexual experiences, was taken up at the moment by the development of a software system for use in the freezing of embryos. He did have a sort of girlfriend – Stephanie – but he considered her more of a hanger-on than a companion. A stalactite which he could not be bothered to prise from the plastic inner lining of his life. It was at Stephanie's insistence that Felix had bothered to come to London for his mother's funeral at all, his work was all-consuming. He had chosen Manchester because of the superiority of equipment in its Low Temp department, and also because one of his professors held a consultancy position with a large American IVF company. Felix, unlike either of his parents, approached each season with deliberation and well-laid plans.

Verbal communication had never been one of Felix's main skills, particularly when it came to his mother's younger live-in boyfriend, Oliver, and as the two of them prepared to leave Rylance Avenue together on the morning of Andrea's funeral, thoughts of the day ahead had induced in them both a sort of glacial insensibility.

'How is your course going?' asked Oliver with only a modicum of genuine interest.

Absolutely no response at all, which one might expect in a fifteen-year-old, but Felix was twenty and should by now have developed the rudiments of social skill. They remained silent for a few seconds until Oliver could no longer wrestle with his own feelings of mounting anxiety. He had always thought that somehow it was his job to try and 'get through' to Felix, and that, if ever he did succeed, this anxiety would be dissipated. In fact, like Nature, Oliver merely abhorred a vacuum.

'I'm really nervous about today,' he said with a jocularity which seemed pathetic to him even before the words left his mouth. 'You OK?'

There was an indecipherable grunt from Felix which could have meant 'yes' or 'no', but which undoubtedly contained the subtext 'What's it to you? You are merely one of the many mistakes my mother made.' Oliver's usually tireless compulsion to try and make people feel better abandoned him in the face of Felix's frigidity and, after fruitlessly asking how long Felix intended staying in London, he gave up, sliding into his own thoughts in the back of the black cab.

The only remark Felix addressed to Oliver all that day was 'Why did HE have to come?' in reference to his father. Oliver told himself again that he had done the right thing in inviting Barry, despite Felix's hostility and even though Barry was a high-risk guest at any gathering on account of his tendency to swill alcohol and devour picky bits, shout incomprehensibly in Latin and fall noisily asleep in inconvenient places.

Possibly because of the bitterly cold weather, Barry Fox didn't actually misbehave too much at his ex-wife's funeral. He spent the outdoor part of the day with his woollen scarf wrapped around his face, pulling it down only to take a more than occasional swig from his engraved silver flask. Seeing father and son together, or rather in close proximity to each other – they had only one brief exchange – further convinced Oliver that it was right for Barry to be there. There could never have been the slightest question over Felix's paternity – they looked so alike. Barry would never have felt the need to ask for a corroborating blood test as some modern fathers are inclined. Felix had the same endomorphic frame, albeit with less stomach and more hair. The same bulbous nose and lips, and above all, the same inelegant stance as his father. However much he might try to disguise it with the uniform of a student – lousy jeans, creaking trainers, open-neck shirt with pullover and Oxfam coat – Felix was daddy's boy through and through.

It had been quite gratifying for Oliver to see Barry and Felix talk, even for those few seconds back at Rylance Avenue where everyone had congregated for a short while after the cremation. Oliver was someone who needed, daily, to feel that he was in some way making the world a better place. Had he gone into politics, this vanity might have been exposed to ridicule. As an osteopath and dietician he was safer in that the harm he was capable of doing was on a smaller scale. He felt a tiny sliver of pride in this minor filial reconciliation as he washed up the glasses and put the empty bottles in the bottle-bank.

All the guests but one had gone. Since not all the bottles were empty, Barry Fox had found it difficult to leave and was slouching on the couch in the living area, smoking a Gauloise with a long tower of ash hanging off it. Since it was Andrea's funeral, Oliver had allowed guests to smoke in the house – it was what she would have wanted, being a sporadic Silk Cut woman herself. But as soon as they had gone, he had removed and cleaned the ash tray, putting it back in its place by the patio window.

'She was a corker that gallery girl, wasn't she?' Barry shouted through to Oliver, tipping his ash on to the Peruvian rug and massaging it in with his foot. 'What was her name? Forgotten it. Blast! Got her phone number though!' Barry chortled and then wheezed. 'Here!' He pulled a torn-off scrap of funeral-service paper out of his top pocket. 'Not bad, eh?' On the page in front of him were the words 'Piss off grandad'. 'Oh God! I'm in love with her already!' he said.

'Oh, you mean Rebecca,' Oliver called back as he wiped the kitchen surfaces. 'Yes, she's very nice. Very good at the figures evidently, Andrea always said. Got a degree in history of art as well as being a registered accountant.'

'Can't think why she'd bother to work for Andrea with all that. Must be able to get a proper job. What's the matter with her?'

Rebecca, the only person to cry at the funeral, was a

tiny, dark woman of twenty-seven who'd been working for Andrea for five years. Barry was right: with her qualifications and abilities she could have taken a job at a more prestigious gallery in the West End and have been paid more and more regularly, for less time and less effort. Her intelligence, which was keen, far exceeded what was required of her. She had performed all the tasks at the gallery which Andrea's affected scattiness left undone. Her administrative duties ranged from booking Andrea's taxis and plane tickets to helping with Andrea's wardrobe choices and relationship counselling. Frequently she would be called upon suddenly to work weekends, and sometimes – if Andrea was abroad, for instance – at night. Where Andrea had been extrovert and flirtatious, Rebecca was cautious and reflective. Andrea was tall and posh, Rebecca the opposite, and the only real explanation for her staying so long in a job where she was so patently being taken for a ride was that she was in awe of Andrea. That she too found her 'magnificent'.

Just how magnificent Rebecca found Andrea had once been a cause of some jealous speculation from Oliver, which he had voiced in a roundabout manner one night in the car. The thing which never ceased to surprise Oliver about Andrea was that the gentler or more understanding his approach, the more explosive was her response. On this occasion she had opened the passenger door of their ancient Volvo estate and jumped out of the moving vehicle. This was just after her shouted assertion that sex with another woman did not constitute infidelity because it was non-penetrative. Oliver had blamed her subsequent broken ankle on himself for bringing the subject up.

'It was so good to see you finally talking to Felix today after all this time,' said Oliver, who was beginning to wonder when it would be polite to ask Barry to leave. 'That's one good thing at least to come out of today. I know he's not very forthcoming, but I think he'll need some reassurance now, that's all.'

'Nothing wrong with him. Seems to be doing rather well actually,' said Barry, holding up his cigarette butt. Apologising, Oliver fetched him back the ash tray, which was a Spanish peasant pottery piece embossed with tin.

'It's important for him to "fix it" with his dad, I think. I know he finds it difficult to express himself.' If Oliver took any pleasure in life, it was in feeling that he was instrumental in some way in healing people – whether it be relieving their lumbar pain or reuniting a son with his father. He also believed that talking things through was a panacea for all interpersonal problems and had often run into conflict with Andrea over this credo. Sometimes he used to follow her around the kitchen while she tried to make a cup of coffee, or into the bathroom when she was washing, to try and resolve a particular disagreement to his own satisfaction. This was not necessarily productive with Andrea, who had the irritating ability to decide when a conversation was over by getting up and leaving the room. As far as talking to Oliver was concerned, Andrea held the philosophy that building more roads would only increase traffic congestion.

'I think Felix tends to bottle everything up, you know?' he said, sitting down on the Arts and Crafts chair opposite Barry.

'Bloody good thing too. Don't want all those messy adolescent feelings splurging all over your beautiful home, do you?'

'Well,' said Oliver, 'all the same, I think it's a shame he's gone straight back up to Manchester like that. I think it would have done him some good to get to know you a bit. Let some of whatever's in there out.' He felt drawn to the challenge of softening Barry's intransigence.

'Thing about Felix is – and I've known him all his life – everybody's got a secret place where they hide all their bits, you know, secret diaries under the knickers in the underwear drawer, love letters in an old biscuit tin under the bed. Usually the first place you'd look, isn't it? It's almost as if they've been hoping somebody will notice.' Oliver's mind raced immediately and guiltily to the piece of Filofax paper with Mrs Baldry the whip woman's number on it, which he had quite unnecessarily stuffed in a disused biscuit tin at the top of a kitchen cupboard. He hoped that Barry was too drunk to notice this momentary shadow flicker across his face. Barry continued, pouring himself a glass of cheap Chardonnay from one of the opened bottles on the hurricane-wood coffee table.

'Like your average serial killer, see? Leaving little clues and signs everywhere in the hope of being caught and exposed. The pleasure of having the secret is greatly enhanced by the potential torture of being suddenly discovered . . . or is it the other way round? The torture of having the secret is enhanced by the pleasure of discovery? I can't remember which now, but my point about Felix is . . .' Barry was looking straight at Oliver now, his sonorous voice deep and commanding, '. . . he's not like that. He wouldn't accidentally leave the bed-covers untucked in the appropriate spot as a sort of marker, you know, for the naughty biscuit tin. No. He genuinely doesn't care whether anyone's interested in him at all. His hiding place is much better than a com-partment under the floorboards, his hiding place is in his own head. Very good hiding place for a man, that, if you're strong enough. He's a great kid.'

What would you know of Felix? Oliver wanted to say. You're not the one who took him to school most mornings when he was eleven; you didn't have to go to parents' evenings, put up with his mind-numbing taste in music all those years, smell his bedroom when he hadn't cleared it up for weeks, pay for his aborted piano lessons, teach him how to drive. What would you know?

But instead he said, 'Would you like to stay for some pasta? It's no trouble, I'm making some anyway.' As if responding to an insult, Barry looked at him with a witheringly quizzical expression which seemed to say, 'Don't you know *anything* about alcoholism?' But then he thought better of it. Even though swallowing food at this stage of the evening would be a virtual impossibility for Barry, it was important to him that he remain here with Oliver and try to steer the conversation as delicately as he could towards the matter of the house. He was hoping to avoid mention at this stage of his various debts, one in particular, of seven and a half K, to his unofficial landlady, the charming Sophie of Chelsea.

'Pasta?' he said on a burp. 'Yes, yes, that would be, er . . . delightful, old chap, if you're sure you have enough.' Staying around for a bit longer would also allow time for completion of his self-appointed duty to finish the opened bottles of wine which were singing to him from the table.

It was a hauntingly melancholic experience for Barry, to sit in the house he had bought and lived in, had argued in, had had plates thrown at him in. On furniture some of which he recognised from his student days, or from richer times when he had had a proper income. This house was what he had provided for a family which he had thought he was to be a part of, but despite its four

bedrooms, twin reception and kitchen/breakfast conser-
vatory, it had still, somehow, not been big enough to
contain him. There was much in it, of course, that had
changed: the colour, the style and, above all, the
artefacts. For the last few years, Andrea had been
collecting ethnic and primitive pieces of art, and the
room in which he sat contained several African phallic
sculptures in dark wood, as well as four silk-
embroidered wall hangings from Kashmir, and a small
circumcision table from Papua New Guinea, with a
Balinese flower vase wedged into its deep blood runnels.
In addition to wanting to advertise her affinity with the
archetypal and mythic, the things she bought had given
Andrea genuine pleasure and she had often described
her reaction to these works as 'free mind space'.
Looking at them when stoned was the nearest she ever
got to a mystical experience.

The first time she had become aware of the power of
a piece of art to induce a trance-like state in her was in
1983, when she was still married to Barry Fox. It
happened while she was on a visit to an old school friend
in Melbourne. She'd been to see the exhibition of
Papunya aboriginal artists at Melbourne Fine Art gallery
while extremely stoned on Thai sticks. Later, after
several more smokes, she had watched an ATV
documentary on Geoff Bardon, the first man to give the
indigenous Papunya people boards and acrylic paint, and
had found him incredibly sexy. He'd gone out to the red

centre of Australia in a big four-wheel-drive wagon, wearing masculine boots and a rugged Ozzie chin, and suggested to the local artists that, rather than drawing their traditional Dreamtime pictures in the sand or painting them on to bits of tree bark, they use modern materials, thus making their culture more durable and, of course, ultimately much more saleable. By the late eighties, aboriginal paintings were fetching thousands of pounds in galleries all over the world, and one aboriginal artist had even made a dot picture called *Amsterdam Airport Dreaming*.

Andrea had started by buying a couple of small pieces by Tommy Possum Tjupurrula and selling them almost immediately to a buyer in Paris. But the Australian government were quick to realise their new asset and put withholding taxes on items leaving the country, making it difficult for her to gather financial momentum. This, coupled with the explosion of interest in aboriginal art from the big galleries in New York, London and Chicago, meant that Andrea's antipodean connection was a short-lived one.

However, the experience had given her a taste of what her new life without Barry Fox could be like. By 1989 she was alone, careerless and bored. She started to travel to Latin America, India and Africa. She saw herself as an international envoy for the Third World. She bought embroidered marquee tents in Rajasthan and sold them to a rock star in Wiltshire, she bought a sequinned voodoo flag in Haiti and sold it to a novelist in Hampstead. As her list of fashionable contacts grew, Felix became more accustomed to staying with friends, or cooking alone.

She met Oliver, the osteopath, through a mutual client, the publisher Jane Purcell, who as well as having sacro-iliac problems, was interested in doing a book about the Keralan dung sculptures of Chas Aurubundulam. Oliver, then twenty-six and just qualified, was looking for a room to rent, and Andrea needed a little extra cash and some company when she was in town. The book never materialised, but in a matter of weeks Oliver went from creeping past Felix's bedroom in the night to sharing Andrea's bed full time. He had only ever paid the first month's rent, preferring once they were a couple to contribute to the bills, do the cooking and housekeeping and baby-sit Felix when Andrea went out to openings and parties, which was often.

In the beginning it was good for Andrea to have someone to whom she could recount the various crimes and awfulnesses of Barry Fox, but she soon tired of this. After a while their relationship seemed to hinge on the fact that, as an osteopath, Oliver gave a superb and thorough shoulder massage.

'So how's the faith healing going then?' Barry followed Oliver into the kitchen and perched his wide bottom on the narrow seat of one of the unfamiliar Conran stools. 'Done any laying-on of hands recently?'

He wanted to find out where Oliver thought he stood with regard to the house, and a man-to-man talk about money might lead them there.

'Well, it's not exactly faith healing, what I do,' Oliver replied, half laughing to turn the insult into a joke. 'Although a positive attitude does help in many cases.' He got out a large saucepan and filled it with water.

'Oh God!' said Barry, 'Well, I'm afraid that counts a self-respecting alcohologram like myself out for a start. Not very good on positive attitude.'

'Well, an attitude of hope, you know?'

'Talking of which, do they have to take all their clothes off?' asked Barry, sniggering. 'That must make it hard, if you'll pardon the pun.'

'It depends,' said Oliver, deliberately ignoring Barry's leeriness. 'Some people are more relaxed that way, take pride in their bodies, whereas others just seize up completely.' Oliver was used to fielding these kind of questions about his profession and so it was not Barry's crassness that was irritating him particularly. It was the actual physical presence of the man in his kitchen which was causing the trouble. The man he had spent so much of the last eight years talking about in derogatory terms with his partner. The first thing that had had to be established between him and Andrea – their founding principle – was his absolute agreement with her that Barry Fox was a shit, and the cause of most of the world's major problems. 'I've converted the front room into a surgery, actually. Just let me get the pasta on and I'll show it to you if you like.'

'A woman walked into a bar and asked the bar tender for a double entendre, so he gave her one,' said Barry, and waited for Oliver to laugh. Barry had often wondered why the making of puns appeals so much more to men than it does to women. He could think of no connection between double meanings and other usually male activities such as drinking to excess, sports obsession and cars. Nevertheless he could not think of one woman of his acquaintance who punned, whereas every bloke he knew would pun if allowed, or at least appreciate the puns of others. But Oliver had not reacted at all. Must be a woman, concluded Barry as he followed Oliver across the hall to revisit his former front room.

On entering what was now the surgery, Barry was suddenly struck by an overwhelming gloom. There was nothing in there that he recognised. Nothing. The feeling of displacement buffeted him like a strong wind. He put his hand on the wall to steady himself. The walls were white and covered with skeleton diagrams, the carpet was beige, the desk was a light green self-build from Argos, and Barry's cheap old Belgian chandelier had been replaced by black-coated steel wall lights.

'So this is where it all happens, eh? The miracle cure centre . . .' He tailed off as memories which had been dormant for many years suddenly and insistently woke up inside him. The two men stood in silence for a while.

'I slapped her once, you know. In here. In this room. Smacked her, hard. It was a terrible thing to do. Only across the top of the head, not in the face or anything. On the other hand, it was when she was pregnant, of which I am deeply ashamed. And. . .' He paused, gazing sightlessly at the acupuncture meridian poster on the wall, '. . . I pushed her over once, not twice as she claims. From a standing position into a hedge. The other time we were sitting on the floor anyway so it was more of a rollover. But I did threaten her a couple of times and there was a lot of shouting. Terrible times. God, when I think about them now . . .'

Barry considered for a moment what it was that had turned his marriage into such hostile terrain. He remembered Felix, as a baby, crawling at speed across this room towards the plug sockets to try and stick his fingers in, hauling himself up to a standing position on the bookshelves, which toppled on to him. It was the arrival of Felix that had put the kibosh on it, he concluded. The nipper had definitely shunted Barry down a few notches on Andrea's priority list, and that had been unbearable to him. Initially he had tried to share with her the joys and hard work of bringing up the little shit, but was soon feeling as if his involvement with the child, though apparently desired, demanded even, by Andrea, was in some way making him less attractive to her. He feared that his pre-parental ruthlessness and male insensitivity had been the petrol that had fuelled her now-subsided passion for him. She seemed to have wanted an exclusivity clause over their offspring and would have preferred, he suspected, a man who couldn't care less about family matters, an unhelpful one about whom she could complain to her female and gay friends. Within a couple of years, Barry had taken the path of least resistance, abdicating his role as the father of the family. Abrogating to Andrea all responsibility for matters concerning the emotional organisation of life; not just looking after Felix, but anything to do with the home – from the choosing of curtain fabric to filling the social diary. After the first eighteen months of this, he had felt like a stranger in the hotel that his home had become, and would frequently go to the pub or for a curry rather than spend an evening with the not-so-young mother. She was no longer in love with him, it seemed; she was in love with Felix, and would detail the bloody infant's every bowel movement.

'I know all about your violence,' said Oliver, turning out the lights. They left the surgery and returned to the hall. 'And I know it's natural as a man to resort to that when you start to lose control, but it really is the bottom line. The point beyond which you must never, ever go.'

'Natural, eh?' said Barry. 'I would have thought you would have approved of that, old boy. You know, natural herbs and holistic mumbo-jumbo and all that.' Barry was finding the emotion of the evening intolerable and had an uncontainable urge to leave the house and its memories immediately. Any discussion regarding ownership of Rylance Avenue would have to wait. He who fights and runs away, and all that. He decided to forego the delights of pasta with the osteopath, made his apologies and hovered by the front door.

'I didn't mean natural like that,' said Oliver, opening the door for him. Barry noticed that the chunk he had taken out of the skirting board with his bicycle in the days when he had owned a bicycle was still there. Covered in pale-ochre eggshell paint now, but still recognisable. This place was stirring him in a way he didn't want to be stirred.

'Tell me, I've often wondered,' he said on the doorstep now, 'what does it mean, then, when they say that some little bottle of vitamins or seaweed tablets or whatever is "natural"?'

'Oh, I suppose, not chemical, coming from something made by nature rather than man. Safe.'

'You mean safe like LSD, which derives from a mould found on ears of rye?'

'Well, yes . . . well, no.'

'Or the first antibiotic, penicillin, another of nature's moulds? Or aspirin, say, which comes originally from the bark of the willow tree?'

'No. What I mean, I suppose, is not chemical, not made in a laboratory.'

'So, made in a shed or a back room somewhere. Basically anywhere that can't afford to keep to the standards of hygiene required by a laboratory.'

Barry was wicked in debate, and had once been famous for it, making occasional appearances on radio and TV. A germ of a concept of an idea of a possible angle was beginning to tickle his consciousness. It just needed sprinkling with some light Italian white wine to grow into a thousand-word article for the Saturday *Express*. He'd pick up a bottle on the way home. Trouble was, round here the off-licences would no doubt only have more bloody CHARDONNAY, the favoured gulp of the whingeing classes. The Chardonnay grape was not, by a long soak, Barry's favourite; he found its flavour too acrid, too clarty for his sandpapered palate, and when drunk in quantity it left him with sinusitis. Nevertheless, it was Wednesday night and needs must.

'Well, goodbye,' he said. '*Naturam expellas furca, usque recurret*. Which means: you can drive her away with a pitchfork, but Nature will always return.'

Oliver, too, was hovering in the doorway. Like Barry, he felt a dread of returning to the memories that the interior of the house would revive. He could not tell whether this was his own fear or one he had picked up from Barry over the last few minutes, but he was suddenly uncomfortable at being left alone there.

'On Tuesday nights I have a sort of men's group here,

if you'd like to come along one time. We talk about things like . . .'

'Like shagging. I'll bet you do.'

'Well, yes, naturally we do talk about sex, but not just that. It's more for men who want to try and change, you know. Stuff like you were talking about just now in the surgery. Just men.'

'A biscuit club? At your age? We used to do that at school. All stand around a digestive and wank on to it, last one to come has to eat it. Ought to be ashamed of yourself, my dear fellow.' The sky was a black sheet. There was no moon or stars. Oliver shivered in his shirt.

'No. It's nothing like that. We talk about gender issues.'

'Superiority over women is what all exclusively male groups are about. They teach xenophobia and bigotry. Brotherhoods, clubs. That's what they're there for. Always have been. Haven't you or your chums clocked that yet?' Barry really wanted to get away, he was finding Oliver clingy.

'Well, you're welcome to come along anyway. I mean, we could talk about Andrea, you know.'

'You know what I think your little group's about? It's a bunch of chaps who feel chippy when women get too demanding or successful and who secretly fantasise about docile bottoms which love to be punished and spanked.'

'It's every Tuesday evening. You'd be very welcome.'

★

As he trotted off down Rylance Avenue, Barry considered his column. He was eager to return to the one-way conversation he was in the habit of enjoying with his Toshiba laptop at this time of a Wednesday night. Whatever has happened to that poor word 'natural'? he thought to himself. How it has become abused. His piece would begin with a round-up of all the supermarket products with the word 'natural' on them, and he could think of several off the top of his head, from toilet paper to low-fat chocolate bars. Then it would move on to a coruscating critique of what he called 'fad' medicine, possibly concluding with a joke about the phrase 'might get run over by a bus tomorrow', which people use as an excuse for avoiding looking after themselves. He might even afford himself a flight of fancy in which turquoise-uniformed air-steward types were posted at every bus stop with laminated safety cards, miming to pre-recorded road crossing instructions. It might not be the most relevant or hilarious piece ever to arrive on the fax machine of the *Express*, but he felt he could get away with it. He relaxed a little for the first time that week, knowing that with an hour or so to nip and tuck, he was most likely in the clear again until Sunday night.

As he lay in the double bed that night, Oliver contemplated masturbating, as he used to do most nights when Andrea was out, if only as a soporific. But the thought of Andrea in her New York hotel room kept invading the screen of his fantasy, followed hard by the picture of her lifeless face at the mortuary. Mrs Baldry and her bruised behind could not shift it, nor could any number of images or embroidered erotic memories. He found himself wondering what Andrea had really thought of him, what, if anything, she had felt for him. He could not imagine that she had had any feelings at all for him. He didn't see why she should, after all. He wondered whether he would ever be able to masturbate again.

FOUR

'That is good news, BF darling. Not good that the poor old thing kicked the bucket, of course, but then again I never knew her, so . . .' Sophie giggled over the straw of her vod and slimline. Her teeth were perfect and extra large. She could have gone on telly to advertise dental floss. 'I mean about the house and everything. I'm so pleased for you. We do so like our best, best friends to be happy and rich!'

Barry had been summoned to an audience with Sophie, known as the Class Tart, in the foyer of the Conrad hotel in Chelsea Harbour. She had an apartment in the harbour complex which had a partial view of the river, looking downstream towards Battersea Bridge, the green and gold one, colours of Harrods, she liked to say. One could just see the lights of the superb Albert Bridge beyond, if one stood against her cloakroom door. Not that Barry had ever been into her sanctum, the exact number and block of which was a secret she kept from all but her closest female friends and her wealthiest male ones.

She sat amongst the maroon upholstery of the almost

empty hotel cocktail bar as if posing for a lifestyle photo-shoot in *Hello!* magazine. Her posture and presentation were at all times self-conscious and flamboyant: shoulders back, stomach held in, lower back arched and bottom muscularly wedged into the back of the chair, allowing her long brown legs, which were currently crossed and wrapped in expensive shiny tights, to be the eye catching centrepiece of her display. Her skirt, which was skimpy when standing, was made breathtakingly short by the adoption of this sitting position. Not easy and relaxed, but quintessentially, professionally female. The sort of woman drag artists aspire to be.

On first sitting down, Barry had commented slyly on the gorgeousness of her legs and received a delightful smack on the back of his hand; just hard enough to imply that she would know how to deliver a proper spanking should the need arise, but not so hard as to dislodge any of her beautifully enamelled fake fingernails.

'You are a naughty old tiger!' she'd said, and ordered him a G and T from Bernard, her favourite waiter. This welcoming ritual over, Barry had stumbled straight into his prepared speech about the death of Andrea and the possibly invigorating effect it might have on his finances once the house at Rylance Avenue was sold. Unusually for Barry, he found himself searching for the appropriate words, even after the arrival of the G and T. 'Seem to have lost my *copia verborum*,' he stammered. Owing someone seven and a half thousand pounds was an unnerving and tongue-tying experience, even if that person was as charming and delicious as Sophie the Class Tart. Barry's confidence and relaxation were not helped either by the presence of her young companion, Carla, an over-made-up blonde from High Wycombe, to whom Sophie conspicuously turned for a conspiratorial and confirming giggle every time she finished a sentence. Sophie liked to have acolytes around her at all times.

Through the window beyond Sophie's shoulder, Barry could see the desolation of the harbour itself. A few expensive-looking gin-palace cruisers in white fibre-glass bobbed up and down against the mostly empty mooring pontoons. An obviously American elderly couple were the only people to be seen on the neat grey quayside which runs around the small marina. Built in the early eighties on the site of the old gasworks, Chelsea Harbour has never really taken off. The recession arrived shortly after it was completed, and many of the apartments remained unsold for too long, which has meant that there was a swift turnaround of shop owners in its cleaner-than-clean mall. The ambitious atrium now contains mostly specialist interior-design studios and tourist gift shops. At one point it had three Belgian chocolate shops but no chemist, no tobacconist, no bank and no grocery store. Its distance from any suitable public-transport outlet and the fact that it is not on a through route to anywhere mean that none but the super-rich and a smattering of agoraphobic media folk actually live there. Its three storeys of underground car parking remain virtually empty, the only cars to be sporadically sprinkled in there being the Porsches and Mercs of the wayward sons of the few remaining arrivistes of the eighties boom.

It does however sport three sprauntzy restaurants and a five-star hotel with its own gymnasium and ozone pool. A great place to be sent on a company expenses junket, but not so well known for its strong community links, its history, or village atmosphere. Barry Fox would have been breathing more easily in one of the more typical haunts of Old Chelsea: lovely old Finch's on the Fulham Road, for example, or the Cross Keys, the Front Page or the Phene. But he owed Sophie more than just the seven grand, he owed her friendship and respect. He was one of the loyal subjects of her court. They had had some outlandish evenings together, and besides, she owned the lease on his flat in Phoenix Mansions in Tite Street. He was, in many ways, her serf.

'Oh, it all sounds so terribly serious, darling,' she said, after allowing Barry falteringly to calculate what kind of sums he might have at his disposal after the sale of the house. The timbre of her voice, the accent and manner of her speech had forced some small-minded people to quickly reassess their preconceptions about women of colour. Either she had been to Roedean, or she had taken elocution lessons from someone who had.

'We do hate funerals and gloomy things, don't we, Carla?' Carla backed her up on this. 'I'm sure it's going to work out just hoodledy-dandy for you, BF. But those nasty probate thingies always take so long, don't they? All the horrid solicitors and tax men and everything. Urrgh!' She affected a mock-shiver which rattled her Grant and Cutler earrings. Then, instantly returning to her award-winning smile, she put a hand on Barry's knee and told him what they were going to do about the situation.

It so happened, she began, that Carla, the bombshell sitting next to her, had once been married – a foolish mistake, as Barry would no doubt appreciate. The chap's name was Eco, he was Venezuelan, and evidently he was not the sort of person we like.

'Oh my God, Sophie, you're not going to ask me to bump someone off, are you? I really don't think I'd be . . . at my age . . . how should I put it? Capable of . . . not really made of the right stuff and all that? Well, sort of pickled actually . . .' Barry was drowned out by honking laughter from Sophie and Carla.

'Goodness gracious no, darling BF, you sweet, sweet man, you're far too old and far too nice,' Sophie squawked.

'Not really,' said Barry, 'I'm a sort of nefarious swine, actually. I can't help it. Famous for it, in fact.'

'There you go again!' Sophie squealed with delight

like a little girl who had just caught sight of her first pony. She turned to Carla. 'I told you he was sweet, didn't I?'

Eco, Carla's macho spouse, was temporarily in England and, being a jealous man – a hot-blooded Latin type, as Sophie put it – he would undoubtedly be looking for Carla in order to do things to her which might include romance but would more likely involve bouncing her face against a table. Barry noticed a small and not unattractive scar on Carla's upper lip. The resolution was that Carla needed a safe house, so she was going to use Barry's flat in Tite Street for a while – days or weeks were not specified – until the bozo went back to Venezuela. This proposition was not put to Barry in the form of a request, nor was there the slightest suggestion of a begged favour about it. It was presented to him as a fait accompli. He took it graciously. Sophie thanked him as if it had been his idea. 'How clever and generous of you, BF!' she said. Barry would have to check into the Chelsea Arts Club, where he was a member of some twenty years' standing. The rooms were cheap and a mere staircase away from the bar, which had a late licence. Things could have been worse. He explained to Sophie that he'd have to drop by Tite Street every now and then to pick things up and drop things off; like his laptop and his mail, clean underpants and socks, etc. Privately he was panicking over the volume of paperwork, books and empty bottles the place housed. He took his leave, kissing both of them on both cheeks. They were going for a steam and a dip in the ozone pool. Sophie had already provided Carla with a key to the flat, Barry didn't even need to have one cut.

As he left Chelsea Harbour, Barry felt sorry enough for himself to pop into the Firkin pub on Lots Road for a Dog-bolter. He sat on the wooden bench with the in-house copy of the *Telegraph* unopened in front of him on the table, and cursed his luck. Four Gauloises and two Dog-bolters later, he felt ready for the walk home up the King's Road.

Of all the boroughs of London, historic Chelsea must surely be the one to be used most often adjectivally: Chelsea Pensioners, Chelsea Flower Show, Chelsea Porcelain. There is a Chelsea Football Club, the Chelsea Shed, a Chelsea Arts Club, Chelsea Physic Garden and, of course, the famous Chelsea bun, which in the eighteenth century was a cinnamon cake considerably more refined than the lumpen twirls of dough now available under that name in sandwich bars. Barry considered, as he plodded slowly through World's End – deciding against a visit to the Water Rat for a quick chaser – whether Sophie should accurately be described as a Chelsea Tart. Chelsea Harbour, where she lived and conducted her affairs, is technically speaking in Fulham, but Barry was willing to overlook this inconvenient detail. As far as he was concerned, Sophie epitomised the very essence of the historic Royal Borough, a legacy going right back to Nell Gwynn's days, and should, if there were any justice, receive a fucking GRANT from English Heritage.

Although she was known by all as Sophie the Class Tart, she was in fact one of what are known in the trade as 'industrial debutantes'; amazingly good-looking women who have friends rather than clients, who can adorn powerful men at conventions, clubs and soirees. Women who expect their coats and doors to be held for them, who can often get away with the mere unspoken promise of sex in the future, and whose idea of a good time in bed is an early night in alone with their childhood dolls. 'Outlaws', that is to say, pimpless, they do not do 'tricks', but rather deign to receive 'gifts', which can, if one picks the right man, run to apartments, cars, hockable jewellery, and weeks in the Caribbean on private islands. Sophie was no flatbacker and prided herself that she had never had to hawk her fork for mere cash. She lived in a world where the men with the lucre preferred living out their James Bond fantasies in restaurants and at posh do's to a twenty-quid face-fuck in a back room with drawn curtains. Sophie was Top Trophy Totty, her finest asset being her conspicuous femaleness. She advertised this in the way she dressed, sat and walked. To be seen out with her could mean only one thing, that you were a man, and surprisingly, some of the most powerful men in the world are a little uncertain on this one.

Of course Barry Fox did not qualify as a man on any of these counts. He was not one of her gentleman friends; he was not even an also-ran. His relationship with Sophie was more that of 'hag's fag', with the proviso that he was not a homosexual. He had been her official walker on a few occasions in the past, when she had either been let down by someone more alluring or was attending a function which required a certain intellectual credibility; a book launch, say, or an awards ceremony. Sophie loved awards ceremonies and would block-book tables for all the big ones months in advance. The Oliviers, the BAFTAs, the Booker, the Whitbread; there was something about the tension in the air when the gongs came out which made Sophie tingle, and of course she was a slave to champagne. It is also at awards bashes that one tends to meet the high and mighty at their most emotionally charged and vulnerable. Many a winner had only realised how bored he was with his wife in the ecstatic afterglow of achievement, clutching his heavy statuette on his lap and stealing sly glances at the delectable Sophie on the next table. She always smiled back.

Barry decided he would take 'lunch' at the Arts Club and sort out his accommodation there first, then return to Tite Street to collect a bag of things. He crossed at the Beaufort Street lights, passing the VILE Bluebird complex on the other side of the road. Conran's newish all-purpose yuppie café did not appeal to Barry any more than did Richard Rogers' River Café or Norman Foster's glass mirror building at the bottom of Beaufort on the other side of the river. If it was reactionary to despise the magniloquence and ubiquity of post-modern design, then Barry was content to consider himself an old stick. And anyway, he'd always thought that Donald Campbell's record-breaking *Bluebird* high-speed car was built in Lots Road, where the auction rooms are, not at the petrol station at the bottom of Park Walk where the eponymous restaurant/shop complex now stands. 'What does Terence Conran know, the CUNT?' thought Barry, and then, on reflection, 'Probably a lot more than I do about post-modern design, actually.' The prospect of moving out of Tite Street, even if only for a few days, had put him into a grump, and he snapped at Max behind the bar at the Arts Club quite unnecessarily.

There were three main pictures in the window display which caught Oliver's eye. Two were of beautiful women in their underwear sitting in aeroplane seats with their safety-belts buckled up, the other showed a sweaty man with a washboard stomach standing high up on some scaffolding in just his briefs, which tightly encased an unmissably large bulge. Oliver wondered whether most women would find the sight of this muscular male torso and bulge as overwhelming and disturbing as he found the multitude of sexy images of girls and their underwear that he had been bombarded with since leaving the house only three hours ago. And the girls were all so pretty – that was important – and healthy looking. It wasn't that these displays necessarily made him instantly tumescent, but they commanded his attention at every bus stop and tube station. He felt them drawing him towards them. The seductive, dreamy eyes. The perfectly sculpted pelvic curves. He wondered, too, what these models were thinking; were they only there for money and their happy expressions merely good acting, a trick of the light? Or did they derive some pleasure from their exhibitionism and the inverted power that it gave them? These were not frowsty top-shelf suspender-and-garter people, but extremely fit young models with lambent complexions and luscious smiles. They were pedigree.

He walked stiffly past the Knickerbox shop at Waterloo station, trying to avert his gaze from its window display, hoping that the magnetic effect these pictures had had on him was not conspicuous. It was only twenty past four, but already the rush hour was homogenising commuters. None of the trains back to Clapham yet had departure platforms designated and so there was a large crowd of heavily coated passengers standing beneath the announcement board with their necks craned. The news stand billboard proclaimed it the coldest December day since 1973 and Oliver was wearing his embroidered Afghan hat. The speakers from a Save the Children market stall were distorting Christmas carols at high volume, and the clinking noises from shaken charity boxes competed with the garbled train delay announcements. Oliver decided to buy a cup of tea at the bagel stand, which took him reluctantly back past the Knickerbox shop.

His Tuesday group had once discussed the exploitation of women in advertising, and although they had collectively decided that it was simply another symptom of the disease of male oppression, Oliver felt sure that – as in the best democracies – not one individual opinion was entirely in agreement with the consensus. Privately, he suspected that the difference between erotica and porn is merely one of production values.

Oliver's journey to and from Old Street, where he had met with Rebecca to discuss the future of Andrea's 'Gaia' gallery, had been disturbing in many ways. Apart from the unwanted stimulation of the twenty-foot-high photograph of a perfectly rounded breast cupped in see-through black lace above the caption 'Move On Up!' on Old Street underground station, there were the middle-shelf magazine covers in the newsagent's and the plethora of 'brass-cards' in every phone box he walked by. Unwillingly, he had imagined phoning Mrs Peter Baldry, whose number was still burning a hole in the biscuit tin at the top of the kitchen cupboard. He was appalled to realise that the number was also still warm in the front of his mind. He had memorised it by mistake and tried to budge it out of place by thinking of other, nobler matters.

Rebecca and Oliver had sat in the tiny office booth of the gallery with only the warmth of a one-bar electric heater between them. The rest of the old warehouse space remained unheated in the half-light of the rapidly darkening December afternoon. Rebecca was hunched on the one modern piece of furniture in the room – the Hardicot Lewis orthopaedic chair which Oliver had bought for Andrea's forty-fourth birthday. Rebecca's feet not did not quite reach the floor. Oliver crammed himself into the nineteen sixties Rover car seat opposite her. Strewn around the floor were box-files and papers, amongst them a few remaining unsold exhibits, including a thunder twirling stick from Tasmania, and a frightening collage of rope and glue wrapped in charred cellophane made by a mental patient in New Orleans.

At about three thirty, when the sickly English semi-light from the ceiling window had faded, Rebecca turned on the anglepoise on the grey steel desk so that Oliver could still see the figures on the sheets of paper she had put in front of him. The Gaia gallery – it would have been plain even to a space cadet – was not doing well. Rebecca had been busy amortising in the two weeks since Andrea's death. Partly because it was something she knew how to do, but also because – as she explained to Oliver immediately on his arrival –

Andrea owed her some four months' salary. Rebecca had already given statutory notice on the lease of the building and cleared outstanding debts. These were thankfully few, but on the other hand, the list of potential credits worth calling in was also very small.

Oliver had been hoping to find Rebecca filled with some passion to keep the work of the gallery going, and had imagined, on the train journey there, that she might have a brochure of new exhibitions that had been planned by Andrea before she left for Chicago. Certainly Andrea had always led him to believe that Rebecca's enthusiasm for the project was second only to her own. He was surprised and disappointed to find instead that this reedy young woman in an old black suit and cream blouse seemed if anything to emanate a superior distaste for the place. Her manner during their conversation was formal and icy. When he asked if she had known that Andrea would be visiting New York as well as, or maybe instead of, Chicago, she stopped for a moment and then, avoiding his eyes, said, 'Please don't raise your voice to me like that. She hardly ever told me what was going on. And anyway, it's none of my business.'

Even though he had not shouted at Rebecca, Oliver felt it best to apologise. He could sense her anger searching for a home and it made him feel better to be the one who could contain it. As their conversation moved on to the subject of Andrea's outstanding tax liability, Oliver found himself thinking how a gentle jolt of the facet joints of her cervical spine would be good for her.

'I've applied to the Probate Registry for a Grant of Letters of Administration on your behalf. Unless you want me to execute it, that is. I'm assuming she didn't make a will. Unless you know of one. Do you know of one?'

She was racing ahead of Oliver now. He wished she'd offered him a cup of tea or something to warm up the atmosphere.

'Erm, no. I'm pretty sure she never made one,' he said.

'No. Not really the will-making type, was she?' said Rebecca in a tone which reminded Oliver of a maths teacher he'd once had. 'So, in fact, she's left a complete mess.'

Oliver had visited this gallery many times, and Rebecca had always been there. If not entirely cheerful, then at least amenable. But today he was finding her very difficult. Even with his overcoat still on, he could feel himself seizing up with cold in the awkward Rover car seat. The white-painted brick walls beyond their little room had a ghostly glow to them now, but the spirit of Andrea was not present. Her nightmarish administrative legacy was all that remained of her in the place.

'Intestacy is a pain in neck,' Rebecca went on. 'If you

don't sort it out, the Crown end up taking most of it. As Andrea's dependant you should make a claim now. I must warn you that I will be making one too. On a modest scale, of course, but she was supposed to be maintaining me as well.'

Oliver had never thought of himself as Andrea's dependant, but now it was put to him so brutally, he supposed Rebecca was right. He had always liked to consider himself and Andrea as equal contributors to the home pot. Each delivered what they could according to ability, equal if not in size then in intention. However, it was true that he had lived rent-free in Rylance Avenue for eight years, and during the first five of those, while he struggled to start his practice, his financial input had been negligible. The car was hers, the child was hers, the crockery was hers, the lifestyle was hers. All initially provided by Barry Fox, of course, as was the deposit on the gallery lease, but it was even more uncomfortable for Oliver to think of himself as a dependant of Barry's and so he quickly banished the thought.

'Even if you had been married, there's no such thing as a widower's pension. You ought to look into all this, if only for Felix's sake.'

Oliver could feel his shoulder blades tensing up like a twisted pair of tights.

'I hadn't really considered any of this,' he managed to say.

'And also, about the old man. Mr Fox. Did they ever actually get that divorce, do you know?'

'I'm not sure, I . . . assumed so.'

'I think not. No decree absolute as far as I know. Which could complicate things further. Who actually owns the house? That's what I don't know. Have a look through her stuff this evening if you're up to it.'

Oliver tried to shift in his seat, but finding himself wedged in, he curled deeper into his overcoat for the meagre warmth it provided.

'Thank you for all this. I'm obviously not doing my share here. I'm just a bit shocked, I think.' Feeling guilty about his lack of application, he told Rebecca he would of course act as the official administrator of Andrea's estate. A distant siren wailed outside, and there seemed little more to say. Oliver searched for the appropriate words to sum up the emotion of the afternoon, something to elevate their talk to the ceremonial. He was pre-empted by Rebecca, who let out a deep sigh and stood up as if she had been an interviewer and Oliver the failed job applicant.

'I hate her now,' she said quietly.

'I feel a bit angry too, if that's any help,' said Oliver as he heaved himself out of the uncomfortable chair and allowed Rebecca to lead the way along the dark corridor to the front door. 'It's almost as if I didn't know her at all, do you know what I mean?'

'No. I knew her all right,' said Rebecca, with

unconcealed bitterness. 'Look, she cleaned us out for this New York thing, and I don't think there's anything retrievable. Basically it appears she bought a lease over there. I'll see if I can put it on the market or whatever, but there may be a wagonload of inheritance tax to pay.'

Oliver stepped out on to the street. 'Well, thanks for all your work, and I'll definitely try and see that you get paid what she owed you if nothing else,' he said.

Stepping down from the crowded train on to the platform at Clapham Junction, Oliver felt a twinge in his lower back. A jarring little pain which ground into his left hip and sparked down the back of his thigh. He'd had this one before, a long time ago, before he became a student. In fact it had been a motivating factor in his choice of work. But it hadn't threatened for several years now. He hadn't yet been for his run that day and thought it advisable to give it a miss. He didn't want to aggravate his psoas muscle, which, since it is positioned between the base of the spine and the top of the hip joint at the pelvis, would be taking the strain on a jog.

Back pain is a hazard of being extra tall – as he would so often tell his larger patients – and good posture is everything. But correct posture is difficult to maintain when you are six foot four and most appliances, furniture and buildings are made for the privileged short majority. For Oliver, basins and sinks were set at a level just above his knees, and standing showers, of course, were almost unnegotiable since sprinkler heads were inevitably fixed to the wall at about his chest height. Cars had either not enough head room or not enough leg room, making him have to splay his knees either side of the steering wheel or cock his head to one side to see out of the windscreen. At parties, unless he found a convenient chair arm to perch on, he could not properly hear conversations going on below and became self-conscious about the perfect view other guests would have of the inside of his nostrils. Rebecca, for instance, who was petite, came barely up past his navel. He was frequently banging his head on low door lintels and had once concussed himself on a beam in a country-house hotel. For these reasons he was largely unaware of the authority and strength attributed to him due to his height, and would spend most of his time stooping to diminish himself in order to communicate with people on an equal basis. Also, being a professional, he knew enough about the psychogenic causes of his own pathology to realise that, apart from the cold spell in the uncomfortable car seat that afternoon, there might be other, more subconsious reasons, connected with Andrea and her death, for the nasty twinge which threatened the return of full-blown lumbar pain.

On returning to Rylance Avenue, he went into the surgery and, stripping to his shirt, pants and socks, stretched out face down on his osteopathic table. Even here, his legs extended over the end by a good eight inches. Hardicot Lewis did not make extra-long benches and he was not yet doing well enough to have one custom-built. The afternoon had flayed him. He tried to stretch his trapesius muscles, but everything there was rigid. Eventually he managed to drift into a sort of half-slumber by contemplating his 'homelodge' cabin, which it seemed was now never to be.

'Oh God oh God oh God oh God. I just want someone to rub my shoulders and tell me it's all right,' mumbled Barry into the mattress at the Chelsea Arts Club. 'I just want someone to hold me.' His brain was cut loose and tossed on a turbulent sea, and he knew that with the amount and variety of his alcohol consumption that evening, he fully deserved it.

Barry would often hug a pillow for comfort at night in Tite Street, and the ones at the Arts Club were lovely old-fashioned feathery ones, like those from his childhood. In fact, the whole place was very evocative if, like Barry, one had been to public school followed by Cambridge. The floorboards creak, the furniture is old and there is a gallery above the main club room rather like a choir stall. At the end of the brown corridor is a first-rate restaurant which Barry had not eaten in since 1994, where guests all sit around one gigantic long table which seems to have been made out of half a galleon from the Spanish Armada. One of the oldest clubs in London, and a devil to get into.

A membership induction night consists of all the applicants and their proposers hitting the bar at about eight, wearing pink and yellow carnation rosettes. There, they will mingle with the panel of the membership committee, wearing blue rosettes, for vetting purposes. These applicants have sometimes been on a waiting list for years. The committee then withdraw to discuss which applicants should be offered a place.

When Barry had arrived with his laptop and bag, just such an induction evening was in progress, so the large bar room with its full-size snooker table and church-pew wall seats was more crowded than on an ordinary night. He hadn't bothered going upstairs for a wash, but, dumping his things in the tangled coats corridor, had headed straight for the club room, whence he could hear the exciting hubbub of drunk people earnestly talking bollocks.

An old committee member of military bearing with a blue rosette on his tweed blazer was chatting to a hopeful cartoonist with a pink rosette pinned to his leather jacket.

'You say you've been here several times as a member's guest, and you got to like the place?'

'Yes, I feel very at home here.'

'Tell me, any misbehaviour?' The older man cocked an eye at the younger. 'Ever been so pissed and disorderly you had to be carried out of here and dumped in the street?'

'No. No, absolutely not.'

'Ah. Pity,' said the committee member, and imperiously moved on to his next interviewee.

Barry gently elbowed his way to the bar and ordered a large brandy from the lovely Mary, shouting slightly above the louder-than-usual hum. A voice from behind him bellowed in his ear and a crumpled fiver was pushed into his palm.

'Order me a pint of Freedom, you old git.' Another house custom is that only members are allowed to order from the bar. Behind Barry stood Tara, the flower girl, in a moth-eaten trench coat, with her hair in multi-coloured ribbons. She did not sport a rosette of any kind on her lapel and was not on any waiting list to join anything. She'd managed to gain entrance as the guest of some besuited elderly media man who was now lost in the mêlée, and she was drinking Freedom, a jumpy little lager brewed in Fulham. Barry pushed the fiver back to her and ordered two pints, one for each of them.

'It's ironic, isn't it,' she said, as they downed the first of many draughts, 'that I'm the only real artist here and they won't even let me buy a drink at the bar.' Officially, a condition of membership is being a visual artist of some kind, but in reality journalists, actors, poets and independent producers are numbered among the most illustrious of the club's members.

'You're also the youngest person here by several generations, my dear,' said Barry, flattered to be the gentleman of her choice for the evening. There were no seats available and so they clung to the bar.

'All the art here is pathetic,' she said, rolling a cigarette from her creased packet and then cursing as it fell into the spilt beer on the bar top. Barry bought her new papers and a half-ounce of Old Holborn. Personally, he liked the familiarity of the paintings on the walls at the Arts Club, some of which had been there for millennia, it seemed. He also liked the newer ones. Every now and then there was an exhibition, but he couldn't truthfully say he'd ever given them much of his attention.

'Looking nice on some wall is not what it's about. That's just lazy. You can't take things out of their social context and expect them to have some kind of independent merit any more.' Tara saw herself as a cutting-edge installation maker.

'Ah,' said Barry, pleased to have an appropriate quotation for every occasion. 'Today, it goes without saying that nothing concerning art goes without saying. Theodor Adorno, nineteen sixty-one.' And he knocked back his brandy in one.

'Exactly,' said Tara. 'The meaning of a piece of art cannot exist independently of its political content.' Tara's last show had been in a bakery, where she had painted long loaves of bread with multi-racial flesh colours, then let the dough rise in the oven. Not many people had come to it, but she had had a mention in the *Evening Standard*, most probably because of the piece's title, which was 'Penis Rising'. More drinks were ordered and paid for by Barry, while Tara told him that she would love to be allowed to take over the Arts Club for a day and put on a conceptual art exhibition.

'Somehow I don't think the old place is ready for the contents of your bin liners laid out symmetrically across the floor, or whatever,' he said. 'Although I for one certainly relish the thought.'

'Painting is dead,' Tara said.

'Or at least, as Foucault would have it, mere "idle visual pleasure",' quoted Barry, 'which in the overall scheme of evilness in the world has a fairly low ranking.'

Barry enjoyed Tara's company and her zeal, for which he held a considerable respect. However, his main motive for this dalliance was his own need, during waking hours, to massage the stimulus of abstract debate as a way of avoiding the more perilous ground of conscious introspection. It kept the engine of his thoughts ticking over, without the danger of them suddenly reversing up the cul-de-sac where his feelings resided. A murky place he preferred to avoid.

After an hour or two of badinage with the entertainingly aggressive Tara, Barry had steered himself out of the bar and pulled his now swilling body up the old stairs to dorm and lights out. After clinging on to the sink in his room for a few minutes of dizzy breathlessness, he'd dumped himself on the bed and dragged off as many clothes as he could manage. It was an hour later, when the swell from the bar below was beginning to subside, that he had suddenly thrust himself out of the bed again and stumbled across to double-lock the door. The thought of someone accidentally discovering him in the morning with his arms around a pillow like a soppy arse-wipe BABY had startled him awake. He returned to the warmth of the bed, and held on tight to the pillow again. He frightened himself with the sudden realisation that it was Andrea's magnificent back he was missing. That was what the FUCKING PILLOW had represented all these FUCKING YEARS and now she was a FUCKING PILE OF ASHES. Reassuring himself that the door was definitely locked, he kissed the pillow and fell asleep.

FIVE

'It might seem strange to you that we meet here every Tuesday, but let me try to explain. For too long a system existed where women were oppressed, lived in fear – even in their own beds – where they were forbidden to express their sexuality, relegated to a subservient role. Now women have changed. It might seem obvious to say, but traditional masculinity has had its day. We men have got it all wrong for thousands of years and now we have to change too.'

It had required a considerable amount of courage for Barry, he felt, to go back to Rylance Avenue the next Tuesday and face the awfulness of an evening of worthy psychobabble with a bunch of rope-sandalled melioristic lefties. He congratulated himself on his stoutness of heart as he rang the doorbell and stood on the step in the chill moonlit air. It was the last Tuesday before Christmas, which fell on a Thursday that year. Barry's bravery had been abetted by the fact that it also happened to be the night of the Chelsea Arts Club's Christmas party, and as a man with acute Noel-phobia, this was an event he was keen to avoid. Had his flat in Tite Street been available to him, he might, at this time of year, have cocooned himself in a duvet with a bottle of Cragganmore single malt and tuned in his old-fashioned Roberts radio to a Turkish station.

The door had been answered by a good-looking man in his mid-forties, Barry guessed, with neat silver hair. He was dressed entirely in dark blue, with his tie-less shirt buttoned to the neck.

'Hello, yes, I recognise you,' he said. 'Oliver told us you might be coming, well done!' He held Barry's arm rather too tightly and steered him towards the back of the house, indicating on the way that he should leave his scarf on the chair in the hall. Barry was, as usual, not wearing a coat.

'I'm George. Happy holidays!'

'It may be a holiday to you, mate, but the presses never stop in Grub Street.'

'Oh, do you still write for the papers?' said George. 'I didn't realise. Which one?' Barry gave him a brief résumé of what he had once dared call his career. If there's one thing worse than people full of Christian Christmas cheer, it's those politically correct ROD WALLOPERS who deny it its true and hideous nomenclature, he thought. Happy holidays? My dropped gut!

'I brought this little, erm . . . contribution,' he said, proffering up a bottle of Famous Grouse. No duvet or Turkish radio, but it would have been pointless to do without all three ingredients of the festive season.

'Oh, that's very kind of you,' said George, mistaking it for a Christmas gift, having failed to notice that the bottle had already been opened and relieved of a quarter of its contents. He put it down on the floor under the hall table. Although not forbidden, drinking was not something the Tuesday group usually indulged in, at least not until the halfway break. But as an appropriate gesture of Good Will Among Men, Oliver had put out a few glasses and some bottles from Sainsbury's New World selection. In addition to this, there were a couple of offerings from the other members. Barry was unaware of the fortuity of his timing; on any other Tuesday but this, there would have been maybe one bottle of Riesling between all six of them. However, there was evidently a fair amount of verbiage to get through before the alcohol would be touched. Barry sat on the sofa, trying to direct the focus of his attention on to the group discussion and away from the cluster of bottles on the sideboard in the dining area.

'It is sometimes difficult for us to realise, as men, that this systematic discrimination against women actually does mean that all men abuse all women. And I'm not just talking about the obvious fact that violence is almost entirely committed by men, always. There are other kinds of abuse.' It seemed that general discussion by the group was something which would have to wait until after George had finished his introductory monologue. 'There are a myriad of other ways in which this abuse happens. Like mocking, put-downs, twisting her words, not helping in the home enough, withholding emotionally, changing the subject, demanding sex, going on about money. These are all ways of trying to dominate your partner.'

Robert, a fat man in a suit and tie, shifted in the Arts and Crafts chair, making it creak. 'God, I do that,' he said, giving a self-conscious chuckle and looking around at the rest of the men for recognition.

'Which one?' said John, a miserable-looking bearded man who had moved a dining chair over to the window to have a discreet and non-invasive smoke.

'Well, all of that actually. That's me really, everything George just said,' replied Robert.

Barry took out a Gauloise and lit it, tossing the match into an empty coffee mug on the table. Oliver got up and brought the ash tray for him, removing the mug. 'We don't usually allow smoking in the main room, but since it's your first time we'll make an exception,' he said. Barry grumbled some words under his breath which could have been mistaken for 'Thank you, I appreciate the concession' but were in fact 'Bed-wetting little pansy.'

'And it's not an excuse to just say, "But as a man I have to be competitive and predatory, it's in my nature" ' George carried on, pleased with the self-flagellating reaction he was getting from the men. 'It's just not good enough to have a world where half of the species preys on the other half. That can't be natural, can it?'

There was that 'natural' word again. Apparently, George had once been an actor with the Royal Shakespeare Company – Barry had been told this within minutes of meeting him – and he had a very pleasant voice with clear diction and perfect vowels. His expression was earnest and his skin looked almost too healthy. That can't be natural either, thought Barry. Voice training and moisturiser. He wondered how long it would take for George to perfect his technique and become a politician.

Apart from Robert, there was only one other man in the room who was wearing a tie, a quiet black man called Michael, who sat smiling and listening. The average age of the group must have been thirty-five, Barry guessed, older if one discounted Claude, who was dressed in street gear and had too much gel in his tinted hair.

'Yeah, but it's still up to the guy to make the running, right?' said Claude. 'Which is unfair, because girls don't like this new-man thing. They don't find it sexy, right?' Claude was usually dating two or three girls at the same time. His life was complicated in this respect. The group envied him his insouciance, while covertly enjoying the stories he had to tell. George would often use him as an example when trying to prove the male backlash theory.

'That's just your well-known fear of commitment rearing its monstrous head again,' intoned George with a charmless smile. 'The only relationship you're interested in is the one you have with your own penis.' There was a small but general laugh.

Barry found that he was incapable of applying himself to empirical thought. He knew there were things – clever things – that he could be saying, no, ought to be saying, but the desert that his throat had become was making his tongue feel like the hide of a dead crocodile. He was breathing heavily and his gaze had begun to thrash around the room.

'Are you feeling OK?' Oliver asked him.

'To be quite searingly honest, I need a drink. *Nunc est bibendum.* So unless you chaps want to bury my dehydrated body on the patio, I think I should have one *in praesenti.*' He got up and stood swaying momentarily.

'We should wait really, someone else might turn up,' said John, the miserable-looking one, who had carefully wrapped his cigarette butt in the silver foil from the packet, but remained sitting on the dining chair by the window which he had left open to let the thick stench of Barry's Gauloise out of the room.

'No point in waiting for Keith,' said Michael, speaking for the first time. 'He's minicabbing again tonight. He said he'd drop by if a job brought him south of the river.'

The absent Keith, whose complicated timetable and financial difficulties meant that he was only a part-time member of the group, was a motorcycle mechanic whose live-in partner had left him with twins aged five.

At the moment he was working nights to pay for a two-year legal battle with Her Majesty's Government to be allowed parental responsibility over his own children. 'Where's Mummy gone?' they'd asked initially, and since she'd left no forwarding address and never rang, he'd told them she was with the Angels. The Hell's Angels, Nottingham Chapter.

'You must be wondering what the bloody hell you're doing here,' said George to Barry. 'And personally I wouldn't blame you, it does seem a bit odd at first!' His laugh was irritatingly high-pitched. Barry looked over his shoulder to see if there was a joke behind him which he had missed.

'Since the Industrial Revolution, we men have really missed out on the company of other men,' George continued, oblivious to Barry's need for the company of a bottle. 'Football and the pub,' George mimed inverted commas around the words 'football' and 'pub', 'are poor substitutes for the warmth and approval of men around you. Hairy men, real men. This is one of the malaises of so-called Western civilisation and didn't happen in so-called primitive cultures, if you'll excuse the word primitive.'

'And also if you'll excuse the word civilisation,' corrected John from the window, 'because that's only our white, male, Western value judgement.'

'And if you'll excuse the word excuse,' said Barry, joining in, 'which I personally find feeble to the extent of offence.' He swung over to the sideboard and grabbed the bottle of Côte Rôtie Chapoutier '96, the only expensive wine standing there. He was a man who could pick out the best bottle of red from seven paces, 'Might as well get this one down us at kick-off,' he said, 'because later on we won't be able to tell the difference, hopefully. Where's the corkscrew, old boy? Any guesses?'

'Oh, it's on the sideboard there,' said Oliver, after glancing across at George for approval. Barry was beginning to sweat a little with the delay.

'Just because our fathers didn't come across to us and give us a great big hug doesn't mean we have to be like that with our sons,' said Michael, who had not apparently taken any offence at being included in John's generalisation about white male value judgements.

'It was the nineteen fifties, for Jiminy's sake! Or in my case, the forties,' Barry choked. 'People didn't DO that kind of thing then, hairy, shaved or otherwise. Never mind fathers not doing it, mothers didn't do it! Fuck it, LOVERS didn't do it, if you'll excuse the word love in this context. And by the way, I definitely do not excuse the word hug. Disgusting New Age implications, don't you know.'

On the sideboard in front of him was an aeronautical-looking device in chrome, about the size of a Moulinex juicer. He concluded, rightly, that this must be the corkscrew and picked it up. It had moving arms and a hinged silver trap-door.

'Ah,' he said, examining it, 'the designer strikes again.' He inserted his finger into the cavity behind the trap-door to try and ascertain its bottle- and cork-receiving capability. He waggled its shiny wings and twiddled its unscrewable porthole. 'What the FUCKING HELL am I meant to do with this?'

New technology, particularly when combined with innovative design, was bad for Barry's blood pressure. He was proud to consider himself fogey enough to deplore invention when it interfered with the primary function of an object. Since the eighties, he argued, this tendency has become an epidemic. Indeed, in 1994 he'd run a campaign against all such devices in his column of the time, which had gone on most profitably for several weeks. The primary function of a toilet-paper dispenser is to give you toilet paper with which to wipe your arse. Yes, it runs out sometimes and the roll has to be replaced, but this is not reason enough to design a perspex tube in which the next three months' supply is stacked above the roll in use so that their combined weight makes it impossible to get one perforated square of tissue out, leaving one with little shreds under the fingernails. Nor is it an excuse, Barry had raged in print, for making millennium-wheel-sized toilet rolls housed in steel cabinets from which one has to coax the leader tissue by sticking ones fingers inside and whizzing the whole thing around like a giant roll of stale sellotape. Among other innovations, he had also successfully trashed those tape-mangling forward-reverse mechanisms on cassette players which prevent one from ever finding one's favourite track; double zips on jackets – intended for easy inside pocket access – which leave one exposed in the wind whilst staying irretrievably fastened at the neck; and even men's toiletry products which are so minty-spicy you can't even see yourself in the mirror when you shave – like rubbing Vicks vapour into your eyes. In every case, the secondary function destroying the principal reason for the object's existence, rendering it fit only for the museum of sad mistakes. He'd had many letters of support at the time, and someone had even printed up some stickers saying 'First prize, Neasden Institute of Crap Design' for use on any offending articles. Heady days. Barry enjoyed the privilege of his position as an armchair anarchist.

Robert, the overweight man in a suit, must have empathised with Barry's booze predicament, because he too had got up and was standing now with Barry trying to work out what to do with the silver rocket-ship corkscrew. The Chapoutier '96 had been his contribution to the evening's refreshments, and had cost him over twenty pounds. He had bought it from a specialist wine merchant on his way home from the City, and had no intention of leaving it entirely in the hands of a man who so evidently knew a cracking little red when he saw one. Finding the flow of discussion impaired by this activity, Oliver joined them at the sideboard. His long fingers quickly swivelled the thing on to the bottle, whipping the cork out with a low whistling sound.

'It works by a sort of suction,' he said, passing the bottle back to Barry.

'Hm,' said Barry. 'Just like my cock.' As the dank aroma wafted out from the bottle, Barry felt his saliva glands waking up, ready to receive the beautiful dark liquid. He snatched the largest of the assorted glasses he could see and poured himself a goodly goblet. He had glugged a dog's bellyful before the bottle was even back on the sideboard. About three pounds fifty's worth.

'You have all made the mistaken assumption, it would seem, that if you give a woman what she asks for, things will automatically go well for you, but I fear rather the opposite is the case,' Barry said, and waited for Robert to finish carefully pouring himself a glass before taking the bottle back off him for a refill. The first trickle of wine had acted like a quick spurt of WD40 on his rusty tongue.

'In my humble opinion, marriage is like a prison,' he went on. 'There's the slopping out, the dogs, the searchlights, the barbed wire. And that was just the honeymoon.' Claude, the younger man, laughed. George, who as the only one with any counselling experience was the unofficial leader and facilitator of the group, paused and gave a nervous smile. He tried to hide his displeasure at the disruption Barry was causing. Oliver was still standing next to Barry at the sideboard, so Barry poured a glass for him too, even though he had not asked for it. The bottle was nearly done.

Barry continued: 'No, it's worse than prison. At least you get time off for good behaviour in jail. In a marriage it's the other way round: the better you behave, the longer it goes on.' Barry's spinnaker was out now and there was no stopping him with the warm gurgle of the grape in him. He proffered the bottle around, and Claude got up to join them at the sideboard.

George took a deep breath and considered how he might gently guide the group back to its purpose, and his own agenda. 'Oliver tells me that you beat your ex-wife, Barry,' he said, with a slight lump in his throat.

'Does he? The little turd. The weasely turncoat ferret.' Barry shot a glance at Oliver, who sat back down with his glass of wine.

'Don't worry, everything we say in this room is totally confidential. We all agreed that before we started,' said Oliver by way of excuse. 'John once smashed his partner's front door in, didn't you, John?'

John nodded miserably from the window. 'Yeah, she was taking my kids away without telling me. All the same, that was no excuse . . .' He would have continued, but George glided across him.

'Is this violent abuse something you'd like to share with us, Barry?' asked George, the confident resonance of his voice returning.

'What is this? Maoist China during the Great Purge?' said Barry.

'It can be self-inflicted, and that can be just as bad,' said Michael, the quiet one, referring his remarks partially to George for agreement. 'Hitting your own head against the wall, smashing the furniture, drinking, taking drugs, even getting ill. Those are all kinds of abuse. That was my problem. I don't drink at all, or take drugs or anything, but I kept damaging myself and getting ill until I realised that what I was doing was just like rape . . .' George nodded his approval of Michael's confession while interrupting him.

'Yes. She only has to feel threatened for the finger to be pointed at you,' said George. Oliver pushed his glasses up his nose.

Barry poured the remainder of the wine into his glass, but stayed standing with Claude and Robert by the rest of the bottles. 'You all seem to be labouring under the illusion that my darling ex-wife, young Oliver's live-in share-partner, was a good person. She was not. Didn't stop me loving her. Still loving her actually, God damn her.' He took another large bolt of wine to quell the mawkishness in his tone. 'What's the matter with you all? If truth be known, she was an arsehole. A lying, cheating, narcissistic, self-centred, talentless shit. I'm sorry, Ollie old chum, but I'm sure you'll back me up on this. You may have been able to turn a blind eye to Andrea's ghastly need for constant attention and physical gratification, but I certainly couldn't take it. Her frequent trips to the Caribbean for what she liked to call 'banana research', her unrelenting search for multi-ethnic sexual experiences. That's probably why she got bored with me. I just wasn't capable of the she-worship she demanded as a fucking right.'

'She was a very insecure person I think, yes,' said Oliver weakly. Privately, he wondered how much of Barry's tirade was based on fact. 'I think she had a lot of emptiness inside.'

'You're telling me,' said Barry. 'When she went to the gynaecologist for a check-up, he looked up her and said: "Cor, I've never seen such a big one, cor, I've never seen such a big one." And she said: "there's no need to say it twice," and he said: "I didn't." '

Claude, the young lad, laughed loudly at Barry's joke. None of the other men in the room even cracked a half-smile. There was a short silence in which George inhaled thoughtfully and put his index fingers up to his lips.

Robert, who was miffed at the demise of his vintage wine, walked back to his seat and said quietly to the others, 'You know, I really do think I find this offensive. I mean, how much more of this do we have to listen to? I don't see it as very constructive for us as men to hear this. George?' George inhaled again, this time to speak, but he was interrupted by Barry.

'And by the way, the time she says I pushed her into

the dresser and she bruised her shoulder is a lie, as are any of the other accusations she freely hurled around to anyone who could be bothered to listen, and who will of course choose to ignore the constant stream of abuse she ladled on to me, including thrown plates, telephones and a hot steam iron. Insults and put-downs in public – something I never reciprocated, by the way – frequent full-on punches to the mouth, jaw, eyes, shoulders, stomach and groin, kicks to the shins, arms and ribs and a one-off attack with a pair of scissors for which I completely forgave her because at the time I really was asking for it and the whole thing was very funny anyway. In terms of unreasonable behaviour, if that's what you want to call it, I would say she matched me cut for cut, blow for blow.' Barry was spitting rather unpleasant dark brown saliva over the pastel Kashmir chair-throw now, and seemed to have lost all sense of where he was. Claude backed away and sat back down with the others. Barry stood a moment, out of breath and blinking.

'Yes,' said George, summing up, anxious for control of the group dynamic, 'I think you should look at what you've just said and think about it, and then maybe take responsibility for your own actions. It's amazing, and a tribute to Andrea's spirit, that she wasn't permanently damaged, psychologically.'

'Andrea? Not psychologically damaged? Come off it, old bean! The woman was damage incarnate, a veritable

Medusa; go within a five-yard radius of her and you'd need therapy! That was the attraction! That was what was so magnificent about her, don't you GET IT?' Barry was shouting now.

Michael rose awkwardly and walked slowly to the kitchen area. He was visibly upset by the discord and had decided to make a cup of tea. He asked meekly if any of the others would like one, but no one responded. Barry fumbled in his pockets and lit another Gauloise, this time tossing the used match into the empty Twiglet bowl on the sideboard. 'I'll say one thing for her though,' he muttered through the cough of his exhalation, 'she was a good housekeeper. After the separation, she kept the house.' Young Claude stifled another giggle.

John, still sitting at the window, tut-tutted. The space between his eyebrows knotted even further and he was chewing the trails of his moustache with some vigour. 'You're the kind of bloke,' he said slowly, 'for whom we should all hand out baseball bats, go round to your house and beat the living daylights out of you to keep you in line. If this was an African tribal village that's what we'd do. It would be up to us, as the men, to go and make sure that none of us got away with it.'

'Got away with WHAT?' shouted Barry. Realising he had finished the remaining Chapoutier '96 in his glass, he rummaged around for the next half-decent bottle and tried to figure out the corkscrew. He was abandoned to the confrontation now, and pulled a garish drunken face at George.

'I think what we're saying is – it's more a question of what you haven't done, actually, Barry.' said George with an annoying kindly smile. 'Like face up to your own actions. That kind of thing.'

'I gave her my NAME, which incidentally she still has. I gave her this bloody HOUSE, for fuck's sake, gentlemen, in which you meet to HUMILIATE each other every week. I gave her my SOUL, my BALLS on a PLATE.'

Robert picked up again. 'I . . . I . . . can't take any more of this. I really don't think we should allow this kind of . . .' He stood as if about to leave.

George looked across at Claude, the one least under his control. Claude felt he had better side with the winning team. 'Yeah, calm down, mate. I mean, OK, she might have been a bitch, but it's like you hate them all.'

'On the contrary, it seems YOU don't give the ladies much credit, come to think of it.' Barry was addressing his remarks to George now, although it had been Claude who had spoken. 'All women for the last two millennia were just simpering little GIRLS, were they? Incapable of acting in their own best interests until my lovely but misguided friend, Germaine, came along and told them how to THINK? Is THAT what you believe? You don't give women much VOLITION, do you, don't give them much RESPECT!' Barry was spluttering now, and red in the face. His attempts to manipulate the corkscrew into bottle-opening mode were contributing to his apoplexy. He was banging the thing on the sideboard. 'How d'you get this CUNT OF A CONTRAPTION to fucking WORK?' he yelled.

'Don't you think you've had enough to drink already?' said Michael from the kitchen.

'Of course I have! I've had enough drink to last me several reincarnations, that's the point, you BUTT-PLUNGING PISS-ANTS!'

George sighed. Managing to stay calm in the face of Barry's performance was giving him a kind of self-satisfied glow. 'Claude's right, Barry. I think you should sit down, take some deep breaths and think about all this. We're not having a go at you, or persecuting you. But equally, I think it's fair to say that we're not here to rake over the coals looking for excuses for your violent and abusive behaviour.'

'No, exactly, EXACTLY. That would be too hot for you to handle, wouldn't it? Go on, pick up one of those coals, pick it up, I DARE YOU! And hold it glowing in your hand. Whoever can hold it the longest gets to shag all the birds. That's what being a MAN is all ABOUT and you don't like it because it isn't FAIR, it's too much of a competition and you're afraid you might LOSE. You want to make up new rules so a shower of HALF-PINT TINHORNS like you can get a turn. You can't control sex, you know, it's a fucking CAULDRON.'

'It's a question of evolving . . .' George began, but Barry careered into his sentence.

'Don't you evolve any more, you're OVER-evolved, you lot. If you're not careful you'll evolvulate up your own VULVAE.'

'I don't think this is getting us anywhere,' said John. 'The man is completely out of order. Oliver?' He looked to Oliver, who he felt as host should be doing more than cowering silently in his seat.

'Yes?' said Oliver, looking to George for guidance. Robert intervened.

'I really don't need this,' he said. 'It's nearly Christmas, and if we're going to have this kind of . . . offensive evening, I might as well be at home with my wife.'

'Gentlemen,' said Barry, recovering a modicum of composure, 'I can see my palaeolithic attitudes have caused offence. You would like me to leave, I shall. I need to take a leak in any case. Anyone else fancy coming to siphon the python? Or perhaps a bout of arm wrestling on the patio? No? Very well, I shall abandon you to your tendentious ratiocinations.' Grabbing the nearest bottle, which happened to be an inferior Italian white, he sashayed out of the room and into the hall, colliding with the architrave of the intervening door before closing it with gentle aplomb.

On the front doorstep, the cold of the night air

slapped Barry's hot cheeks, giving him a surge of bracing pleasure. Breathing deeply, he shivered and spun the top off the bottle of Famous Grouse. He had retrieved it from the front hall on his way out, leaving behind the unopenable Italian white along with his scarf. He tossed the lid of the whisky bottle into a rosemary bush and gulped down the equivalent of three doubles like a seagull gobbling herring. Then, stretching his arms wide above his head, he gave a triumphant howl at the moon. Somewhere a confused blackbird was singing in the orange glow of a street lamp, but apart from that, and the ambient hum of traffic on the Tooting Road, it was quiet and still. Without putting the bottle down, Barry undid his fly and, with his right hand, fingered his cock out of its warm nest and into the icy-crisp night. The wee came easily and steam rose off the patterned Edwardian tiles on the front doorstep. He was losing heat fast.

'The trouble with most men is that they get together with a woman first, and then grow up later, if at all. Which of course is the wrong way round,' Michael was saying, back in the warmth of the room.

'Yes, they strut around, thumping their chests, exploding their weapons in an endless contest for status. A hopeless quest for proof of their superiority over women,' added Robert, whose superiority over most of the population had been assured since birth.

Oliver was uncomfortable with the way the group had moved on so swiftly after Barry left. George deftly changing the emphasis with a quick: 'You can't force people, you know, it has to come from them. He knows where we are when he needs us, it has to be his decision.' Michael had made his tea and Robert had been persuaded to sit down again and stay. John had said, 'Pathetic!' as Barry closed the door, Claude successfully put Barry's outburst out of his mind by saying, 'Poor old git,' a sentiment they had all seemed to agree with, and the men had moved forward as one. Except for Oliver, who felt that since he was responsible for bringing Barry, he was also in some way responsible for his departure.

George picked up on a point which Oliver had mentioned earlier. 'For instance, I think, funnily enough, that a good example of controlling behaviour is Oliver's worry over Andrea's being in New York rather than Chicago.' He had not been made aware of the exact details of Andrea's demise. 'She was on a business trip, right? For thousands of years it's been men in that position. It's hard for men to give up this control over the means of power, but give it up we must.'

'All in war is SO cold! The future none can SEE, I toss my coin to SAY, in LOVE with me you'll stay! Because ALL IS FAIR IN LOVE!' On either side of the three shallow front steps were low grey-stone walls, no more than a foot high, forming a sort of banister, with two tubs containing small cordyline trees at ground level by the front gate. Having kicked off his shoes, Barry was standing in his socks on the left-hand wall next to the rosemary bush, singing his favourite Stevie Wonder song. Invigorated by the keenness of the sudden temperature drop, he had just decided that life was a marvellous and exhilarating gift when he toppled into the hedge, scratching his face and winding himself. He sat there out of breath, tangled among the winter twigs, and felt the wet of the frosty earth seep through the seat of his trousers.

Excusing himself from the others, Oliver walked into the hall and, noticing the scarf still on the table, went out into the street to see if Barry had gone far. He found Barry's shoes on the path, and as he bent to pick them up, spotted the man himself. 'What are you doing?' he said. 'Are you all right?'

'I may be pissed as a three-day-old fart, but the brain still works like this, you know. In fact, it works better.' Oliver tried to help him up, but Barry grabbed hold of his lapel, pulling him down, and challenged him to a mud-wrestling match. They grappled noisily on the ground for a few moments. A woman in a white raincoat walked past like a ghost, her high heels clicking on the pavement. Her pace quickened once she was past the men; they must have frightened her. With his neck in a head-lock it was difficult for Oliver to get his opponent on to his feet, but he managed, with effort, to escort Barry and his shoes back into the house, where the dry warmth from the central heating immediately nuzzled up against them like a lazy cat.

Hearing the commotion of their re-entry, George came to the meeting-room door, shortly followed by Robert, who pushed past him. 'Look, I really am going to have to go, you know. No offence, Oliver. And Happy Christmas everyone.' He grabbed his City coat and briefcase from the hall and almost ran down the path, slipping slightly on the step still wet from Barry's urine. Claude followed him immediately, no doubt thinking of more suitable and romantic ways to spend what remained of his evening. It looked as if Barry had successfully dispersed Oliver's biscuit club.

Barry had gone blotchy with the second sudden temperature change, and his cheek was bleeding slightly from the fall. By chance, or the instinct of the experienced, he was still holding the now nearly empty bottle of Famous Grouse. Oliver tried to relieve him of it and sit him down in the hall chair, but he was lurching uncontrollably. 'Let go of me! I'm all right!' Barry slurred. 'Stop fussing!' Both men smelled like a lamb roast from the rosemary bush outside. Barry, however, was looking unsavoury, and George suggested making him a cup of black coffee. Michael went to the kitchen to see to it, while John stayed in the back room by the window.

'At least she was hot!' Barry said, looking as fiercely as he could up into Oliver's eyes. 'She was passionate. If I went out for a night with her, I could just relax because she would do all the fighting, she would wind people up who deserved it. Like HIM!' And he indicated George. 'He'd have lasted five seconds with her – proselytising SWELL-HEAD.' George gave a studied sigh of resignation at this insult. 'She'd show off, she'd dance on tables. I adored her, she had espr . . . espr . . .' He was swaying now. '. . . Spirit. She had spirit. I could just sit back and watch the trouble she caused. I admired her . . . her . . . what's the word?' He tried to draw himself up to eye level with Oliver and belched involuntarily. '. . . Her . . . what's the fucking word? Edmond Rostand, *Cyrano de Bergerac*. You know . . .' Failing to finish his sentence, he seemed to rally himself. 'And now if you'll point me in the direction of the little boys' room, I think I need another slash.'

Oliver had installed a small understairs macerator-toilet in the front hall for clients. Leaning on the stair banister for support with one hand and slurping from the whisky bottle with the other, Barry ducked into it and closed the door. It had a brass swing lock on the inside which, with a little fumbling, he managed to slide shut.

'I'm really sorry, George, I had no idea he was as bad as this,' said Oliver. He and George had moved into the kitchen to join Michael, who was looking through the cupboards for the instant coffee. 'It's in the drawer by the cooker,' said Oliver, and found himself checking to see whether Michael's search had taken him to the biscuit tin where Mrs Baldry's phone number lurked.

In the small compartment under the stairs, Barry's breaths were longer and deeper than he thought himself capable of. Standing in the only full-height part of the tiny room, he thought of himself as a felled bull lying in the sawdust waiting for the thrust of the matador's sharp blade. And then it came. Yow! A sudden tightened knot in his upper left arm followed immediately by a streaking, burning arrow of pain across his chest. He let out an incoherent croak, which was instantly stifled by the stabbing in his neck. He felt as if a watermelon was being crammed down his throat, and his legs gave way. He slumped on to the toilet seat, banging his knees against the pipes of the mini-basin and dropping the bottle, then toppled sideways, knocking his head on the flush handle. The engine of the macerator started up. Barry's eyes rolled up into his skull, and then bounced back. 'Panache!' he managed to gasp. 'That's the fucking word! Her PANACHE!'

SIX

Carla was not having as chic a Christmas in Chelsea as she had anticipated. She had found the inside of Barry's flat totally disgusting, and for the first couple of days had concentrated on clearing all of his horrid old books and bits of paper into the top of the bedroom wardrobe and locking it. Then, holding her nose, she had removed all the hippy throws from the creaky armchair and the sofa and dumped them underneath the shoe rack in the hall cupboard. She'd been up the King's Road to buy bleach and polish and carpet shampoo – all of which had been absent from Barry's undersink space for some years – and spent the rest of the week putting her back into awkward positions to eradicate any recumbent traces of nicotine- and tar-enhanced grime. As far as she was concerned, Barry was an animal and she set to her work very much as a zoo-keeper might spray down the elephant house.

There were a few items which she was unable to improve – a couple of rotten dark-brown cork tiles in the kitchen by the fridge, the yellowing and charred plastic of the lighting rose in the bedroom, a creeping grey footprint of mould on the bathroom wall – but generally by the end of the weekend she was satisfied that there was no trace of Barry in the place – no aftertaste – and on Monday she made a second trip down the King's Road to buy new and colourful throws for the sofa and armchair and some pretty tasselled light shades, which were cheap for Chelsea, to replace the horrible yellowy parchmenty ones. And she hadn't been able to resist a small lacy pillow to put on the bed. She couldn't afford new bed linen, not until the sales, but she'd double-laundered the stuff she found. Barry's remaining clothes and shoes she slid to one side of the wardrobe, closing and locking the door on them so that she didn't have to see them at all. And she stacked his framed pictures of theatre first nights, original Punch cartoons and the odd erotic etching in the hall beneath the coats, replacing these with posters from the Design Centre and the Conran shop.

Her trips to the outside world of Chelsea – to the supermarket, the laundry, Habitat – were always first thing in the morning. After four o'clock she'd stay in, because by that time, she told herself, Eco might be up and about and trying to find her. He was a night person. After all this activity she had become bored and almost felt like going out to The Main Squeeze, or Crazies or the 162, flossed up in a short one and fishnets all by herself and waiting for Eco to hear about it and get wound up and come after her. At least that would be something. She might be able to ruin his Christmas, and ruin it for whatever fat minge he was screwing now. But then he'd be in her life again and she didn't want that. No. No way. Sophie, her so-called benefactor, had seemed to understand that and said she was her friend, but now Sophie had left her here in this dull flat which had smelt like really bad when she first got here. And Carla had not been invited again to Chelsea Harbour, nor anywhere else for that matter; no Christmas Eve party to look forward to, no club opening gala, not even a little lunch at The Brasserie or Thierrys. Bitch. Sophie was meant to be looking after Carla. No cute male admirers, no girlie friend, and Barry's telly was a wobbly old thing with a video machine that must have been made in the seventies before she was born! I mean like, is that sick or is it sick? Carla thought. And she was going to have to get some money in or she wouldn't be able to buy more things. All in all, the whole thing was turning out to be pants.

One of the shops on the King's Road which Carla had visited was Lush. Not a trendy off-licence as one might imagine from its name and location, but a purveyor of extraordinary rough soaps. The counter looks like that of a delicatessen: giant cubes of soap stand there like enormous uncut cheeses and customers buy them by the slice. The smell in there is overpoweringly pleasant since these multicoloured soaps have interesting stuff in them: herbs, seaweeds, pine cone, even garlic. Along the back wall are buckets of ready-cut soap chunks and various novelty products such as Valentine's Day soaps, massage oils with bits of twig in them, and 'bath bombs'. A bath bomb is a sweet-smelling ball, about the size of a large lemon, which when tossed in a hot bath, will fizz and pop itself to nothing, leaving the bath full of aromatic oil and bubbles. Lovely, thought Carla, and bunged three into her wire basket, along with the bergamot and tea tree soap and a kelp and tangerine facepack.

Back at Phoenix Mansions in Tite Street, she had just slipped off her Capri pants, run a bath and plopped the bath bomb into it when the doorbell chimed. She immediately turned off Barry's old radio, which had been tuned to Heart and was now standing in the steam on the toothbrush rack. She stood absolutely still and listened, trying to control her breathing rate. The bell rang again. Her feet were quite chilly on the bathroom floor, but her neck was getting hot. She was afraid. What if it was Eco? With her heart beating fast, she tiptoed to the front door to look through the spyhole, and to put the chain on the latch if necessary. Halfway there, she realised that it might of course be Barry Fox, who had his own key, and she was half undressed. She went back and fetched her silk mini-Happi coat from the back of the bathroom door. In its dying throws, the remains of the bomb sank to the bottom of the bath, still effervescing weakly. Poo, she thought. The whole fun is watching them fizz.

The bell went again, this time more insistently. She returned quietly to the front hall and peered out throught the spyhole. It wasn't Barry Fox, nor was it Eco. She felt a little deflated by that. She had got all scared and worked up in case Eco shouted at her through the door or tried to break it down or something, and it wasn't even him. It was some other bloke she didn't even recognise standing out there. She wasn't going to bother answering the door to him; he didn't look particularly hunky, he didn't have flowers or anything, and he wasn't in uniform. She would have liked to put the chain on now, but he'd hear that and know there was someone in and then not go away, and she'd have to actually deal with him. Which would be a total arse ache.

She sneaked back to the bathroom and took out another bath bomb and dropped it into the bath. You couldn't have too much oil in a bath, could you? As the bomb started to bubble and crack, Carla heard the unmistakable sound of a key in the front door, which then swung open suddenly and a massively tall man was in her front hall looking around.

'Hello?' he called, and caught sight of her standing, startled, in the bathroom doorway in her little silk dressing gown and knickers. 'Oh God. Sorry. I thought there was no one in,' he said, but didn't turn his eyes away from her. 'So I thought it would be OK. Sorry.'

He wasn't that bad-looking after all, quite boyish.

Specs. The lens of the spyhole must have distorted him. Very tall. That was good. A bit goofy. Kind face, but what was that he had on his head? Some kind of turban thing with ear flaps? He was still staring at Carla like a schoolboy.

'I've just come to pick up some of Barry Fox's things, if that's OK. Sorry to burst in on you like that.'

'Ooh, you gave me such a fright just then, darlin',' she said, fanning her flushed cheeks with her fingers. Closing the bathroom door behind her, she came into the hall. 'I was just about to dive into a bath.'

'I'm sorry. I won't be long, he told me where to find everything. Or should I come back later?'

'No, no. Come in.' She was glad of company, especially male, especially tall. 'Would you like a cup of coffee?' She smiled at him casually.

'Do you have any mint tea, or anything like that?' He closed the front door and followed her towards the kitchen. He noticed the silk of her short housecoat clinging to her thighs and getting a little caught up where her knicker elastic curved up above her buttocks.

'Actually, I moved all of Barry Fox's books and stuff into the bedroom cupboards, I hope that's all right,' she said, putting the kettle on. 'It was such a sight in here when I got here, you wouldn't believe it. And it really smelt. I've got decaffeinated instant if that's any good?'

'That'll be fine,' he said. Oliver hated instant.

★

Minutes after Barry's collapse in the toilet at Rylance Avenue, Keith, the minicabbing single father of the Tuesday group had arrived, with apologies for missing the first half of the evening. He had been surprised to find the group in such disarray and it had been he who forced the door of the understairs cubicle, using the Icelandic metal fish sculpture which hung on the wall in the hall. He and Oliver had managed to extricate Barry from the room and carried him immediately to Keith's people-carrier, a Subaru seven-seater. Oliver and George had travelled with Keith to the hospital while Michael stayed to look after the house. John had skulked off home with his depression.

The nearest Accident and Emergency department was five miles away towards Vauxhall, and so Keith drove fast. Although not entirely helpful, George had assumed the role of leader and shouted directions from the front passenger seat. Barry's face had gone a greeny white and it frightened Oliver, who was sitting with him in the back of the car.

St Mary's Hospital, Stockwell, must have missed out on the modernisation schemes which swept through London hospitals in the eighties and early nineties. In its concourse it has no hairdresser, no American hamburger concession, no easy-access financial services counter and no cappuccino-serving cafeteria with large weeping-fig trees in it. The last time an architect was allowed near it was 1912. The part-time florist and sweet shop are housed in a shack by the front gate, after which a maze of one-way roads lead one round the back of its six forbidding buildings and out again by the exit gate without any possibility of stopping the vehicle. The miniature car park is very well concealed, and unless you have the right coinage, your car will be clamped. To keep the hospital traffic slow, there are sleeping policeman bumps every seven yards. Barry let out an inhuman grinding sound as the the four-wheel-drive car jolted over each one. Since his rescue from the toilet, he had managed to say only: '*Plures crapula quam gladius*' – drunkenness kills more than the sword. On their third circuit of the hospital one-way system in search of somewhere to alight, Keith decided to drive into the no-go area of the ambulance bay and argue with the uniformed warden while George and Oliver lifted Barry out of the car and hovered with him waiting for help. From inside his hut, the receptionist called for a porter with a trolley and nurse, and then returned to his TV game show.

'You can't leave that car here,' the warden was saying. 'This is a no stopping area.'

'No. I'm not going to. Just dropping someone off,' said Keith, who, having given his seasonal greetings to George and Oliver, got back into his car and drove home to relieve the baby-sitter.

'You can't drop off here,' said the warden to Oliver.

'Oh, sorry. But I'm fairly certain this man's just had

some kind of a heart attack and I think we ought to get someone to see him fairly soon or it could be really quite bad for him.'

Barry had indeed had some sort of aortal malfunction or angina pectoris. Either way, his arteries, which over the last decade had become like the inside of a works' canteen kettle, had given up, leaving his heart muscle to cope. And that now resembled an overstuffed pâté. He was ten pounds of sausage meat trying to get into a five-pound skin. After some minutes an almost antique wheelchair arrived and Oliver and George were directed to take Barry through to see the triage nurse, who would decide – rather like in *Alice in Wonderland* – which door he would be going through. On examining an incoming patient, a triage nurse has three questions to ask her – or himself – hence the name 'triage': one, are you ill, but can wait twenty-four hours or so for treatment? Two, are you critically ill and immediate treatment will benefit you? Three, are you so ill that treatment is not a priority? Unfortunately the triage principle was invented before the days of dissolution and disillusion in the National Health Service and so there is no fourth question; are you very ill but going to have to wait a year or two to have diagnostic X-rays of your condition to tell us what treatment you might have needed had you survived? And there is certainly no fifth question: what's the point of it all? Why not give up this ridiculously underpaid job and run a bar in Spain instead? Barry, it was decided, was in need of instant attention. Oliver had been right.

George was beginning to irritate Oliver. He kept using his resonant voice and self-important attitude to make it look as if he was in charge of the three of them, while not actually doing much of any consequence. It was as if he believed that merely by being reassuringly authoritative he could lessen the awfulness of events, relaxing those around him. The opposite was true, of course: the more he tried to control, the less communicative people became. Oliver pushed Barry in his chair into the large, bed-carrying lift, where George made much of pushing the floor buttons and asking the way.

'You needn't stay if you don't want,' said Oliver. 'I'm sure Barry'll be all right now.'

'Bollocks,' mumbled Barry. 'Definitely not all right, going to die.' Despite Oliver's hints and Barry's hostility, George stayed with them during the electro-cardiograph tracing test, where wires were attached to Barry's arms, legs and chest.

'Oh dear oh dear oh dear,' said the frighteningly young white-coated doctor. 'Overdoing it a bit, have we?' Barry's eyes ranged wildly around the room. Oliver felt sorry for him, he looked scared and vulner-able. George asked intelligent questions about the rolling graph paper on which the automatic pen scratched the alarming bunch of blue wiggles which mapped Barry's chances. Oliver put his hand lightly on Barry's shoulder to reassure him. It was like touching a central-heating radiator. The doctor took some blood and Barry was given a clot-busting injection, and then they were told that he would have to stay in for forty-eight hours to be monitored with further sequential blood tests to see if his cardiac enzymes had been raised.

'You've had a sub-endocardial infarct, I'm afraid, mate,' said the doctor. 'Which just means a heart attack.' His accent was a perfect Surrey-Cockney mix. 'We're going to put you on aspirin, seventy-five milligrams a day, and ask you to come back in six weeks to see how you're getting on, maybe do another ECG, put you on a treadmill, and if you're very lucky we might give you an angiogram, which is a kind of X-ray to find out what's going on in there, to see if anything more needs to be done. But you've got to stop smoking and go easy on the drinking, mate.'

Barry managed a barely audible 'Fuck off.' Oliver made sure that it was he and not George who took the paperwork and forms when the doctor had finished, although George had reached for them. This had made Oliver feel proprietorial enough to put down Rylance Avenue as Barry's address. Had Barry possessed private medical insurance, he might have been fitted with a self-inflating tube – or stent – to help his heart valve, or even given bypass surgery that night. As it was, he would have to join the queue of those waiting up to a year for a diagnosis. Barry's main worry at this point in time was that the forty-eight-hour sojourn in hospital would take him through to Boxing Day and hence would mean enduring two days of unbearable hospital Christmas jollity, helplessly pinned to the bed while nurses, health visitors, do-gooders and QUAKERS even, were allowed to foist their obscene positivity and goodness on him. He was feeling fragile, and even he was aware of how ripe he smelt. His excessive sweating earlier had left salt lines in every crevice.

Oliver had gone all the way to the exit of the hospital with George, and even said goodbye to him as if he were going home himself, seeing him into a taxi before turning round and going back up to where Barry was. He didn't want Barry to lie there all night thinking that all of the Tuesday men despised him, that his group had somehow brought on the attack. He had seen Barry frightened and vulnerable and found that difficult to bear. He drew up a little stool by Barry's bed and sat there for a short while. Barry looked exhausted now, and his eyes were drifting in and out of focus.

Sitting next to Barry, Oliver felt something of the nervous anxiety he had experienced as a boy when addressing his father, whom he had idolised until, when he was twelve, his mother had taken him and his sisters to live in Kent. From that point on, any talk of his father was forbidden and Oliver had seen the man infrequently for ten years and then not at all for the last thirteen. The initial interchange of letters had become pointless and eventually dwindled to nothing.

Oliver couldn't think of anything to say or do. He wanted to encourage Barry to survive, to be happy even. He thought of taking his hand, but did not do it. That would probably have given a man of Barry's sensibilities and generation another attack. Oliver felt now a smaller amount of that same yearning he had had in his father's absence: for approval, for disapproval even. Just for some acknowledgement of his own existence.

Barry was playing his part in this well. He scowled disdainfully at the display of human philanthropy spread before him. 'I want my radio,' he rasped, 'and I have to write a piece for the *Express* by Thursday morning, so I'll need my laptop.'

Oliver tried to persuade him to forget work. He took the name and number of a contact at the newspaper and promised he would tell her of Barry's condition in the morning. Barry had various other requests for items which Oliver wrote down on a scrap of hospital paper, along with the address of the Chelsea Arts Club. He took the keys out of the pocket of Barry's trousers, which were hanging in the bedside locker, and left the ward. He had been happy to be of some use.

By the time he got back to Rylance Avenue after his jaunt to Chelsea to collect Barry's things and his meeting with Carla, Oliver was in a state of anxiety. For the first

...he ever, it seemed to him, he had met a woman – one with whom he had managed to have twenty-five minutes or so of ordinary, pleasant conversation over a cup of coffee – who was not a client, who was wearing very little, and who was extremely, unbelievably, wildly attractive to him. His heart rate was up, his sphincter had tightened and he'd had an erection all the way home on the 38 bus. Everything about her had turned him on: the curve of her spine, the muscles above her knees, even the slightly glazed, stupid look in her eyes. The curl of her mouth, the crackling huskiness in her voice.

It was Christmas Eve, and although he had remembered to buy a tree, it remained undecorated in the corner of the front hall. Christmas cards lay in piles on the sideboard, not displayed across bookshelves or strung on lines as they were most years. There hadn't seemed any point, with Felix staying in Manchester and Andrea gone. In fact – Oliver dared to think – the house and everything it stood for was pointless now. For eight years it had been he who made sure they had some kind of celebration at Christmas, despite Andrea's preference for paganism or a holiday in the sun. Oliver had thought he was doing all this for her and Felix's sake – to keep them all glued together. Now he could not think why he had bothered.

He left the kitbag with Barry's things in it by the front door and went to the kitchen, but he could not settle. He went to his practice room to listen to any messages;

there were none. He felt Andrea watching him reproachfully. Not only was he allowing Felix to stay away, but he was not bothering to have a Christmas at all. The fact that an alive Andrea would in reality have been delighted to skip Christmas completely did not change his feelings of guilt and responsibility. He sat for a while on the sofa in the living area of the back room.

Now there was nothing to stop him ringing this woman he had met today, this Carla, if he so chose. He didn't have to hide his interest in her from Andrea or anyone else. He didn't have to qualify it by saying the girl was dumb, or had naff taste, or was tarty, tacky, dopey, dizzy, piggy or politically incorrect. He allowed himself to remember the plunge of her breasts beneath the dressing gown, the placement of her neck when she laughed, the flatness of her belly. He felt ashamed at his relief that he would no longer have to banish these thoughts from his mind, no longer have to claim to be uninterested in flat bellies and muscular legs, in the shape of waists and thighs. He would never have to pretend again that he didn't mind about stretch marks, hanging underarm flesh and nipples like prunes. Never have to pose as that rare – almost impossible – man in love with the whole person, not just the appearance; a man oblivious to all the signs of Andrea's seventeen years of seniority over him.

The shame of these awful, ungrateful thoughts only increased Oliver's excitement and agitation, and, inevitably, his erection returned, more insistently now than on the bus. He got up from the sofa and roamed around the ground floor. He went halfway up the stairs and gazed out of the window on the landing. It was a bright day with enough light on the bare trees to inspire a French Impressionist painter. A tingle of freshness tripped along the surfaces of Oliver's flesh. He could not settle, he just could not settle. It didn't seem right to him to be in this house at all today. Not right at all. Only a week ago, it had been an ocean liner of which he was, if not captain, then at least first mate. Now it was untethered and had drifted into strange waters where he did not have to go, where he did not want to go.

He dialled 141 before ringing the number, so that if it went badly he would be untraceable. He coughed while the phone rang, and hummed a little to make sure his voice would be neither croaky nor too high-pitched if he had to speak. He was as tense as a teenager arrested for drugs. The pain at L4 returned and his mouth went dry. His tongue felt like a pebble in the sun. After many rings, the phone at the other end was picked up, but no one said hello. There was a silence, but it was the silence of a room in which someone was holding a phone receiver and not speaking, not an electronic line-dead type of silence.

'Hello?' Oliver said in a croaky, high-pitched voice. He was sure he could discern breathing from the other end. 'Hello?' he said again. 'Are you there? It's me,

Oliver, the bloke who came round earlier today?'

'Oh, hello. Sorry about that, darlin', the phone just went funny,' Carla lied. Always let them speak first, find out who it was, then you could hang up if you didn't like them, or if you wanted to make them mad at you. 'Yes?' she said, and waited for him to explain why he'd rung, as if she didn't know. Might as well make him work for it.

When Oliver asked her if she wanted to go out for a drink with him, she feigned enormous surprise, but asked when. He hadn't expected to get this far and so hadn't planned any suitable dates. Falteringly, he suggested that very evening, Christmas Eve, but then immediately apologised and rescinded the offer because he assumed she would have other, grander plans. He explained that the only reason he happened to be free was that his partner had just died and her son had decided to stay in Manchester for the whole Christmas holiday. In his nervousness he said too much that was true and not enough that was charming.

'Aaaah, you poor thing. I might be able to meet you in the early part of the evening, but I'm going out with friends later on,' she lied again. Always best to leave yourself with a get-out. Carla could only relate to people properly when there was a figurative taxi waiting for her outside.

Putting down the phone, Oliver's exultant feelings accidentally manifested themselves on the Tibetan candle-holder on the phone table, one of Andrea's very first acquisitions. It fell to the floor and the handle section broke off. As he went to pick it up, an impulse overtook him and he trod on the thing, breaking it into several shards before he gathered up the bits and dropped them into the bin. He couldn't claim honestly that the breakage was an unavoidable accident. Ashamed at this, he went to take a shower and consider his wardrobe choices for the evening.

There is something 'almost opera looking' about Chelsea, as Thomas Carlyle, one of its many illustrious literary inhabitants, once said. Whether he was referring to the architecture, the grandeur of the river, or the enormous number of eccentric old ladies in gigantic hats, garish make-up and leopardskin leggings is not clear. But certainly, the King's Road and its environs has a far greater proportion of these feathered octogenarian rock-chicks than any other borough of London. It is a place of ostentation and pose, of overpriced antiques and shamelessly expensive interior design, of old money and young bodies. This is the groovy spot which flaunted itself in the sixties and then forgot to stop flaunting through the sourness of the seventies and eighties. A place where a donkey jacket is always 'such fun' with PVC shoulders on it, and never something a docker wears to keep warm. The quintessentially hippy Granny Takes a Trip, the first punk emporium Boy, and the weird World's End, with its wonky floors and backward-running clock, are all clothing shops which could have existed nowhere but Chelsea. It's a show-off place for people with open-top cars, where the slightly naughtier younger sisters of ski-chalet girls go to hang out with unshaven photographers, and where art students don't mind that they are not at Goldsmiths. Georgie Best, Oliver Reed, Terence Stamp all gave the area a façade of louche glamour, and unlike Notting Hill Gate, Islington or even Hampstead, Chelsea is proud of its reputation for seedy splendour and privilege.

Over seventy per cent of London's commemorative blue plaques are on houses in Chelsea, from Bram Stoker, the author of *Dracula*, up by the barracks, to Sylvia Pankhurst down on Cheyne Walk. And many famous artists made their studios there. Sometimes, on a foggy morning, one might think the river at Chelsea Reach reminiscent of a painting by Turner, and one would be right, for this is where he spent much of his time, particularly looking back towards the three bridges from the yard of Battersea Church, where, incidentally, William Blake was married.

As well as disproportionate amounts of plaques and genteel bag ladies, Chelsea has always had more than its fair share of fashionably beautiful people. Four of the top model agencies in the country are based there, including the camply named So Dam Tuff agency for boys with washboard tummies and gelled hair. Any coffee bar on the King's Road will have its ration of immaculately presented girls with their portfolios under their arms.

For Oliver, so long cocooned in the beer-and-rugby suburb of Clapham, south of the river where the anoraks live, the allure of Chelsea was intoxicating. From the top floor of the bus he looked down at the river, wide and magnificent here, with its black surface constantly shimmering in the fancy illuminations of Albert Bridge. But even now his excitement was tinged with a bitter seasoning of self-abnegation. What would George and the rest of the men in the group think of his walking on to this gaudy stage in his clean jeans and best shirt to meet with a woman just because he fancied the look of her? Especially so soon after the death of his life-space-partner. He decided that he would probably keep this new-found Neanderthal tendency from them, only admitting to it if asked directly.

After alighting from the bus, he realised he was early and strolled up Oakley Street on to the King's Road, his eyes pulled to left and right by the sheer swank of the female passers-by in their designer froth. The shops were mostly closing now, but still swelled with light and flagrant displays of marked-up goods. Even vegetables cost three times more in Chelsea.

He had arranged to pick up Carla at Phoenix Mansions, not out of gallantry, but because he had no knowledge of anywhere suitable to meet, didn't even know the names of local pubs. Oliver was not good at asking someone out for a date. This was not just lack of practice, having lived with Andrea for eight years. He had never really been good at it. The few girlfriends before Andrea had sort of happened to him; either they had been at college with him and hence going to the same functions anyway, or, like Andrea, he had chanced on them and they had pounced on him. He had never been pro-active in his mating habits, and found the idea of asking for a date embarrassing in its brazenness and sexist in its implication of predation. In fact, he considered, as he crossed the road at the Town Hall and looked at the beds and glassware in the Reject Shop, he could not remember ever being so brazen-faced as to have simply rung a woman up and asked her out. It made it so obvious that you fancied her, that you had turned her into an object of desire, there was no getting away from that. He was quietly pleased at his new-found swashbucklery.

The evening itself was hard work. Oliver couldn't understand Carla's bemusement at him; she just seemed to laugh at everything he said and did. She couldn't understand why Oliver kept asking her where she wanted to go, whether she was hungry, what she felt like doing. She'd never met a man who included her in the decisions, and she didn't like it much. He'd asked her out, for goodness' sake. It was up to him to entertain her, not the other way round. He should have worked all that out and then she could decide whether she was impressed. Impressed enough to let him proceed further. That's the way it goes. Whereas this bloke didn't seem to be playing the game, or any game at all. He was not showing off, he kept telling her things that were actually true. Maybe he was gay. All the same, she stuck with it, because he did make her laugh with his earnestness. He was funny. Not as in cracking jokes or making dissy comments about other women's clothes. No. Funny, as in bumping his head on the light hanging over their table and then, hilarious, apologising about it. Funny, as in thinking you could walk anywhere in these heels rather than get a taxi everywhere, even the one hundred yards from Sydney Street to Paultons Square. As in not wanting to get completely plastered on tequila Red Bulls, as in never having tried a Dime Bar vodka cocktail, nor any kind of chocolate vodka mix.

By about seven thirty she was having enough fun and made up her mind to lose the invented other engagement, so she got her mobile out of her bag and pretended to get a message on it. They were in the basement at Jerry's Bar and still hadn't eaten anything. Carla tottered upstairs to the Ladies' to 'call her friends back', she said. Oliver watched her behind swing up the spiral staircase. He was drunk, but not as drunk as her, and the smoke from her Marlboro Lights hanging in the unairconditioned basement was making his eyes and nose stream. She was wearing a short skirt and knee boots with a fluffy lamb's-wool cardigan over a black T-shirt. Her leather coat with fake fur collar was slung over the back of the ironwork chair, and she'd left her bag where she had been sitting. Although she was dressed and made up for the evening, she did not a have a petite suede evening handbag, but a bulky white canvas shoulder bag which lay half open on the seat by Oliver's knees. In the top of it, amongst the usual junk of make-up pouch, scarf, cigarettes and lighter, was what looked to Oliver like a shop's credit-card swiping machine. Strange, he thought, that someone should walk around with something like that – something as large as that – in their handbag.

'You know what, babes? My friend who I was going to see tonight? His mother's been taken ill so he's got to go to Brighton.' Carla was back from the Ladies' and stuffing her mobile into the bag, ramming the card swipe down to the bottom. 'So I been stood up. All on my little own and nowhere to go, and it's Chrissy Eve.'

'Oh dear. What are you going to do?' said Oliver, oblivious to even the most over-syruped hint.

'Whatever you tell me to,' she said, and laughed. She had a loud and dirty one. The air was hot and damp and smoky and, feeling uncomfortable, Oliver suggested they leave. On the wall by the bottom of the spiral stairs were a couple of posters for West End theatres and a rack of free advertising postcards which had been covered in fake snow and holly. To the side of this was a shelf with various flyers for local clubs, shows, and events. Oliver picked up a couple of these on the way out.

'There's a club where they have live jazz seven nights a week,' he said, reading one of the cards as he followed her out into the street, 'but only if you don't mind jazz music. Some people really hate it, I know.' A memory of his father being shouted at by his mother for endlessly practising the saxophone flickered for a moment in his mind's eye.

This time they did get a taxi. The 606 Club, which originally got its name from being at 606 King's Road, is in fact situated in Lots Road, down by the wharf and the old power station. Noise and steam were emanating from its cavernous entrance at the bottom of the stone steps beyond its clanking prison-style iron gate. Big Fergus let them in, but it was Christmas Eve and all the tables were taken. They squeezed into the back-room bar where the old sofas and chairs were draped with drunken couples and the bar stools supported old men with ponytails. The ceiling and the lights at the 606 are low. On the tiny stage, a young saxophonist stood to one side, tapping his foot while the ancient drummer jammed something as incomprehensible to the average ear as the inner workings of a steam engine. Some of the audience clapped and the saxophonist, with his accompanying bass and keyboard player, returned the evening to some semblance of recognisable melody.

Oliver was still trying to gain the attention of the

itinerant bar staff when Carla suddenly stiffened and gripped his forearm. Instinctively, he looked across to where she was staring. Two or three bronzed and suited men sat at a table with their fancy women. For a moment, one of them looked coldly into Oliver's eyes. Carla turned quickly into Oliver's shoulder, saying, 'I don't really like this place. Shall we go?' She was tense and looking at the floor now. Patiently, Oliver followed her out of the club again, weaving through the tables, past the front of the stage, past Big Fergus, up the steps and out of the iron gate on to Lots Road. Once on the street, Carla pulled an opened bottle of white Rioja from under her coat, took a long swig from it and, cackling like a witch, passed it on to Oliver. Then she set off down the street, wobbling on the heels of her knee boots. Oliver quickly checked the club entrance behind them to see if anyone had noticed her theft. Then he took a swig himself and set off after her.

'Sorry you didn't like the club,' he called out.

'It wasn't that. It's just I saw someone I know,' she said, and then, 'Taxi!' as a cab drove past. It was already taken and didn't stop.

'Where are we going?' asked Oliver innocently, as he caught up with her.

'Who cares? It's Christmas Eve, darlin'. And we gotta have a good time! I know where we might be able to get some Charlie. You got any money?' She tried to hail two more occupied taxis, which drove on by. She was very drunk now and put her arm through Oliver's, more for support than anything. They were walking along the Embankment, past the Chelsea Yacht and Boat Company, where a hundred or so large houseboats are moored. There was a party going on in one, which had its front door open. Carla steered them both to the Embankment wall and shouted down to the boats: 'Merry fuckin' Christmas, you wankers!' An old man in a blazer came to the front door of the boat and closed it. There was a half-moon up high over the river and its beams trilled on the tips of the millions of tiny wavelets on the river's surface. High clouds scudded by the chimneys of the power station, looking like the cold on their breath.

Carla broke away from Oliver and wandered ahead to where a smart BMW was parked. She swayed for a moment, then bent down and, with apparent ease, slipped off one of its hubcaps. She whooped and, staggering back to the wall, flung the hubcap like a frisbee across the boats and on to the muddy banks of the Thames beyond. Looking around nervously for the owner of the BMW, Oliver caught up with her again and, taking her arm, moved her off at speed.

'Oooh, masterful,' she said, and giggled. 'Am I your fantasy then?' She pouted at him. 'Or could I be your nightmare?' Grabbing the bottle off him, she took another swig and tossed it over the wall. It landed in the dark mud with a single plop.

SEVEN

Waking the next morning on the small and cramping sofa in his surgery at Rylance Avenue, Oliver was tugged into full consciousness by a nasty grinding pain which travelled between his right ear and his left hip. His meridians were definitely bunching up. He ran his long fingers down the back of his neck. You wouldn't have needed to be a qualified osteopath to feel the knot; it was the size of a ping-pong ball. Gingerly he extended his limbs beyond the confines of the sofa arm rests and groaned.

The first thought to occur to him was that he had not had sex with Carla the night before, and a small amount of relief stirred amongst the regret. As if he was pleased to hang on to a sliver of his own free will in the face of an exceptional dance of enticement. By the time he had summoned the courage to make an advance towards her it had been too late, the moment was long past its sell-by and Carla had been too far gone. She needed help getting through the door at Tite Street. 'I don't do kissing,' she had said, and then started vomiting into the kitchen sink. Oliver had helped her get clean and let himself out, walking all the way home in a state of reflective excitation.

Plenty of opportunities for him to make a pass at Carla had presented themselves earlier in the evening, but he had never been quick enough off the mark to stop her from flying off into the next diversion. She had only left him a window of a couple of seconds each time. After relieving the BMW on the Embankment of all four hubcaps and lobbing them into the river, she had peeled another hubcap from a Vauxhall on Milman Street and carried it as far as the Beaufort Hotel, where the staff seemed to know her, Oliver thought. Failing to get a drink there, they had then gatecrashed a Christmas Eve party on Bramerton Street and Carla had disappeared for at least twenty minutes, leaving Oliver to explain the difference between osteopathy and chiropractic to a middle-aged woman whose voice should have been logged in the national sound archive as a perfect example of Sloane. When Carla returned, her cheeks were flushed and she was almost vibrating with heat. 'If you want any Charlie, it's up in the bathroom,' she whispered into Oliver's ear. He could feel her hot breath on him and smell the film of sweat on her forehead and neck. He would have tried to kiss her then, but before he could think of slipping an arm around her waist, they were out on the street, with a bottle of gin which had mysteriously found its way inside Carla's handbag.

Oliver's excitement at Carla's antics was that of a

spectator watching a dangerous sport. He was mesmerised by the way she could turn the world around
them into a crackpot place of her own interpretation. He
was also hooked on the look of her. Her hair, which
became tousled and then ruined as the evening wore on.
The weight of her breasts against the fluff of her lamb's-
wool top. While he was with her, he felt he would be
able to live in this alert but sexually frustrated state for
ever. After finding and quickly leaving an uncomfortably
full late bar, they had staggered back to Tite Street,
where there was no lift and he had helped her up the
stairs. As they entered, the phone started ringing and
didn't stop even when answered by the turned-down
machine. It just started ringing again. Oliver felt glorious
in his frustration as he strode back home across the river
at Chelsea Bridge, and the fact that he'd forgotten his
keys and had to break in through the side window only
made him feel more vital. He had gone to his surgery and
fallen asleep in there because it was the only part of the
house which held no memory of Andrea for him.

The second thought to arrive the following morning
was that it was Christmas Day and he should be on his
way to see his mother and sisters in Kent. He'd spoken
with all of them at least once since the news of Andrea's
death and found their attempts at familial support not
only irritating, but actually hurtful. 'You should have
gone with her to Chicago, then this would never have
happened,' said his sister Irene, never one to take his side.

'She was far too intelligent for you anyway. You are a difficult man, you know,' was the nearest his mother got to sympathising with him. Both Oliver's mother and sisters would assume that if there was anything wrong in a relationship it must be the man; hence they could interpret his current predicament only in terms of how he must have let Andrea down.

Oliver usually tried to spend as little time as possible at his mother's annoyingly small house in Frisham, outside Goudhurst, but this Christmas was a record. He'd given up staying the night in his mid twenties, around the time he met Andrea. At Christmas, and maybe one or two other times a year, he would arrive just in time for lunch and leave soon after supper. This year he got there just as they were serving up, and was gone before they'd put the kettle on for afternoon tea.

The house – with its low ceilings and doors – had always been called the Waterhouse because part of it once straddled a brook. It was a pretty Kent house with ship-lap boarding up one side of it and a dovecote in the front garden. Oliver hated it. The traffic noise in the front room was worse than in Rylance Avenue, he contended, because the A4471 followed the path of the now defunct brook right past the Waterhouse's front door.

Oliver had remembered to get presents for both his sisters – Sandra and Irene – and his mother, whose name was Elisa, but who was known to all as Mummy. He had got each of them a gift pack from the Body Shop. Not very inventive, but he had learned not to try to be inventive with his family. Christmas was normal, that is to say formal. Oliver had never quite managed to dispel the disapproval of his family at his living with a woman seventeen years older than him. There was a certain amount of jealousy thrown into their attitude, he was sure. Neither of his sisters yet had children and it was getting a bit late for the older one, Irene, a spinster who worked in financial services and spent a lot of time in the Far East.

During lunch, Oliver managed to perform all the required Christmas niceties, while inside he thought of Carla – of her bending over to pick up her bag, giggling on his arm, vomiting into her basin – and shifted in the uncomfortable, undersized chair. He declined more food and wondered whether people actually do overeat as much at Christmas as they claim to, or just blather on about how full they are because the meal is so acutely boring, especially the plum pudding. Setting fire to it at the table does not make it any more palatable, he thought. Most likely made with pork suet anyway. As he was leaving, his younger sister, Sandra, surprised him by taking him to one side and, asking how he was getting on in the aftermath of Andrea's death, offering to come and see him even though she lived in Southampton. He thanked her but declined. She told him to ring her if ever he felt low. He thought this too would be unlikely since he couldn't stand her husband, Brian, who was a lecturer at the university there.

'I've spoken to Dad,' she whispered to him in the hall at a suitable distance from their mother.

'God. Why?' he whispered back.

'I don't know. I just felt it was the right thing to do. I spoke to him before, a few years ago, and he writes to me every now and then.' It was news to Oliver that his father still existed, and he was surprised that his sister had a contact address. 'If you want his number, just let me know.'

On the drive home, he imagined what it would be like if Carla was Mrs Baldry, the woman with the glowing buttocks. If it were Carla's number in his biscuit tin. If it were Carla who liked a good thrashing. If it were Carla who would, when called upon, come round with her straps and canes to be punished by him. These were the kind of thoughts he would definitely be unable to share with George and the other members of the group. Maybe Barry had been right, it was merely a biscuit club for wankers. Once, when discussing pornography, the group had decided, despite George's contention that all pornography is exploitation, that if an act was consensual then it wasn't entirely wrong. The trouble is, Oliver thought as he drove home from Christmas in Kent, if it's too consensual it might not be so sexy. The thought of smacking Mrs Baldry, in her clichéd Carry On film attire with her easy familiarity and no-nonsense mumsiness, somehow lacked passion. In fact it dampened his ardour, which was probably just as well since he was approaching the South Circular and there might be drunk drivers on Christmas night. No, there was something considerably more disturbing and hence exciting about the thought of smacking Carla. She seemed to be role-playing her life for real. When he thought of her, his fantasy veered out of control, as if she was deliberately teasing him, even in the confines of his own fetid imagination.

That night in bed he frightened himself because the images in his mind seemed to have a will of their own, taking him over and mentally transporting him to places he might have preferred not to go. It began with him lifting Carla's skirt and smacking her bottom, and then moved on to his whacking her thighs and legs with a stick until they bruised. Then he was beating her with his hands. He turned her around and slapped and punched her in the face, but as he wrestled with himself in the bed, he realised it was Andrea's face he was punching, it was Andrea he was hurting and kicking and pushing. The worst thing was that doing Andrea this injury in his secret imagination was the thing that aroused him the most. Shocked at himself, he rolled over and turned on the bedside light, which was mounted in a Cambodian sandalwood carving. His heart rate was up and his breathing was heavy. He decided that it must be the fault of this bedroom. Of this bed. Of this bedside light. He couldn't sleep here, this room was all about Andrea – the rugs, the Moroccan hanging on the wall. Every object was redolent of her. He could feel her all around him, sense her cloying, disapproving presence. He knew what she would have recommended on a night like this; that he do some chanting, that he touch the healing crystal she kept on the window ledge, that he try to think only positive thoughts. Then they might have spent half an hour discussing how they could improve the room's feng shui by rearranging the furniture again.

Oliver got out of bed. He felt certain that he would not be able to sleep in here tonight, maybe never be able to sleep in here again. He thought of going for a run, but the pain in his lower back warned him against it as he reached down for his trousers on the chair. It was cold out of the bed, and on the way to the wardrobe to get his padded jacket which doubled as a dressing gown, he stubbed his toe badly on the corner of the bed. Cursing, he hobbled to the other side of the room and wrapped himself in the padded jacket. It was only when he bent down for his slippers that he realised the damage he had done to his toe. He switched on the main light. The toenail of the second toe of his right foot had been flipped up and away from the skin and was held on only by the joint at its root. Seeing it dangle there, he was suddenly aware of quite how painful it was, and from nowhere he could have foreseen, let alone prevented, he found he had lashed out and swiped all the trinkets off the dressing table on to the floor, where he kicked them with his good left foot. Over the next thirty seconds or so, he could hear his mother's and his sisters' voices: 'Oh, Ollie's having another tantrum, dear oh dear, why can't he grow up? Best leave him to it. Pathetic.' These aggravating inner voices only served to inflame him further, and by the end of a minute, the room was a mess. The curtain rail was down, clothes from the wardrobe were strewn everywhere, the crystal was smashed on the floor and there was a three-inch dent in the wall plaster where it had been hurled. Oliver had become his own poltergeist. God knew what kind of negative karmic energy he had released, nor what chances he would now have of being reincarnated as an enlightened being. But he didn't have time to worry about that, since the pain in his right toe had become agonising. He went to the bathroom and tried to bend the nail back down on to the gummy toe before dressing and binding it. He wouldn't be running the marathon this spring, that was for sure. He had, it seemed, his own particular endurance test to undertake, and it had started badly.

Blue. It was nearly blue. Like the last one. Not more blue, not less blue. She could wait an hour now, until she felt like another wee, and then try again, or she could – should – wait a couple of days, when it would be more definite – and it was still a bit early to tell – and then use the third of the packets she'd got this morning. On the other hand, what a ridiculous concept, waiting a couple of days! No chance. She went to the grimy kitchen sink and poured herself another large mug of water to make her pee. She'd try best of three now. It was eight quid a go, but if this one came out a bit blue as well, then the twenty-four quid spent so far would be nothing compared to the money she'd have to find in the long run.

She picked up the phone to ring Donna, but halfway through dialling put the receiver down. My God, this is a big thing. She wanted to keep this for herself a little longer. She wanted to know what she would do. She would have it. She would have it. It came to her instantly. This was a good thing. A good thing. The only thing worth having so far. All the rest – the reasons and counter-reasons, the practicalities, the money, the people and what they might say or think – were things which might be good at certain times or might not be good. Or might change. But this was the one good thing.

Without realising it, she had rolled a joint. She stopped herself from lighting it, in case, and prepared herself mentally for the possible skunk- and nicotine-free months ahead. She was ready. She wouldn't need them. She lurched to the sink and drained another mug of water. Standing in front of the mirror, she pulled up her jersey, and looked at her tummy. She stuck it out. She rubbed her palms over it gently, then harder. She stood sideways and pulled her jersey up higher to look at her breasts. They had been a bit sore but they didn't actually look bigger or anything. If it was real, this good thing would make her good. Not that she was, or thought of herself, as bad. But now she could actually be made of goodness.

Even Manchester would be a good place to live. The rain wouldn't matter and nor would the fact that there was nowhere to go. There would be no point in going anywhere. The world would be happening right here in her belly. She had something more beautiful and more important than all the sights and experiences the world has to offer. This was her destiny. She was suddenly at the centre of the universe and in touch with the infinite. Her degree, friends like Donna, seeing the Taj Mahal, all could wait. People could either help, orbit around her, or go away. There were no half-measures any more.

Now that she knew what she would do, she was not afraid to tell Felix. Genetically speaking, it was half his after all. But she knew she didn't mind, whatever his reaction. He could either join in or piss off. She didn't want to stop him from doing anything, carrying on being a genius, developing his career, anything. She didn't imagine that he would make the most attentive father and the thought of him as a husband was comical. But that didn't matter, she would be independent. It wasn't as if they were even properly going out together or anything. They'd been seeing each other for ages – at least four months – but she knew he wasn't particularly committed to her. He'd never said he loved her, never said much at all actually about those kind of things. She didn't know if she loved him either, but it was kind of irrelevant now, or might be in a few minutes.

At last she felt like peeing again. She considered, while waiting the interminable ten minutes for the chemical reaction to take place, whether she ought to ring her mum at the home in East Anglia, and decided to wait a while, maybe even until it was too late. And she didn't want to trouble Dad. She didn't want grown-ups stealing this feeling of strength. *Esta fuerza*. She'd left the little white plastic stick on the sideboard in the kitchen and wouldn't allow herself to go back in there until a full ten minutes had passed. She picked up the joint she had rolled and lit it. This might be her last one ever, for all she knew. She dragged the smoke into her lungs and tried to lie back on the sofa and relax. No chance. She cleared up the rolling tobacco, roach ends, stash, jumbo Rizlas – everything, and put them in a Tesco bag, ready for the bin if necessary.

After eight minutes she went back into the kitchen to watch the white stick. Its tip was already the colour of a pale April sky. She stood completely still for the last two minutes, watching as it gained complexion, turning from a light azure to the pellucid deep blue of a hot afternoon in Spain. She binned the Tesco bag and put on the kettle. The whole of life now had meaning, and Felix would either have to grasp that or disappear.

★

'I'm just a piece of shit. Everything about me, everything I've ever done is execrable,' said Barry peevishly. 'If you were to go to an open-air pop festival which had improvised toilet facilities used by thirty thousand lager louts who had existed for a whole week on a diet of takeaway curry cooked by drugged-out hippies, and if you were to shovel amongst those faeces and the attendant maggot and insect life and dig deep to the bottom of that trench, there you would find ME. The real me, I mean. That's where I exist and that's where I deserve to exist.'

'The doctor said you might experience some depression. It's perfectly understandable you should feel this way, but that doesn't mean I have to go along with what you're saying. You're not shit. You're just ill,' said Oliver.

'My body disgusts me. My life disgusts me.'

It was the Sunday after Boxing Day and Oliver was driving Barry to Willis Hall, near Dorking in Surrey, a convalescent home in which he had managed to find a place for Barry using a combination of his own osteopathic contacts and Barry's membership of the NUJ. It was another cold, sunny day and they were coming round Devil's Punch Bowl for the third time, since Oliver had made a couple of wrong turnings after Box Hill. But the prettiness of the scenery and the unusual amount of light were doing nothing to lift Barry's mood.

'If there's one word that could sum up my life so far, it

is SHAME,' he said, transfixed by the steady rhythm of the trees passing on the passenger side.

'Maybe you could get an appointment with a psycho-therapist while you're in there,' said Oliver, trying to help.

'Trick cyclist? No thank you, sir. No. You know what I fancy right now? A big, four-skin, black-hash, two-cigarette conical joint,' said Barry, taking out another nicotine capsule and fitting it into his plastic inhalator. 'This fucking thing's not going to last. I can tell you that for nothing. Can't we stop at a garage and get some proper fags? Or little cigars maybe?'

Oliver said nothing and they drove on in silence for a while. After a few minutes listening to Barry puffing and wheezing on the inhalator, he tried to distract him from his dark, addictive thoughts by asking about his work, but this seemed to stimulate an even more oppressive gloom.

'I am a failure. An absolutely talentless, useless, washed-up, burned-out-at-fifty-four, twenty-two-carat slice of ordure.' Barry glanced over at Oliver. His complexion was chalky and his skin tone flaccid. The whites of his eyes hung below the pupils like a blood-hound's. 'I used to think that I'd been quite good once and had just gone off a bit recently, but in that hospital I realised I was never any good. I'm a disgrace to my profession. A FUCKING DISGRACE. I have existed to write one thousand words of inconsequential drivel every seven days. I'm a disgrace. You know who once lived in Tite Street? Oscar Wilde, that's who. Addison and Steele started *The Tatler* AND the fucking *Spectator* just round the corner from me on Cheyne Row, and Jonathan Swift, the fucking author of *Gulliver's* fucking *Travels*, lived on Old Church Street. And what have we ended up with? The inheritor of this fine legacy is yours truly, BF, Barry bloody Failure. The line stops here. I've squandered a tradition.'

'You make people laugh,' said Oliver, and then, 'And you make them think sometimes.'

'I've done nothing. NOTHING of any value. I earn a pittance from putting people down, from picking little holes in targets wholly undeserving of my attack. I scan the news for frim-frammery; Madonna is buying a house in London. WOW! Is bulimia encouraged by fashion photographers. That sort of CRAP.' Barry went quiet again. He was considering whether it is better to make people laugh or to contemplate their mortality. Then he spoke again. 'Still, it's better than writing one-liners for Angus Deayton or whoever happens to be the latest TV witmaster.'

It was healthier, Oliver thought, for Barry to exorcise his demons by annihilating others, rather than turning his guns on himself. Trying to draw him out further, he asked Barry why it would be so bad writing jokes for television.

'When I was in Footlights, we just did it for a laugh.

Not as a career move. Same with Cleese and Birdie and Cookie, God rest his soul. These young bastards nowadays go to Cambridge in order to get into television comedy. It's all part of their business plan, you see. A step towards owning their own broadcasting franchise.' He lapsed into morose contemplation again and they drove on in silence for a while. 'Anyway, no point in trying to get an answer from Auntie Beeb's finest at this time of year, because they all go skiing together, out on the piste doing their deals. You won't get a reply from any of them until after fucking EASTER. If you're lucky.'

Oliver spotted the sign for Willis Hall hidden among some acacia bushes and made a sharp last-minute left turn into the gravel drive. A lorry that had been following them hooted.

'No. To be honest, I'm just jealous. That's all it is. A touch of schadenfreude, except that instead of taking pleasure in the misfortunes of others, I find I get ill when they do well,' said Barry as they drove up to the main building, which had a small lawn in front. A couple of inmates were crossing it with assistance from a female nurse dressed in turquoise nylon overalls. 'They're just better than me. I'm just a never-has-been old windbag . . .' Barry went quiet as he took in their new surroundings. Oliver noticed a momentary flicker of fear in his eyes. One of the inmates on the lawn had a large dent in his skull, probably the victim of a motorcycle accident, and was learning to walk again. In the main doorway

stood a fat Asian man gazing placidly into the courtyard.
Every few seconds he let out a squawk like a bandicoot
heron, mumbled a few words and shifted his weight on
to the other foot. Oliver got out of the car. Barry
remained slumped in the passenger seat.

'You wait here, I'll see if I can find someone to help,'
said Oliver and entered the reception hall past the
squawking man, who did not register him at all. Inside,
the sudden switch from brightness to dark made it
difficult to see for a few seconds, but as he grew
accustomed, he found that he was in a spacious entrance
hall with dark parquet flooring. He walked over to an
unattended reception desk and a big free-standing
noticeboard with various leaflets and messages pinned on
it. The most prominent sign was written large in orange
magic marker and said: 'Funday afternoon chapel. Come
and meet Jesus!' Other notices included an appointments
timetable for occupational therapy, with a photo of a CD
rack made by a patient in the carpentry room, and a
names list for those wanting to join the Monopoly
tournament.

A frail old woman with a walking frame shunted
herself slowly up beside Oliver to look at the day's menu,
which was badly xeroxed and pinned to the bottom of
the board. Beef or cod with waterlogged British
vegetables, followed by crème caramel with a leather
skin. Oliver shivered. The papers on the board flapped
momentarily in a sudden breeze. Someone must have

opened a door in the innards of the building. Oliver could pick up the distant scent of the meal on the draught which whisked through the sad old hall. He went back to the car.

Barry was slumped, chin on his chest, with his seatbelt undone and bag on his lap. Despite the lines on his forehead and the deep creases down his face to his jowls, he looked about ten years old and pitiful.

'Have you got all the pills you need and everything?' asked Oliver.

'Yes,' said Barry without looking up.

'Right, let's go then.' Oliver started the car again, drove round the lawn, back down the gravel drive and out into the road. 'You're not staying there,' he said. 'You'll have to come back and stay at Rylance Avenue for a while. I'm sorry I didn't think of it before. I thought this would be better. Do your seatbelt up, please.' Barry obeyed.

'Bloody hell! What's got into you, Matron?' said Barry. 'Calm down, old girl.' It was true, Oliver's breathing had become short and his cheeks were flushed.

'Those kind of places make me so angry. Those people don't know anything about health, nutrition, balance or anything.'

'Can we stop at a garage and get some rolling tobacco then? That's not so bad for you, you know. Because they take so long to fucking roll.'

'No, we can't,' said Oliver.

EIGHT

It was an almost otherworldly experience for Barry to find himself two days later sitting working in the box room at Rylance Avenue. The room where he had written all his early material, including his only novel, *The Misandrists*. The room where he used to catch up on sleep on the small single bed when Felix was first born, the only place in the house that he could have called exclusively his own. When he and Oliver looked in it, having returned from their aborted mission to Dorking, it had been full of cardboard boxes, business files from the gallery, a plastic spinal model covered in dust, and some of Felix's early attempts at fridge building. Between the two of them they had cleared it – taking them all of Sunday night and most of Monday – throwing a lot of junk away and dispersing the rest throughout the house. They had had to work slowly, like a couple of old-timers, because of Barry's heart and Oliver's back. 'Can't be good for business, eh?' Barry had joked on noticing the pain Oliver had when lifting. 'I'm sorry, Madam, but I can't click your neck because I've cricked mine and I can't bend down that far.'

Oliver's pinched nerve seemed to revive Barry's spirits and he made repeated references to it throughout the day. The fact that Oliver was also limping due to his bad toe was another source of delight.

For their supper, Oliver made some rice with vegetables and seaweed which, Barry complained, tasted of paper. 'You shouldn't have spicy foods any more, Barry,' said Oliver. 'You'll have to learn to change your diet. It'll be hard at first, but you'll get used to it. You have too much fire in your system – too much of what the Indians call *pitta* – and unfortunately for you, you now have to stop putting fuel on it, which is spicy food, alcohol, caffeine, all those things you are used to.'

'Are you going to keep me prisoner here?' asked Barry peevishly. 'And make me eat dull food until my brain turns into a cabbage and I wear a Marks and Spencer cardigan? Passion, old boy, there has to be passion. There has to be hot and cold.'

'And that's another thing: too much thinking is like a bellows to fan the fire. You need to meditate or do something to calm the thoughts down, maybe take walks. The common is near by. You need a little more *vata*, which means space.'

'Did you know that the renaming of familiar objects is how fascism and cultism get started?' said Barry. 'Let's not call it Monday, let's call it Waco-day. If you mean it'd do me good to get some fresh air for a change, then for God's sake say that.'

'I'm only telling you the basic principles of Indian Ayurvedic medicine, which is one of the most ancient healing practices in the world . . .'

'And it's done a pretty good job healthwise in India for the last couple of millennia, has it? No major diseases hanging around the old sub-continent then?'

Oliver ignored him, 'To put out your *pitta*, your fire, you need earth and water. So from tomorrow, it's fresh carrot juice every morning and at least two litres of water every day. Those people in the convalescence home would probably have killed you by Easter with their diet.'

'Look, it's inordinately decent of you to put me up like this, Herr Camp Commandant, and it's jolly well appreciated and all that, but I already feel it my duty as an Englishman to dig an underground tunnel to the nearest pub,' said Barry, trying to enjoy the bland green tea Oliver had made for him. It was all very well, being on native soil, as it were, but he wanted to pay his debt and get back to the heat of the city. It was too suburban for him here, he would atrophy. To accept a favour is to sell one's liberty – *beneficium accipere libertatem est vendere* . . . and the rest.

'I suppose you'll have to have the odd glass of wine,' Oliver conceded, 'but try making it a spritzer. You have to lose some weight too.'

By Monday evening, Barry was poised over his laptop, looking out of the box-room window on to the rosemary bush where he had scratched his face the week before, the stone front steps and a laburnum tree whose bare branches scooted against the pane in the wind. He felt like a Roman general returning in triumph from a ten-year campaign. And the general had his 'cold-water' slave up there with him on the chariot to whisper, 'Remember you are mortal' in his ear lest he become too arrogant. The events of the last week had reminded Barry Fox sharply of his own mortality, and it was humbling.

But now he had a thousand words to write. Of course he had been unable to hand in anything the previous week, but since it was Christmas, his absence from the pages of the *Express* was not greatly felt. They had filled his two column inches with a 'last year's best male bum' piece by a girl from breakfast television. He slumped in the chair, feeling old. Barry had always had a childish attitude to authority and those supposedly in charge. Which, despite almost all of them being younger than him, included his bosses at the *Express*. He still thought of people such as lawyers and teachers or anyone who wore a suit as being, by their very nature, older than him. He cast himself as the perpetual rebellious teenager. He had also believed that somehow this made him cool. Stuck over the laptop now, trying to conjure this week's slice of sugared dissidence, he felt altogether undignified. His life's work seemed to him to be a pathetic bid by an old and rebarbative troll to stay young. Still considering himself to be against authority, although in fact by his age, colour, education and class he *was* authority. His mind drifted through memories from the last five years. In every replay there he was, an over-weight Peter Pan with impending emphysema, wheezing his way through another post-lunch whisky mac, thinking it heroic, or even macho, to slip and sidle his way out of responsibility. A sad old git with an 'I was big in the sixties' haircut; David Puttnam, Melvyn Bragg, Paul McCartney, Richard Branson, Trevor Nunn, they've all got the same haircut. An ugly boy who just got bigger instead of growing up. A craggy, paunchy nine-year-old in adult clothing. Not a man. Not a real man.

He allowed his thoughts to waft further back, to farthing chews, Matchbox cars and Meccano sets. Suez, and the days when people had blankets not duvets. When the prefix on a phone number was a word – like 'Prospect' or 'Cunningham' – when there were twelve pence in a shilling, when muesli was called 'Bircher muesli' after some mad Swiss doctor. He recalled Tinker toys and windcheater jackets and Pelham puppets and the potter's wheel. And he felt very frail. Barry Fox was alive and unwell. Bloody Jeffrey Bernard, he was another DEMON sent to cause Barry ANGUISH. At least Jeffrey went out in a blaze of glory, had a play written about him, had Peter O'fucking Toole play him, for God's sake, in the West End! With my current luck, thought Barry, I'd get Mr Bean and a small educational film about the evils of nicotine.

He opened a new file and decided for the first time in his life to write, if not from the heart – which considering its current condition would have been unwise – then at least about it. 'I had a bit of a ticker problem last week. All OK now,' he typed, 'but Matron says I've got to go easy on the old fry-ups from now on, and not get too heated up or the whole thing might go conflagrative on me again.' This made him feel rather good. Despite his classical journalistic training on the *Liverpool Echo* in the seventies, he decided he would put himself into his work.

There is a hugely popular trend at the moment, he reflected, having surveyed his first sentence, for ill or dying journalists to document their last months in detailed diary form, describing minutely every treatment, every meal and bowel movement. Perhaps Barry could join that wealthy, if not healthy, throng and produce a book of his own progress, and even a television documentary for Channel 4 about his poor circulation and imminent death. This bit of bad fortune might actually have been rather an astute career move. After considering this for a few minutes with still only a first sentence up and running on the screen, he realised that he was flailing. His brain could not function properly without a fucking drink.

Oliver was out, but he'd left the spare keys on the

hook in the hall. The Magpie had changed in the decade since Barry last lived here. What had been a comfortable grubby hole of a place was now more wine bar than pub, thought Barry, as he carried his glass and American bottled lager back to the newly upholstered seat. On the tables were handwritten menus on which were dishes like sea bass in ginger, and ricotta and spinach ravioli. Salads were served with balsamic vinegar. Desserts contained white chocolate. The serving staff wore uniform green T-shirts with a Magpie logo on them, and all seemed to hail from Australia or New Zealand. Barry grumbled to himself and whipped the cellophane off his panatella.

'Excuse me, mate? But this is the no-smoking area?' said a depressingly good-looking green-T-shirted Australian.

'This is supposed to be a PUB!' retorted Barry.

'Yeah, I know, but, well, people are eating, you know?'

Vodka, Barry thought later that night, now there's the spirit. Not so fattening, and because it's see-through, less likely to lay you out. Fucking DANCERS drink Vera Vodka, for Christ's sake. Odourless, hence less easy to detect on the breath. Altogether the right one for someone in my position. He poured himself a large mugful from the bottle he had purchased at the offy on the way home from the Magpie, added the remains of the carrot juice from the jug in the fridge and padded back up the stairs to his room, where he hid the bottle under the bed. After a small rearrangement of the furniture, he found himself quite comfortably ensconced by the open window with his laptop actually on his lap, and mini-cigars and lighter on the window ledge, with vodka and carrot cocktail refills a mere elbow away. In this cosy and mildly inebriated state he found the words came freely, and when, after a couple of hours, he went to the word-count facility on the laptop, he discovered that he had actually written three and a half thousand of the elusive little buggers. Surely out of that he would be able to extract this week's column? Admittedly, the sudden outpouring was a departure in style for him; contained not one pun nor reference to Greek mythology and paid only passing lip service to what card holding members of the media might call the 'Zeitgeist'. In other words, it had no topical jokes, but was instead a personal account of the bitterness and frustration of a middle-aged man with a dodgy heart. Barry was excited that such a new approach had come so easily, and slipped into bed satisfied that he had done a good day's work under the circumstances, optimistic that there might be a place in the world for him after all.

He was woken minutes after drifting into a vodka-enhanced snooze by the sound of the front door slamming and Oliver stomping noisily into the kitchen. After a few seconds of furniture-bashing and crockery-clinking, there was a series of peculiar rhythmical whooping sounds like an agonised Canada goose. Barry lay awake in the tiny single bed, trying to figure out what was going on below. Had Oliver brought some bird back? A bloody noisy one who could go from nought to multiple orgasm in seven seconds flat? Oh for God's sake, the man was crying in the downstairs room. The strange honking noise which at first Barry had mistaken for a car alarm was in fact his late ex-wife's common-law jiltee sobbing in the living room. Whatever next? What very poor taste! A fully grown man bloody blathering. Barry hadn't heard of such a thing since Stetherington at school, and he was a homosexual. Went to live in Capri, or became a monk or something.

Barry lay awake and wondered whether he should do anything or merely continue to pretend to be asleep. A chap in a state like that likes to be left alone. Barry knew he would. Wouldn't want anyone knowing he'd slipped up. Lucky young Felix wasn't around, he thought. Damn poor example to set.

Downstairs, where he was lying curled on the floor by the sofa, Oliver suddenly stopped his sobbing and laughed. I think I'm all right now, he thought, and stretched out a bit on the rug. Geez. Phew! He laughed at himself for being so stupid. As if crying were a mistake, a disaster thing, like smashing your knee, which might need a quick visit to Casualty, or a bandage or medication. We have no right, we men, thought Oliver, to assume our feelings matter or are even worthy of attention.

If you imagine the earth as being the size of a ping-pong ball, the moon would be a small pea two and a half feet away from it and the sun would be a big globe, nine feet across, three hundred yards away! On this scale, apart from Mercury and Venus, at distances of 120 and 200 yards from the sun, all around and about there would be emptiness until you came to Mars, 500 yards beyond the sun, Jupiter nearly a mile away, a foot in diameter, Saturn a little smaller two miles off, Uranus four miles off and Neptune six miles off. Then nothingness and nothingness except for small particles and drifting scraps for thousands of miles. The nearest star to this ping-pong-ball earth would be 50,000 miles away. So what did it matter? What difference did it make to the overhanging panoply whether Oliver was happy or not? Whether he was bereaved, whether he could or could not get laid, whether he fell in love or in lust? Perversely, these thoughts cheered Oliver up and he was able to get himself to bed.

If Oliver had been one of his own patients, he would have recommended he take some time off from work, but the week after Christmas was always a busy one. Like the suicide rate, which soars at that time of year, people seem to wait for a long bank holiday to do injury to their spines. Oliver called it his elastic band theory. One lives habitually with one's adaptability stretched to the limits of its endurance and one gets used to things that way. One can cope. Then along comes a public holiday with the instruction to relax – let go for a few days – and the elastic-band, having been taut for so long, loses its springback and loafs around, aching and twingeing, now three times its original length, with stretch marks.

Throughout Monday the phone had rung incessantly, and Oliver had fifteen patients booked for Tuesday. A more renowned osteopath might be able to go away for the whole Christmas period to Barbados-on-Sea among all the pop stars, but someone at Oliver's level had to be there to pick up all the last-minute, 'please put me out of this immediate agony' calls. Barry was relieved that, since he would be working late, Oliver had sensibly asked the Tuesday group to meet elsewhere that night. He was nervous about encountering the Men Who Run from the Wolves again. He didn't want them to see him in his current state. Barry was not feeling altogether wholesome and could not face any smug 'told-you-so's from George. The very thought of George set his pulse racing again and it occurred to him that maybe he should be blaming George for his current ill health, and not the twenty years of cigarette and alcohol abuse. Yes, that was it. George's fundamentalist bent was what had blocked Barry's arteries and impacted his heart muscle.

He loosened his shirt; he was becoming hot again. He trembled involuntarily as he imagined George being publicly ridiculed by himself with the assistance of Jeremy Paxman on *Newsnight*. Barry was the studio guest and George had the disadvantage of being on the video screen, and so there was one of those tiny second delays each time before George answered one of Jeremy's piercing questions. This made George look stupid before he'd even begun to speak. Then Barry would wither him with a one-liner and the studio audience would crack up – in Barry's imaginary *Newsnight* there was a studio audience – and maybe at a later date, Barry would formally be invited by the BBC to kick George's head in, live, as a ratings puller. Barry had to sit down and breathe deeply for a few seconds. This childish revenge fantasy had got him all hot and it was only nine o'clock in the morning. He must be careful now, it seemed, of his thoughts and feelings if he wanted to survive. He would have to live the rest of his days in an emotionally temperate zone. Bugger it, what an absolute scum-sucking BUMMER.

The wonderful thing about Oliver's freshly made carrot juice was that it really did make you feel stronger, brighter and healthier when you drank it. The less good thing about it was that this beneficial effect lasted for only thirty seconds and then you craved cigarettes, alcohol and coffee, not necessarily in that order. Barry fumbled around in the kitchen looking for something he could have which would definitely not be so damn good for him. It was this godawful PRESSURE to be VIRTUOUS all the time that was causing all the health problems, the shortness of breath, the sweating. That was what was making the veins in his neck pulsate. Or perhaps now that he was marginally more sober than before, he was more aware of the inner workings of his own system, its weaknesses and warning signals. He was scared by his symptoms, but continued the search. He found coffee and then at last he found sugar. Healthy raw cane sugar admittedly, but nevertheless enough to stave off alcohol craving for an hour or two. He also happened on the biscuit tin in which resided the phone number of the saucy Mrs Baldry, and which contained in addition a light-cerise woman's elastic hairband and a picture torn from a magazine of a girl bending over in red thong knickers. Barry chuckled as he made himself a large mug of black coffee with seven dessertspoonfuls of raw cane sugar swirling around in it.

New Year's Eve for Oliver would normally have been spent with Andrea at some media or art-world bash in Notting Hill Gate or Soho. She would get high and drunk and dance and flirt and he would lurk near the champagne trying to avoid being cornered by inebriates who wanted to discuss their neck and shoulder pain with him, or stoned actors obsessed with the malocclusion in their jaws. Once they'd had a New

Year's Eve party at Rylance Avenue which had gone quite well as far as Oliver was concerned, but that was early on when Oliver still had his own circle of friends to invite. Somehow over the last six years these people had drifted away; whether through Oliver's lack of social application once he was part of a couple, or, as he now suspected, through Andrea's little acts of hostility towards them. So it was a novelty for him to stay in on New Year's Eve, and a novelty, too, to be entertaining a guest. It was also an unusual experience for Barry to have company at this time of year, since 'Auld Lang Syne' brought on the sleeping sickness in him, and at the first sign of public celebrations such as singing in the street he retired to bed until it was all over. Pubs and clubs became unbearable, as did all public places, and the TV was shit unless you are Scottish, in which case it was embarrassing and shit.

'What we need is some female company to entertain us and keep us on our toes.' said Barry. 'To add some lateral tangents to the conversation, to challenge our inventiveness by making us compete with each other for attention, or even, come to think of it, to perform a lesbian floor show on the Peruvian rug over there.' He sipped on his vodka and carrot juice. He was sure Oliver must know of his lacing the health drinks by now, but if he did, Oliver was turning a blind eye and had even offered Barry a glass of Sainsbury's own champagne, which he had considered appropriate for the evening.

They hadn't been able to agree on suitable music for the occasion – Oliver mildly suggesting some eighties soul, while Barry initially demanded Gorecki's maudlin third symphony, and eventually conceded to Bob Dylan's *Desire*, which made Oliver very jumpy – so they left the radio on instead.

'What about that little sizzler I have staying in my flat, eh? A right patootie! If it weren't for her, you wouldn't have to be putting me up, you know. Well, her and the vast sums I owe in what it would be semi-accurate to describe as back rent.' Barry fitted another nicotine capsule to his inhalator. He was allowed a fat cigar later on, and since it was New Year's Eve, he had informed Oliver that he intended to inhale it right to the bottom until he felt sick. 'What say we get her round here for a hootchy-kootchy show? She looked like the sort of cupcake to enjoy a bit of a pageant. No funny business, no special services – of which I fear I am no longer capable in any case – just the excoriating chorine, whatever her name is . . .'

'Carla,' Oliver interjected.

'Oooh! Bit too quick off the mark there, old thing! Giving yourself away, you greenhorn.'

Oliver's nervy reaction to this suggestion told Barry that he had hit on a subject which might pass the time admirably between them until midnight. 'What's the matter, old chap? Hit a bit of a sore one, have I? Don't tell me you wouldn't like to see her peel off to the soundtrack of your choice. Have her undress like a trouper before our very eyes, in our own living room.'

'I really don't think it would be fair on her,' said Oliver, grabbing another handful of pistachio nuts and attacking the shells at speed.

'Well, we'd have to pay her, of course, she is a professional after all. It might be our night off, but it isn't hers.'

Oliver felt a fool. Having failed to get Carla out of his mind since Christmas Eve, and unable to get her on the phone, he had been over to Chelsea on the Monday night and hung around outside Phoenix Mansions in case she emerged. He knew she was in there, because the lights went on and off a couple of times. Before coming home, he'd called her one last time on his mobile. This time she'd answered, but had been ice cold with him, dismissing him as if he were a stranger, as if he had not been there with her when she was vomiting. As if there was and had been nothing between them at all. He had felt a fool then and had stormed home, waking Barry with his wailing, and he felt a fool now for not having better understood Carla and her portable credit-card swiper. Now he gave himself away again by asking Barry too many questions about her: where she was from, how long Barry had known her. Barry apologised that he was unable to satisfy Oliver's curiosity, having only ever met her the one time with Sophie in Chelsea Harbour.

'I'm going to stop you right there, you young panther you, you sexual steam engine. I just want to say that it would be a very, very bad idea for a bloke like you to fall for a butter baby like our Karen, or Kylie, or whatever she's called.' Oliver corrected him again. 'Carla, right. But I can see from your dark look that I am speaking after the stallion has bolted. Oh dear. The boy has fallen for a brass. He's haunted by a hooker. You'll never "save" her you know. Not wishing to be too Dickensian about this, sir, but you are a right plonker and you're gated for a week.' Barry exploded with sudden laughter at Oliver's forlorn and serious expression. 'So have you got anywhere so far? Have you done it yet? You dirty dog!'

Oliver got up to throw away his pistachio shells. 'No I haven't done *it*. As you put it. And I'm not . . .' He ran out of words.

Barry couldn't wait for his cigar any longer. 'You devil,' he said as he lit it. 'You rooster, you swordsman. But a definite mistake if I may say so, for both the heart and the pocket.' He had a coughing fit on his first inhalation and Oliver fetched him a glass of water. 'And also a mistake for the cock, most likely, with that one. Make sure you wear a condom, won't you, if you ever do get anywhere near it.'

Barry Fox did not seem to Oliver like the best person from whom to be taking relationship counselling or sexual advice. Nevertheless he did feel that he could trust him to be honest – unpleasantly so, in fact – and in this sense he was probably a better bet than George or any of the other men from the Tuesday group. Oliver was surprised, though, by his own willingness to listen. He had never thought of himself as being someone who might need advice or help of any kind, only as someone who gave it. The idea of being looked after himself made him feel slightly nauseous.

'You know what my first sexual memory is?' said Barry. 'Well, the first one of a purely auto-erotic nature, which is of course the kind that really matter. Went to see Walt Disney's Pinocchio. Must have been seven or eight years old. And in the story there's this big bad brute of a man with a big beard, can't remember his name, who runs a vaudeville theatre. He forces this poor little cartoon girl to sing on stage against her will. While Pinocchio and fucking Jiminy Whatsit were working out how to rescue her from his evil grasp, I was imagining her being made to perform a little burlesque which consisted of cartwheels and handstands to reveal her knickers and petticoats. I suppose it must have been the extending nose bit that had alerted my child's mind to matters erotic, but ever since that day I've been hooked on the idea of woman as performer. As recipient of the male gaze. Or to put it another way, I like to watch. I find that having a no-touch but gawpable fantasy on the premises is the most compatible way of dealing with her desire to be special and my desire to peek. To be honest, any woman who wanted more out of me than that would be not only disappointed, but also downright stupid. I've got such a tiny one anyway, there's not much point in promising what you can't deliver.'

'That's so awful what you're saying, Barry. What about intimacy and companionship and things like that?'

'And New Labour and Tony Blair. FUCK OFF! I'm not saying I don't like female company. I just like to have some depersonalised voyeuristic sex with the one I love every now and then. Is that so much to ask? Well actually it did seem to be too much to ask of Andrea. She couldn't abide me in bed. I don't know what she was like for you. Hated it with me.'

Oliver was saved the embarrassment of a confessional about his sex life with Andrea by the doorbell ringing unexpectedly. Standing on the front doorstep was a young woman, wearing a very battered man's leather flying jacket and carrying a motorcycle helmet. 'Does Barry Fox live here?' she asked.

'He's just through there,' said Oliver.

'Thanks,' she said and brushed past him, the cold of the night emanating from her hair and clothes. 'Oh, and Happy New Year, by the way.' It was twenty past ten.

Barry hauled himself up to greet her. 'Tara, my dear thing! What an absolutely unexpected pleasure and delight. How on earth did you find me?' It was the florist from Chelsea.

'I've brought you some blow,' she said. 'They told me at the Arts Club that you were half dead so I thought, I know what he needs, a nice bag of weed to help him chill.' She stubbed out her roll-up in Barry's ash tray. Oliver opened the window wider.

'You absolute ANGEL!' said Barry.

'I can't stay long, I'm on my way to a party in Brixton and I thought I'd just drop by,' she said, and then, 'Shall I skin one up then?' She pulled from her jacket a plastic bag which smelt like a student's digs.

Barry looked at Oliver for permission. 'Can you make him one without tobacco?' said Oliver, who had to concede that it would be better for Barry's health to get stoned rather than drunk, especially if he could get used to it without the awful nicotine. Ganga might be just what the doctor ordered for a heart in Barry's condition. Barry offered Tara some of their champagne and Oliver went to the kitchen area to get her a glass.

'How's it going with the house?' she whispered conspiratorially to Barry, as her fingers expertly put together a quick spliff. 'Have you managed to get it off him yet?' Barry shushed her, since there was no separating wall between the living area and the kitchen. If getting Oliver out had been his intention, then having a heart attack had been a fairly thrusting opening gambit, Barry mused. Oliver returned with a glass and poured her a very mean little slug of champagne.

'Oh, don't worry, I'm not driving,' she said. 'I just

carry this helmet around with me to keep muggers and rapists off. They all think I've got a boyfriend or a motorcycle nearby, or both. And if anyone does try anything on . . .' She demonstrated how the helmet could be used as a weapon by holding on to the strap and swinging it. This nearly knocked all of the glasses off the table. Oliver carefully rearranged things away from her and cleared up the little sprigs of grass which she had spilt.

'I met this fantastic bloke over Christmas,' she said. 'He's a stand-up comedian. It's his party I'm going to.'

Barry felt a rush of pleasure scythe through the tensions in his mind and body at the reassurance of being remembered by an old friend. And also at the marijuana sailing into his blood. It was good to hear Tara talk of her sex life again.

'And look, he gave me this.' She held up a video camera which was about the size of two packets of cigarettes. 'Which is already out of date evidently, but I've started using it in my work and I'm getting some really amazing stuff.' She turned the camera on and continued to speak to them while looking through the viewfinder. 'Which is what I wanted to ask you about, actually. And you.' She aimed the camera at Oliver.

As could have been predicted, Tara had a motive other than pure altruism in coming to visit. The only thing more important to her than her sex life was her art.

'I've had this absolutely brilliant idea to do a huge

installation about my sexuality, which would really show how sex needn't be furtive or mechanistic in a typical male kind of way, but can involve the whole of me – mind-body-spirit sex. Except that sounds so crappy, I can't think of a good title for it yet.'

'How about "Who needs art, when you can get a shag"?' proffered Barry, good-humouredly.

'I need, like, a really big space because I'm going to have giant models of all the cocks I've ever sucked – which is something I'm particularly good at – and I'll have videos of guys trying to pick me up in pubs – oh, and loads of photos of me in leather straps, my stand-up comedian guy's got all this stuff, he's really into bondage – and people would enter the whole thing through a massive labia gate made of used pink bath towels.'

Her excitement was alarming, particularly to Oliver, who still had the tiny video camera pointing at him, recording his reactions in close-up. He was envious of her. He knew he had never had mind-body-spirit sex. It sounded good, but the problem, he felt, was finding a woman who wanted all four of them from the same man.

'And I need, like, a really big space, so I asked that woman at the Gaia gallery, Rebecca – and she was really nice – but she told me to ask you guys if it was OK first. It'd only be for two days. She said the place was closing down in three weeks anyway . . .'

Oliver gazed at the floor, having no idea what to say.

'*Ars Longa, vita brevis*,' said Barry, coming to his rescue. 'Art is long, life is short. He'd be honoured and privileged to lend you his huge space for a couple of days, and what a fitting send-off to the old girl, my ex-wife I mean.'

'I'd give you half the takings,' said Tara, 'which could be as much as five hundred pounds if loads and loads of people come.'

When she had gone, Barry quickly applied himself to rolling another tobacco-less spliff. 'What an absolutely sweltering fleshpot!' he said. 'I bet you could fry eggs on her mound of Venus. Now that's the sort of woman you should be after. More sensible age for you for a start.'

NINE

'Get me another drink, now.' Carla got out of her chair and pattered across to the kitchenette, where she mixed a gin and tonic with ice and lemon from the contents of the plastic bags on the sideboard. 'She has a beautiful arse, no?'

Oliver couldn't believe this guy Eco was real. He didn't look real. He looked like the sort of chiselled older male model you might find in an aftershave advertisement, except in miniature. He must have been about five foot five. Everything about him was perfectly formed and essentially masculine – but smaller and neater. His skin was deeply tanned, his brushed-back hair a salt-and-pepper mix, his poise self-consciously relaxed, and his voice annoyingly resonant and deep. His bone structure was good enough to ensure him preferential treatment both in the genetic pool and in the world of photography. His wardrobe and jewellery – for he had a fair number of trinkets slung on him – looked expensive-casual, maybe Ralph Lauren, maybe good copies picked up cheap at Singapore airport. He had an air of the international about him. His accent was unplaceable, but there were traces of German, upper-class English and Spanish laced into the principally North American twang. Maybe he wasn't real, but made up of parts he had garnered from magazines, soap operas and airport novels. Maybe he had decided who he would like to be and then constructed himself by sticking the ingredients together in the oven of his own will-power. It seemed appropriate that he had spent the last year and a half in Los Angeles – home of the invented curriculum vitae – or at least said that he had. He had certainly come with his own supply of charisma, or was that just cheap bravado and coarse acting to add veneer to his self-invention?

Carla gave him his drink and hovered by the chair on which he was sprawled. His fleshy upper lip curled over the glass and he drank without once breaking his stare at Oliver. He was pinning Oliver to the wall with his gaze. 'What? You don't like her arse?' he said.

'No. I think it's . . .' Oliver stammered, adequate vocabulary eluding him momentarily. Then, gathering himself, he tried again. 'It's, it's . . . it's . . .' The words fantastic, sexy, or amazing just would not come out from the back of Oliver's gullet. He decided to sit down. Standing with a plastic bag full of Barry's books – ostensibly the reason for this surprise visit – was making him feel awkward and weak. Sitting down uninvited would, he hoped, show Eco that he was not a man to be dismissed easily. He slid Barry's front-door key back into his pocket. It was hot from being gripped in his palm.

'What about her tits, pretty perfect, huh?'

'Well, I wouldn't know . . .'

'They should be, they cost me a lotta money.' Eco had a laugh which seemed to come from some horror Santa's grotto. 'Lotta, lotta money.' He rubbed his thumb over his index finger to indicate cash. Oliver couldn't believe anyone actually did that.

In an attempt to appear relaxed, ready to take on any challenge the other man might throw at him, Oliver crossed his legs and leaned back in his chair. But his breathing had become unsteady and his neck was visibly tense.

'She is mine, but sometimes, you know, I let her play around a little.' Eco winked and smiled at Oliver, which was possibly meant to be reassuringly man-to-man, but which produced a chilly sweat between Oliver's shoulder blades. 'You want to fuck her?' said Eco, like a host offering a second helping at Sunday lunch. 'She tells me your woman just died. That's sad. Too bad.'

Oliver swallowed and his eyes darted up involuntarily to Carla for guidance. She seemed to be enjoying his discomfort too. Oliver was frightened, but also excited. Of course he wanted to fuck her, that much was surely evident from his behaviour of the past ten days. Of course he admired her physique, had been unable to dislodge images of it from his short-, long- or mid-term memory. Indeed, more than that, he was fascinated by her, obsessed even. He had become aware in the last week of turbulent currents in himself – the desire to hold her fast, to stop her moving, wriggling away from him. Stop her giggling at him. To put his flag in her. Just for one moment to own her. These shameful urges were now exposed on his face. He recrossed his legs.

Eco laughed. 'What's your problem, buster? You don't like my wife? I think she likes you.' He reached an arm out behind him and round Carla's hips, bringing her into the circle. 'Hey, baby, show your sweetheart the honeypot.' Looking straight at Oliver all the while, Carla lifted her skirt and pulled aside her panties to reveal strawberry-blond pubic hair. Oliver blinked at the blatancy of it. His eyes left hers of course and scanned the triangle of her crotch. He was furious with himself for being so susceptible, so easily exploited. He was angry too with Carla for being so compliant, although no doubt she had good reason for her obedience if this Thunderbird puppet was in the habit of beating her. Oliver was disgusted at the situation he found himself in, and also at himself for staying, and yet he felt compelled to see more, to read the beginning of the next chapter. There might be some Big Truth, some life lesson that he would miss by leaving now. This evening, this meeting with this man might be a test of his mettle, an initiation. He also had protective feelings towards Carla. He couldn't leave her in the hands of this semi-extinct reptile, could he? Or were things not as they seemed to him? Carla appeared to be perfectly at ease, and not at all scared. If she did need saving from the dragon, she was certainly not giving off any distressed-maiden signals. No, Oliver had to admit to himself that with his chivalric fantasy, he was probably objectifying her as much as the manicured mini-dinosaur did. In fact he found the cocktail of signals coming from Carla confusing as well as stimulating and was at a loss as to what to say or do. In this increasingly mad B-movie, would a man like Eco be more angry if Oliver came on to his wife or if he declined? And would a man like that be carrying a knife or a gun?

'So, you don't like her pussy?' said Eco. 'Ah, I forgot. But you are English. You like her arse, yeah?' He spun Carla round to display her buttocks to Oliver. Smiling and giggling a bit, she bent over, curving her lower back provocatively, and stood on her tip toes. That position again. She tossed her hair and looked back over her shoulder at Oliver, still smiling. The peculiar thing to Oliver was that although this situation could be said scientifically to be his ultimate and rehearsed sexual fantasy, he was flaccid under his jeans, sitting more in a state of paralysed shock than arousal. As if someone had taken his fetish from its secret hiding place and put it on a TV game show for family entertainment. Once exposed, allowed, discussed openly like a bus route, normalised even, the sight of Carla's hips and thighs in her thong knickers was divested of what numinous quality it might have previously possessed. Oliver realised that it had been his own investment in the images of semi–clad women which had given them such power over him. The garish lingerie a totem for his worshipful projections.

'Well? Do you like her arse or not? Come on, man!'

Oliver managed to scrape out the words 'Of course I do,' but they sounded as if they were coming from under the floorboards.

'This arse is worth a lotta money too.' Eco said the word 'too' as if it were the French *tu*. 'Lotta money, isn't it, baby?' Carla knelt down on the floor beside Eco, leaning the top half of her body over his knees. 'And baby's been a bad girl and been giving it away to Oleever over here for free.' With a completely relaxed hand, he slapped her buttocks.

'No, I never did. But so what if I had done? What you going to do about it?' It was as if Carla was saying badly rehearsed lines.

Eco grinned knowingly at Oliver, and putting his gin down on the floor beside his chair, he pulled the signet ring off his slapping hand and put it in his jacket pocket. He grinned at Oliver and smacked her again. Still not very hard. She made a little 'ooo' sound and nuzzled herself into Eco's lap to be more comfortable.

'Oleever. He was the boy who asked for more, yeah?' Eco smacked her buttocks again, harder this time.

'Please, sir, can I have some more?' In between smacks, he was gently, even tenderly rubbing her buttocks with the palm of his hand. 'Go on, say it, you bad girl.'

Carla pursed her lips, and from the nest of Eco's lap, where her head rested in a swirl of hair, she smiled cheekily at Oliver, saying, as if to him. 'Please, sir, can I have some more?'

'You are a very, very bad girl and you gotta be taught a lesson so you never do it again. OK?' Eco was concentrating now on her behind and smacking on certain words for emphasis. Then he began smacking it regularly on a beat, as if it were a steak which needed tenderising. There was no uncontrolled aggression in these actions, and every so often he would stop and examine her for redness, very softly stroking the buttocks and talking to her soothingly. 'It's OK, baby, it's OK.' Carla made little sighs and calls when she was being slapped, even coming out occasionally with badly scripted and delivered lines such as 'I won't do it again, I promise, I've learnt my lesson now.' However, the noises she made while he was stroking her and soothing her were neither premeditated nor acted. A warm flush was appearing on her cheeks, and every now and then her eyes would flutter up into the lids. She turned her face away from Oliver. Eco was concentrating totally on the job now and Oliver felt as if he were an audience of one at an end-of-pier peepshow.

'Oh, baby. You are all red. You had your

punishment,' said Eco, and stopped smacking her. Both of her buttocks now glowed pink and Eco began again to circle the palm of his tanned hand over them. He rubbed her rhythmically for a while, until Carla's body started quivering. It shook for a few seconds and then she turned her face back towards Oliver and smiled sweetly at him as if she were the sleeping princess recently woken from a hundred-year slumber.

'Tell her she's a beautiful girl, she likes to hear she's a beautiful girl,' said Eco to Oliver before leaning back in his chair to retrieve his drink.

'She's beaooo . . .' Oliver's vocal cords seemed to be covered in desert dust and his voice had dehydrated somewhere between his larynx and his tongue. A noise akin to a door creaking was all he could manage. He was concerned that although the sight of Carla being spanked with her skirt up over her haunches had turned him on in theory, in practice there was still no physical evidence of this between his legs. He wondered if this experience would be one he would frequently revisit in the future in his mind for onanistic purposes, or whether it might not cure him of the need ever to have sex again.

'She's ready for you now. But you can't handle it, can you? Can't handle her, you creampuff. Not really a man, huh?'

'I'm waiting to see what she wants,' said Oliver, trying to sound righteous.

'I want you to piss off, little baa-lamb,' said Carla, half

getting up and scrambling for a Marlboro Light. 'Either shag me, have a wank, or piss off.'

Oliver could feel instant heat rising up his neck and burning his ears, like a sports injury spray. He inhaled abruptly before lurching out of his seat and to the front door of the flat. He let himself out, forgetting to take with him the plastic bag of books for Barry. He heard their laughter ring out behind him as he leapt down the stairs three at a time.

It had taken a long time for Oliver's latent fury to find a target. Until Andrea died, he had been unaware of how much unexpressed rage he was in the habit of cramming into the holdall of his unconscious. Even after her funeral he couldn't unpack it in case it spilled over on to the great-guy image he was keen to preserve. He suffered that chronic condition of terror at his own temperament: he dared not get cross with anyone, even mildly, over a late payment or spilt drink, lest releasing the small top layer of his anger might unleash the boiling torrent of igneous spleen which lurked beneath it. He had been afraid until now that he might wake one day from a berserk frenzy to find blood on his hands and veins in his teeth. Afraid that unless he kept a tight control over himself, he would do irreparable damage to someone. Certainly his mother and sisters had done nothing to disabuse him of this.

But now, limping furiously on his bad toe through the streets of Chelsea, he felt at last connected to the furnace below his navel. It crackled like a deep-frier and, had a tourist stopped him to ask the way to Harrods or Sloane Square, he would no doubt have incinerated them with the flames belching from his belly. Oooh, he was cross. He was walking fast up Flood Street and into Royal Hospital Road towards the river, hunched and stiff, with his neck sticking out horizontally in front of him like the barrel of a tank. He would have made a fine example of bad posture for a poster on his surgery wall. As he walked, he cursed and spat. 'Arsehole! Who does he think he is! I'd like to get a large metal drainpipe and heat it up until it was glowing red and then shove it right up his arse with a mallet!'

There were actually several people Oliver could have been angry at, now that the beast was out. Not least the magnificent Andrea for the lack of respect and consideration she had shown him during the eight years of their relationship. Or Barry Fox for abusing his hospitality and concern and plotting to take his home away from him. Oh yes, he wasn't stupid, he could see what Barry was up to. Resentment towards Felix or the men in his group might have been justified to a greater or lesser extent. But it was the Venezuelan smoothie and his wife who were the ones to light the touch paper of his ire.

Oliver reached the bottom of Royal Hospital Road and crossed to the Embankment. The river is big and wide here and it whipped a wind into his face which made his nose go snotty. It was a cold night, but his agitation kept him warm enough. A Porsche sped by. Oliver imagined it being driven by Eco, and spat at it. Then he imagined Eco, tied by the heels to its bumper, being dragged like Achilles around the Trojan camp. He imagined Eco's bloodied face and chest like purple scrambled eggs. He imagined kicking the shaking body, Eco begging him to stop, Eco crying. A bewigged and authoritative judge telling him that it was all right to kick and stab Eco; better still, a bewigged and authoritative female judge saying that it was actually his duty to trample Eco into dirt. He roared at the black expanse of the river.

By the bottom of Queenstown Road, the enforced and painful rhythm of his stride had induced in him a kind of fevered reflectiveness. The person to be angry with, of course, was himself. Eco and Carla were right, it seemed to him: he was, despite his size, a half-man, a shrimp. Otherwise he would surely have been able to perform, or at least participate in their game. He shouted abuse at himself as he passed under the Queenstown Road railway bridge, but the echo of his cries came back at him like the pathetic yelp of a neglected puppy.

'Where the hell have you been? I've been worried sick about you. I couldn't sleep.' Barry, in his dressing gown and trainers, was standing halfway down the stairs. 'Are you OK? You look terrible. Have you been mugged or something?'

Oliver was looking manic; his eyes were ablaze and his breathing was febrile. He was struggling with his anorak in the hall and getting angry with the sleeves.

'And what on earth have you done to all that stuff of Andrea's?' Barry had been in the bedroom earlier that day and discovered the mess left by Oliver's recent loss of control. 'I know it's all a load of irritating tat, but all the same it must be worth something.' In fact Barry had been in every room in the house that day. With a tape measure. And he had submitted his findings over the telephone to two local estate agents, who, after making appointments to pop round the next day to do proper valuations, had both come up with similar guesstimates of the current market value of the house: around eight hundred thousand pounds. Barry was pleased with these figures, having bought the place for a mere seventy-eight and a half thousand in 1979 with only a fifty thousand mortgage. Possibly, these estate agents were being optimistic, hysterical even, considering that even a gain of ten per cent per year would only bring the house up to six hundred thousand. But Clapham has been gentrified and BBC'd since 1983. With Battersea it is indeed, the Gold Top Double Cream of the urban gentrification which has spread like a chest infection through the outer London boroughs in the last twenty-five years.

Six hundred thousand pounds, let alone eight hundred, might seem like a gigantic amount of money if you were to try and raise or earn it, but – as people will never tire of saying at middle-class dinner parties throughout the capital – it means nothing because the next house you move into will have gone up in price commensurately. Unless of course you do not intend to buy a next house. Unless, like Barry, you intended to pay off your debt to Madame Sophie and continue to rent a small apartment and live off the lump sum, like a pension, until you died. Even Barry's mental-arithmetic skills, which had always been shaky, could work out that if they shared the house between them – he and Oliver, and Felix if necessary – he might end up with a quarter of a million pounds in his fist, which would do very nicely. He reasoned that he'd prefer a definite two hundred and fifty than a lot of lawyers' bills and hassle to clear the beloved son and the amorous osteopath out of the equation and claim any more of the pot for himself, even though technically speaking the house was his. He felt that an amicable gentleman's let's-split-this-equally-between-us-chaps agreement would be his best shot. This generosity and magnanimity suited the new post-cardiac Barry Fox rather well, he thought. Life would be so much easier, and he would bear no grudges. He had even worked out how many years his clean quarter-mil would last him, and could foresee a deliciously stress-free decade or two ahead. If his heart held out that long.

He had been waiting for the right moment to broach these matters with Oliver, and this evening he had cut back on his clandestine vodka consumption in order to remain mathematically accurate and not lose his temper or pass out or anything like that. This was more likely to be the reason for his current insomnia than his paternal claim to concern over Oliver's safety and whereabouts. However, there was one other matter which had brought Barry's thoughts regarding the house crunching into fiscal focus. And this was his tenuous position as a Chelsea man of letters, upholder of the Royal Borough's literary tradition, which included, amongst its alumni, the Johns Betjeman, Osborne, Galsworthy and Donne. He had lost his job.

Of course the *Express* hadn't printed Barry's sincere account of his week in hospital and its attendant fears. Neither did they intend to give him a second chance. And as a freelance there were no pleasant extenuating circumstances such as redundancy packages, or months in lieu. Just an ansaphone message saying, 'I don't think it's really working, do you?' They didn't pay him to write genuine. They paid him to write snidey British politics-of-envy gags, no matter what the cost to his self-esteem. If they wanted genuine they would have hired a better-looking writer, preferably one who does telly, preferably with a slight Scottish accent. They had probably been looking for an excuse to let him go anyway. All doubtless under the age of TWENTY-TWO, the frilly-knickered FISH QUEENS.

'I just couldn't stand it, trying to sleep in there with all hat stuff of hers. Reminding me of her,' said Oliver, walking past Barry and into the kitchen, where he opened and banged shut a few cupboard doors. 'Why don't you sleep in that room, Barry? I can't take it in there, I'm using Felix's now.'

Barry followed him through. 'What are you looking for?' he asked.

'I'm going to bake a cake. I feel like doing some baking now. I might as well.' Oliver was slamming doors and shunting drawers closed. Barry stood clear of him by a few feet. Generally people did this when Oliver expressed his feelings; he was a very tall man, and, though usually quite placid, a small amount of aggression from him seemed to have a larger trajectory than a blast from shorter men. When he was a teenager, his mother and sisters had once locked themselves in the back room and called a neighbour to come and calm him down. He sometimes felt as if he were Dr Frankenstein's monster. The closer he got to people the more likely they were to run away. Unless he play-acted the part of the soft guy, the nice one who listened, the quiet shy boy. There was no one, he felt, who could really empathise with him, let alone contain him.

'If it's that pretty girlie this is all about, I can tell you now, old boy, she's not worth the candle. Even a vibrating one. You're better off with an undipped wick. You could do loads better, and probably will.'

Some pans clattered from a cupboard whose door

Oliver had not properly closed. He turned on them and kicked them across the floor. Their skidding and banging against the skirting made a satisfying cacophony and so he kicked some more.

'Dear oh dear oh dear,' Barry said above the clonking noise. 'It seems to me you could do with a drink. It's a pity that this house, like those of all genuine alcoholics, contains not a single drop.' There were still two or three shots left in his third hidden bottle of vodka, and he was hoping that this might be a good opportunity to bond a little over a bevvy and still have time to discuss the subject of the house.

'I'm angry, OK? I don't need anyone stopping me being angry and making it all all right because it's not all right. I'm right to be angry, OK?' Oliver found a new packet of wholemeal flour and tore it open, spilling gobbets on the drainer and floor.

'Would you like me to leave you alone then?' said Barry.

'No. Thank you. It's enough that someone is here. Thank you. I just can't face being told what I should be feeling any more. I'm sorry. It's not your fault. I'm just angry.' Oliver took the unsaturated margarine and free-range eggs from the fridge.

'Did you ever hear the one about the two bulls walking down the hill, an older bull and a young bull. And they see a field full of gorgeous cows. And the young bull says, "Look at that! Let's run down there and we might get to shag one of them." And the old bull says, "No, let's WALK down there and shag the lot of them."' Barry looked hurt at Oliver's lack of response.

Oliver had found a mixing bowl and was feverishly kneading dough. 'Incidentally, there's a bloke living in your flat now too,' he said. 'A really slimy little shit.'

'Is there, by gum.' Barry replied. That was bad news. 'Tell you what, why don't I put together a wee spliff – and I promise to make it with no tobacco – that'll douse the flames of your ardour a tad, and then we could maybe have a chat about these things at our leisure.'

While Oliver shredded some carrots into the mix and poured it into a baking tin, Barry went upstairs and fetched the wherewithal so kindly donated by young Tara. He felt sure that Oliver would be in a more conducive state of mind with a couple of puffs of skunk whispering through his veins, and hoped that he would, on this occasion, break his abstemious regime. With the cake in the oven, Oliver agreed to try it, and because he was unaccustomed to marijuana, it had a noticeable and instant effect on him. He slid into the sofa, losing his customary disciplined posture, and let his face subside into an expression of relaxed indifference. He told Barry about Eco and the events of the evening which had so disturbed him. It was hard, however, for him to elicit much sympathy from Barry.

'You mean you got to watch a gazoopie show like that for free? And you just left in a huff? What IS your problem? People pay serious money to sit where you were sitting tonight! What are we going to do with you?'

'The whole thing was just too much for me, I suppose,' said Oliver, beginning to lose sight a little of what it was that had upset him so.

'You mean, you didn't whip the old wire out and give it a twang? How rude. They were probably deeply offended. Whatever happened to etiquette?' said Barry. The grass idea had been a good one. Oliver was certainly looking and sounding more laid-back now. 'And this unwholesome chap is actually living there now, you believe?'

'Well, yes, it looked like it. I think he's her husband.'

'Funny how everything is sort of linked, don't you think? I'm staying here, you went over there, he's over there. Like water flowing downhill to fill an empty space. Wow.'

Barry was already halfway through rolling a second joint, as if the first had not done the trick. He was searching for a way to bring the conversation around to Rylance Avenue and the fact that two estate agents would be coming around in the morning. 'Like the ecology of the coastline. Irrigation in one place may dry up an entire sea further on down the line. Like the Aral Sea. Flood protection in Clapham may cause premature erosion in Chelsea, if you see what I mean.'

'Except we're talking about men and women, not the

level of the flood table, Barry. You're imagining that there's a limited amount of love to go round.'

'Well, in my experience real love is a pretty rare commodity, yes. Pretty fucking precious. Just have to learn to recognise it in time, before it goes sluicing off somewhere else.' Barry lit the second joint and made himself choke. 'You don't think you're in love with this girl, though, do you?'

'How do I know? I thought I fancied her until just now. How can one tell?'

'Well, when you go into a newsagent's, do your eyes still flit involuntarily up to the top shelf of the magazine rack, or are you saved that indignity by thoughts of her?'

'Going on that definition, I didn't even love Andrea, and I stayed with her for eight years.' Oliver managed a laugh.

'Yes. Messy business, love, eh? Much better off thinking of women as cabaret like I do. Helluva lot cheaper too. You don't have to buy houses and cars for an evening's worth of entertainment.'

While Barry was talking, Oliver concluded that he never had loved Andrea. Not properly. By the top-shelf-magazine test or any other. It had been more a question of not getting round to leaving her. When she died, what he had felt was a few minutes of relief, followed by three weeks of guilt at feeling it.

'The reason female prostitutes are so much more numerous and successful than male ones is that they can satisfy four men in an hour, whereas a male prostitute has to take his clients out and tell them they're beautiful. Women need to be told they're beautiful before they can do it, you know.' Barry passed the wacky baccy stick to Oliver, who accepted it without a second look. It made him cough too. He was not listening to Barry.

'I don't know what I'm doing here really,' said Oliver after a few seconds of further reflection. 'I didn't love Andrea. I'm just a sham.'

Was this the very moment Barry had been waiting for? 'How about selling the house and walking away from the whole thing with a clear quarter of a million?' were the words forming in his now-stoned brain. But something held him back. Whether it was an old fashioned Englishness, or an altogether more calculating streak in him, he could not, at this point, tell. But the tantalising thought that Oliver might just be unstable enough at present to fuck off completely, leaving him with everything, did occur to Barry. He decided that, like a Japanese expert in Zen and the art of war, he would withdraw his front-line troops at this point.

'Well, it's a shame, but it was never going to work, you and Andrea, was it?' he said. 'I could have told you that at the time. Come to think of it, I probably did tell you that at the time. Older woman, younger man, you see, biology stacked against them. Can't have children. Did you want children? *Do* you want children? Of your own, I mean?'

Oliver hated being asked that question. It was what everyone had asked within days of his meeting Andrea. His mother and sisters had asked it, his friends had asked it. Even patients had asked it. As a younger man living with a woman seventeen years older than him, the consensus seemed to be either that he was a toyboy who needed mothering or that he was really gay, or both. He was not considered normal. A deviant. In the first years he had nonchalantly claimed that their ages made no difference. But that was before the stone-walling chill had set in between him and Andrea. After a couple of years of going over the same material, the same complaints and shortcomings in one another, most couples devise some system that will enable them to survive if that is what they are going to do. In Oliver and Andrea's case, this took the form of Oliver cutting himself off; staying, as he thought, out of harm's way. He knew that in any negotiation she would win eventually, and so he stopped negotiating. He conceded before the heat was turned on. He knew he would never be listened to, and so he had stopped bothering to say anything. The passion went cold. She and her friends had different concerns from him, remembered different pop music from their teenage years, worried about different diseases, became heated over different political issues. He had managed to salvage some territory for himself: his surgery, the kitchen, and many evenings alone, baby-sitting Felix when he was younger, while Andrea plied her trade at clubs and openings.

So, as far as Oliver was concerned, age had made a difference. And he imagined that it was harder in a partnership like his, where the man was the younger, than in the more traditional older man/young filly combo. He knew this shouldn't be the case, and would undoubtedly not make this claim on a Tuesday night with George and the men, but he knew how difficult it is to wriggle out of the assumptions people make. Blondes are dumb, old ladies are kind, men who sleep with older women are either soft or bounty-hunting. At least the usual man-as-provider-woman-as-carer roles are not usurped when the woman is younger, he thought, and that would be one less thing to worry about. And then, Barry was right, then there was the impossibility of having children. Not that he wanted them particularly, he used to say, especially when you see what overgrown monsters they can turn into. But this was merely a way of defending himself from snooping busybodies like his mother and sisters, who wanted to hang on to the idea of woman as prize, man as champion, despite all the evidence. Staying with Andrea, it now seemed to him, far from being a noble and caring thing to do, had been just another way of avoiding or delaying commitment. A way of getting out of having to have children.

'I think I'm going to go to bed,' he said, and dragging

himself upright from the sofa, he realised how much his body hurt. Right up between the shoulders, down in the sacro-iliac, and his toe was throbbing again in his shoe. He stretched, and shuffled across to the hall. There was still one framed photo of Andrea on the hall table. On a dappled hillside in Tuscany, looking down on the Hangku Panchen Buddhist centre with its purple and yellow banners fluttering in the warm Italian breeze. He turned it face down. He would like to have a child, he thought. He would like a child. A baby of his own. Not the intransigent Felix but a whole other load of trouble which would be *his* trouble. Not Andrea's.

'Oh, by the way,' Barry shouted casually up the stairs after him, 'there's a couple of estate agents coming round tomorrow morning to value the house.'

'OK,' Oliver called down sleepily, and closed the door of Felix's bedroom behind him.

Barry thought he would roll another quick one. He complimented himself on his social skills, and dared to allow a glimmer of optimism to enter his head space. He lit the spliff and inhaled. Things could work out OK if he bided his time. He sat back and smoked in silence. In fact he felt so cosy with himself that he thought he'd do some drawing. Something he'd not done for many years. He rambled into the kitchen to look for a suitable scrap of paper and implement and was hit by an over-whelmingly delicious smell. Oliver's cake was doing well in the oven. Using his dressing-gown sleeves, Barry whipped the thing out and on to the table. Without letting it cool properly, he picked a few nuggets off it. Just the ticket. Scrumptious for a man with a sudden sugar-munchy on him. This called for another joint. Little bit of baccy in this one maybe, since Matron had gone to bed. It was warm as hell in the kitchen now. He sat down at the table with a beautiful blank sheet of paper in front of him. Almost too beautiful to draw on, but not quite. He let his biro sketch a garish cartoon of Andrea as he remembered her on the night she had danced a drunken tarantella in the nude on the refectory table at a parents' evening for Felix's stuck-up school. Her hair swirled into a galaxy of stars and meteorites in the top left corner of the page. The cake would have been good had it been allowed to become a cake; it was sublime as a pudding. Barry went to the fridge and found some half-fat cream to put on it. Nice.

TEN

Since the international success of the film *Notting Hill*, property has been changing hands very swiftly in what is sometimes politely referred to as North Kensington – an area which stretches from Ladbroke Grove up to Kilburn – and the increase in value at each resale has been enhanced a couple of percentage points by what local estate agents like to call 'The Hugh Grant Factor'. Towards the top end of Ladbroke Grove and all around the Harrow Road, people in damp basement flats have been covering their mouldy walls with a quick coat of magnolia emulsion, hurriedly installing the cheapest foam-backed carpets wall to wall, bunging an extra ten thousand pounds on the asking price and skedaddling while this purchase fever lasted. One-bedroom hovels with malfunctioning toilets and dodgy wiring being passed off as sexy bachelor pads to trendy first-time buyers who thought that Notting Hill Gate would be a good starting point from which to make their first independent low-budget films. Also, the easy availability of copious amounts of marijuana in the area has helped to make owning a property in this former mud swamp a very attractive proposition to a whole generation of would-be bohemians – or 'trustafarians', as those intent on spending their inherited wealth on appearing street-wise are known.

All of this should have been very good news to Bob Verbier, for twenty years the owner of Eezy-Lay, definitely the cheapest and probably the fastest carpet-fitter on the whole of the Harrow Road. He could have an old, cold ground-floor maisonette shag-piled in less than half a day and would only touch you for three hundred, four hundred and fifty quid max. Less if cash, obviously. As well as being the fastest from warehouse to living room floor, Bob's carpets were also the fastest to fray, ruck and pull away from their fastenings. At his prices, this was understood, and so most of his clients were those selling up and leaving the area in a hurry. He nurtured drinking-partner relationships with three or four local estate agents and so he stayed ahead of the game.

But this recent upsurge in demand was wearing him out. He had no particular ambitions, no plans for expansion, and had long ago given up the idea of taking on staff. There were plenty of part-timers, jailbirds and dope-heads he could call on if a particular job required extra hands. His problem was that he seemed to be spending all of his time on the phone nowadays, dealing with wankers, and the paperwork was getting out of control. All of which was beginning to interfere with the main relationship in his life; the one he shared with his saxophone. Oh, there was a woman – Pauline Grindley – but their long-standing affiliation had dwindled to an occasional stop-over with sex once every two or three months. He was fairly sure she had a couple of others on the go, and this didn't bother him unduly. She didn't come to see him play any more, and in fact avoided the pubs where he and the boys had regular spots, which suited him fine. She didn't like him drunk, and since this was seven tenths of who he was, he was happy to keep her as a part-timer. In any case, at fifty-eight, the vibrations he felt all through his body after a couple of hours of blowing his sax were far more satisfying than anything conjugal, and he was not a man to crave meaningful conversation. Certainly not the kind of conversation afforded by Pauline Grindley, who worked in the dry cleaner's on the Golborne Road and whose concerns outside of her job seemed to range from clothes to the weather. As a person, she was as interesting to him as the front page of the *North Kensington Gazette*.

Bob lived above the shop in what some would consider squalid circumstances. There had been no concession whatsoever to interior design, the only slightly pleasant aspect of his dwelling being the fact that the building backed on to the Grand Union Canal. Sometimes he would be woken by the sound of the squabbling Canada geese outside his kitchenette window. Narrow boats and freight barges would regularly chug past the double windows of his TV-room-cum-office, the noises from the canal providing a pleasant distraction from the endless hum of traffic from the Westway flyover which loomed large over the whole area. But canal water is not tidal like river water, and urban waste matter tends to accumulate there rather than be washed away. The pilot of even the shallowest-keeled cruiser would have to steer a careful course along this section of the Grand Union to avoid scraping the hull on any of the broken fridges, bicycles, washing machines and derelict cars which lurk under the dark, still surface of the water from Wormwood Scrubs to St Pancras.

From the dilapidated brown swivel chair in his office by the canal at the back of the building, Bob could survey the front of the shop, which was a cavernous, high-ceilinged room, piled high with rolls of second-rate carpets in sludge greens and beiges, and the glass front door, which gave him his only view of the Harrow Road beyond. For lunch – his only meal of the day – he would go across the road to the Jamaica Pasty take-away, where Marge would serve him up jerk chicken or rice and beans in tin containers which he would chuck in a bin bag after he'd finished eating. The bin bag was tied and put out only once every ten days or so, and so his home and his carpets tended to smell like a Caribbean kitchen. Most evenings he would spend wnstairs, the upstairs containing only his cluttered and uncarpeted bedroom and a small shower room with a serious creeping-damp problem. On his arrival here two decades ago, he had slung a full-sized Second World War parachute across the downstairs ceiling, not for decorative but for sound-proofing purposes, and some of its folds and creases now sported dust and grime layers as thick as a Jeffrey Archer novel. To disturb it for cleaning now would not only ruin his stock, but also probably inflict some kind of lung infection on him. Besides, the accumulated dirt enhanced the parachute's capacity as a sound absorber. The combined effect of it and the rolls of carpet made Bob's front room into a more than adequate rehearsal studio for his part-time career as a pub musician. There was not a day of the week when he didn't play to himself for at least an hour, cocooned in this acoustic haven.

Bob hated the phone. He hated everything about it. From the noise of its ring to the little dark deposits of congealed saliva in the mouthpiece. He particularly hated the cataract of new services and time-saving devices with which British Telecom customers had been deluged in the last five years: BT Callminder, which unnecessarily calls you to the phone when you have a message; memory callback, which calls you to the phone when you have eventually got through to a number you had given up on hours ago; and worst of all, the BT call-waiting service. 'The person you are calling knows you are waiting,' says the computer voice repeatedly, 'but rather than let you leave a message or try again later, he or she prefers to waste your afternoon keeping you pointlessly on the end of the line.' For someone who had to use the phone for two or three hours in every day in order to keep his business running, it seemed to Bob as if there was a conspiracy afoot to trash his nervous system. He was in the middle of trying to persuade a prospective customer that to carpet the kitchen of her ground-floor two-bed dump in St Charles Square would be a mistake when the little red light on the cradle began flashing, telling him that there was another caller on the line.

'Can I call you back? There's a very important call on the other line,' he lied, and pressed the call-holding button. There were a couple of seconds' silence after Bob's 'Yeah? Eezy-Lay Carpets?'. He hooked his feet up over the dividing banister between office and shop.

'Hello. It's Oliver.'

'Who? Who's that?'

'It's me. Oliver.' The voice on the other end was tense. 'Is that Robert Verbier?'

There were three or four further seconds in which neither of them spoke, while Bob flung open the memory files of his brain. Then he said, 'Fuck me. Fuck me rigid. Oliver? That Oliver?'

'Well, this one, yes. Me,' said Oliver.

'Bugger me twice with a bratwurst. Oliver. To what do I owe the . . . er . . . ?'

'Just thought I should get in touch, you know. Make contact and . . .' Oliver ran out of words.

'Are you in trouble? I don't have any spare cash or anything.' Bob was sitting upright now.

'No. Well, not like that. No. I'd just like to . . .' Oliver couldn't think what it was he would like. To get in touch, that was now done. To remind his father of his existence, that too was now done. '. . . I'd just like to give you my phone number, that's all.'

'Oh, is that all? Hang on, I'll get a pen then,' said Bob, clearing a space on the desk to write. 'Fuck me, for a minute there I thought you might be ringing to have a meaningful talk about what happened between me and your mum. Finally hear my side of the story. That's a relief. Fire away, I've got a pen and paper.' Oliver gave him the number and they fell silent again. The little red light on Bob's phone started to flash again. He ignored it. 'Well fuck me,' he said again. 'Are you still there?'

'Yes.'

'Well, that's that done then. Anything else?'

'Could I see you some time, maybe?'

'Oh. Well, if you want to come and see the best fucking jazz band in the whole of West London strutting their ugly stuff? Tonight. The Prince Albert. We usually have a few pints after and the beer's not bad there. Bring a few mates.'

'OK,' said Oliver. The power of coherent speech seemed, again, to have deserted him. A pub gig was not quite what he had meant.

Oliver had never consciously considered that there might be a side of the story of his parents' marriage other than the official version, his mother's: that his dad was irresponsible and had abandoned them, that his dad was lousy in bed, that his dad was an emotional retard. A waster who was too weak to take any responsibility. That his dad was the exact opposite of a role model. That if one wanted to grow up and become an adult male, then the way to do it was not only to avoid all contact with one's father – all thoughts of him even – but also to eradicate any atavistic personality traits from one's behaviour. This of course was harder for Oliver to achieve than it was for his sisters: he pissed standing up like his dad had done, his voice had broken just like his dad's had, and he had started getting crushes on girls based entirely on their appearance, just like Dad. In fact, the phrase 'you're just like your father' was one his mother would save for particular naughtiness. The idea that there could be another interpretation of the events in his childhood had never occurred to him, and to have phoned his father at all could be seen as a gesture of defiance. As far as he knew, his father had lost all rights to a side of the story by not being there at all through his teenage years, and being but a ghostly shadow before that. Gone to work before he went to school, invariably home from work after Oliver's bedtime, or out at a gig or on tour.

Oliver couldn't think, as he put down the phone, why he had rung. He wanted to push a brick into Eco's face and then swing away on a vine with Carla under his strong arm. He wanted to beat his chest and yodel and stamp on the jungle floor. He didn't feel that these were sentiments he could exactly share with George and the members of his Tuesday group. Perhaps Barry was right. George and Keith and John and Brian were merely wankers and their dialectical circle just an enormous digestive biscuit on which to toss off. He certainly didn't want to be the one to have to eat it. He had rung his father after twenty years, it seemed, because he had run out of alternatives. Despite telling himself that he expected nothing from the man, a suspicion crept over him as he hung up the phone that he was heading for a disappointment.

The Prince Albert pub on Ingrams Street is situated at the boundary where Notting Hill Gate becomes Acton. North of Shepherd's Bush and its market, south of Willesden Junction and Cricklewood. From outside its large, purple-painted front door one can see the enormous soggy meadow that surrounds Wormwood Scrubs prison, where model-aeroplane fanatics contribute to the noise pollution and serious dog-owners from the neighbouring estate daily add to the smell of shit which pervades the whole area.

If Oliver was looking for some kind of cathartic reunion, then the evening was – as he had feared – a total wash-out. Maybe that was what parents were supposed, inevitably, to be. 'You always love your children more than your parents' was a maxim which, as a common-law stepfather in a childless partnership, had caused Oliver discomfort in the past. He couldn't think whether he had ever loved anyone at all, and was certainly unsure as to whether anyone had actually loved him. So maybe he had seen the idea of going to meet his father as some kind of rite of passage. Certainly, you can't say 'Bye, I'm off to the Big World to become a Big Man, so don't try to stop me' to someone you have hardly even met.

As he entered the Prince Albert, fifteen grizzled male faces turned to him. There were only two women in the place: the short-haired battleship of a barlady and an elderly peroxide gorgon perched on a bar stool, smoking menthol cigarettes. Everywhere else sat or stood gnarled men in paint-spattered jeans, checked shirts and padded bomber jackets. Although there were one or two men under thirty, everyone else was in their forties and fifties. White hair yellowed with nicotine, baldness badly concealed with comb-overs, bellies and arses crammed into clothes which hadn't been upgraded for decades, rolling-tobacco tins on the tables and bar, and lager in straight glasses everywhere.

Oliver could feel the eyes of the whole pub staying on him as he walked to the bar and quietly asked the prison governess of a barmaid for a half of shandy. The conversations around him started up again, but in more subdued tones now. He paid for his drink and looked around for somewhere to sit. He could not see anyone resembling his memory of his father, but it was obvious to everyone that he was looking for someone.

'Haven't seen you in here before, officer,' said one of the younger men sitting at the bar. 'Can I get you a proper drink?'

'No thanks,' Oliver replied. 'I'm meeting someone.'

'Is there any way I can be of any assistance?' said the young bloke. His two mates were keeping their faces turned away from Oliver. 'Who was it you were looking for?'

'Well, do you know what time the band start? I've come to see the saxophonist.'

'Sorry, mate. We thought you was filth.' Another, older man, walking back to a table with his drink, shouted, 'It's all right, he's all right,' across the room to the company in general. Oliver had never been mistaken for a plainclothes policeman before; this was a first for him. Apart from his height, he didn't think he really fitted the old bill. He found a seat close to the Gents' and sat down, self-consciously.

It was nearly an hour before anything was due to happen on the little rostrum stage. A long-haired roadie was rearranging the positions of a couple of the speakers and tapping the microphone. Oliver looked at his watch. It was after nine and he was not enjoying himself at all. It was also draughty and cold in his corner of the room. Every time someone went to the Gents', they had to brush past his knees, and every one of them greeted him with an 'All right?' which he felt impelled to reciprocate. A couple of men tried to involve him in a conversation about engine capacities, and one rather sinister bloke insisted on buying him a pint of lager and winking at him from the other side of the room. The smoke in the atmosphere was bunging up his sinuses and his bad toe was throbbing in his shoe. At half past nine, some men drifted on to the stage and started to fiddle with the equipment. One of them made an anouncement to say that the band would be arriving in about five minutes and then they disappeared, carrying pints of lager with them. Oliver waited the full five minutes and then, since there was still nothing happening, he left. He was drunk by now, on lager. Something he hated to be.

The more he thought about it, the less he wanted to know who had done what in his parents' marriage. It was irrelevant to him who had fucked whom, thrown what at whom, who had been better at tidying up – who was terrible at cleaning, who had used whose credit card for what. What mattered was the growing waywardness of his own behaviour and the question of whether his father might be useful in any way in sorting it out. Was it perhaps genetic? He had actually rung the Home Office immigration department, intending to gather information with which he might be able to get Eco sent back to Venezuela or Toy Town or wherever he was from. He had given up, of course, while waiting on the line for an operator to deal with his enquiry, listening to Vivaldi's *Four Seasons* go round and round. But the alarming thing to Oliver was that he had actually got as far as making the call before realising it was a stupid thing to do. He was beginning to split at the seams.

Of course, having a good old blubber would be the right thing to do under these bereaved circumstances, the politically correct thing to do even. And that was certainly what he would advise a patient to do. But the thought of expressing grief over Andrea made him so resentful of her that he shuddered. Why should he? He knew he ought to be sharing the experience with the other men in his biscuit club, but he also knew that he was a fake. Like the other night, his tears, if they came, would be angry, violent ones, not proper, deep, dignified mourning sobs. He feared he might slobber and shout aggressively at passers-by. An outpouring of emotion from him, he felt, would be seen as threatening, offensive behaviour. He might be accused of assault, he might be arrested. Certainly, at six feet four his presence was difficult to ignore.

When he got back to Rylance Avenue, the lights

were all on and there was a serious mess everywhere. Barry had been smoking pot again. Not only was the washing-up not done, but there were tepid half-empty cups left on surfaces all over the ground floor – and upstairs too, Oliver suspected. In the sitting room, slung over the sofa, were a blue anorak he had not seen before and several bulging plastic bags. An orange nylon rucksack was spewing its contents over the floor. Books and clothes and toiletries all in a muddle. Whoever had packed this was not a smart traveller going on an expensive island cruise.

Barry was standing in the kitchen, waiting for the kettle to boil. 'My dear fellow! How MARVELLOUS to see you! Fancy a Rolo?' There were two chocolate toffees left in the tube, which looked as if it had been in someone's jacket pocket for a year. Oliver declined the offer.

'Felix came,' said Barry, joyfully.

Oliver scowled. 'Oh, really?'

'Yes, but he's gone away again. Back to Manchester. Flying visit.'

The macerator engine of the understairs toilet started up. The door opened and a girl came out and into the kitchen.

'But he left Stephanie behind. This is Stephanie,' said Barry, beaming. 'Stephanie, this is Oliver, the bone-cruncher – Andrea's ex-toyboy.'

'Hi,' she said. 'I was thrown out of my hall of

residence, and Felix said it would be OK if I stayed here for a bit.'

'And I'm afraid that in your absence, Ollie – *in loco PARENTIS* as it were – I said that that would be absolutely fine.' The kettle boiled and Barry made three mugs of tea, putting four teaspoons of sugar in his own. He had found that the craving for alcohol was less acute if he kept his blood sugar level very high, and staying high on marijuana ensured that he craved sugar. He even felt he was achieving some kind of 'balance', as Oliver had put it. The nicotine addiction was harder to conquer, of course, but he had managed to break his brand allegiance to the woody tang of French cigarettes – which was a start – and he was now putting a small amount of rolling tobacco into the joints which he smoked all through the day, beginning before breakfast – at which he had actually managed to eat a piece of toast for three days in a row now. He was running low on weed, though, and must see about replenishing his supply.

Stephanie was wearing typical student clothes: sweatshirt and jeans. No make-up, and her hair looked like it needed a wash.

'How is Felix?' Oliver asked her, accepting his tea from Barry. He had no intention of drinking this milky supermarket brew, but he took the mug anyhow and began to clear the empties from the surfaces in the kitchen and put them on the drainer.

'He had to go back to Manchester because he's so close to finishing his thesis. It's really exciting. And he's got these people in San Francisco who are really interested in it. It's really, really important.' Stephanie had a beautiful voice. Low and mellifluous, like a bowed double bass. It put Oliver in mind of the underwater recordings of cetaceans which Andrea used to play to calm her nerves.

'My son is a total shit, to be frank,' said Barry. 'He's left poor Stephanie here in the classical lurch. Bunged a little bun in her oven, brought her down here to the grime on the chuff-chuff and then buggered off back to the land of flat caps and rain to single-mindedly pursue his glittering career.'

Oliver, who was now doing the washing-up, stole a glance at Stephanie. She had a pretty, boyish face and fresh, soft skin. She was attractive, but not to Oliver. She looked honest, patient, pleasant, sweet even. And pregnant. This was a disaster. The thought that he could become a step-grandfather before he had even reached his own personal sexual starting-blocks irritated him intensely.

'Actually, the fecundity of young Stephanie's condition has given me an idea, Oliver,' Barry went on, 'regarding the house. Don't you think we should sell it? My horrible offspring may be a bit of a cunt – if you'll pardon the gratuitous use of the C word in this inappropriate context – but I most certainly am not. Young mother's going to need a nest, going to need a super-duper washing machine and all the accoutrements. Felix could buy her a nice little place with his share of the takings. Do the little creep some good to take some responsibility for a change.'

And what would you know about responsibility? thought Oliver. You who abandoned your son. You who spent more money on cigarettes than you ever have on your own child. What sort of an example have you set?

Stephanie explained that she only intended to stay until she had sorted out somewhere else to live, that she had no intention of relying on anyone, especially not Felix. There was no sense of panic in her voice; her words came out steadily and evenly. 'I want to be totally independent,' she said.

'I see,' replied Oliver stiffly, and walked through to the sitting-room area to collect the rest of the empty cups. There were biscuit crumbs on the hurricane-wood table and a plate with half a piece of toast on it on the floor.

'With the greatest respect, Stephanie, nobody is totally independent,' said Barry. 'How did you get here? On a train built by Italians. What did you eat for your tea? Some rather nice wholemeal waffles I found in the fridge, made of American wheat, prepared yesterday with considerable know-how by our friend Ollie the osteopath over here. No one – from a wandering saddhu to Ken Livingstone – is totally independent. We are all part of the giant interconnected alphabet soup of life.' There was a time, Barry thought, when he would have felt compelled to expand this theme until it became a vessel capable of holding one thousand words of vitriolic wit: 'Mick Jagger might be able to do as he pleases somewhat more than most of us, but even he is dependent – on Keith Richards, on the lazy off-beats of Charlie Watts, on his wardrobe stylist, on his sperm count.' That sort of thing. He suddenly felt an over-whelming sense of relief that his days as a jester at the court of the Saturday *Express* were over; he could hang up his stick of bells for good. He sat down beside Stephanie and began rolling another joint. Oliver made a tutting noise. Rylance Avenue was becoming a student squat.

'And you're sure it's Felix's?' asked Oliver on return-ing to the kitchen sink. He could not look Stephanie in the eye.

Barry took exception to this remark. 'Not even my ghastly son stooped as low as to question the paternity. Anyway, they can do blood tests these days. And before you insult the poor girl further; no, she does not intend to have an abortion, she is one hundred and ninety-nine per cent committed to popping the little sprog. Aren't you, my dear?' Stephanie nodded.

'Look, if it's a problem me being here, I'll leave tomorrow,' she said. 'I just didn't have anywhere else to go. My mum is a schizophrenic, she lives in a home, so I can't really go back and move in with her, and my dad runs a bar in Ibiza.'

'The Balearic island famous for its trannies, lager louts and all-night Ecstasy jamborees. Not exactly the place for a Madonna and child. There is definitely room in this inn. In fact, I suggested she sleeps in what is anachronistically known as the "master bedroom". We're not exactly making use of it, are we?'

Oliver could almost physically feel Andrea's displeasure at this suggestion. The thought of a young, pretty, pregnant girl sleeping in her room, touching her art, her furniture, created a waft of cold air which seemed to breeze through the kitchen at ghostly speed. It did nothing, though, to cool Oliver's agitation, but rather fanned his grumbling anger into a flame.

'Why don't you just leave?' he said suddenly. 'Both of you. Why don't you just fuck off and leave me alone? I've tried to be fair and show you kindness all along and all you've done is use me and take advantage of me and . . . and, oh just FUCK OFF! And take all this rubbish with you.' He threw a Mexican skeleton puppet which was hanging in the hall at Stephanie's head. She moved out of the way. 'Get out of my house! Get out!' He grabbed at Barry's sleeve and tried to tug him towards the front door. Despite being a lot shorter, Barry was heavier than him and not so easy to shift. 'Go on! Get out! Now! And all this junk! You can take it with you!'

He tore an Egyptian hieroglyphic papyrus from the wall and threw it at the front door. Stephanie retreated to the kitchen.

'Steady on, old chap,' said Barry. 'There's a baby in the house.' Oliver lunged at him and, grabbing for his neck and missing, snatched a handful of Barry's thinning hair. They toppled over together on to the circumcision table, which collapsed under their weight, snapping one of its stout ebony legs at the hilt. 'My heart! My heart! I have to be careful of my heart!' Barry managed to say from underneath Oliver.

Stephanie reached for the washing-up bowl, now empty of cups, stepped forward and sluiced the water suddenly over Oliver's back. 'Come on, boys, it's time to stop now,' she said gently. In the momentary pause when Oliver stopped his attack to register the temperature of the water, Stephanie knelt down and put her arm around his shoulders. 'It's all right,' she said soothingly. 'It's all right. It's OK.' Oliver's breathing was still charged with energy, but Stephanie's calm voice seemed to have begun to untie the knot of his agitation. He tried to slow his breathing. 'Come on, let's get up now,' she said, her arm still firmly around his shoulders. With her other hand she held his elbow. Barry was impressed. It seemed to him as if Stephanie had some invisible balm which she was passing through her fingertips into Oliver. Like the aroma from an essential oil. And it was quite deliberate and determined what she was doing, as well as brave. As Oliver rose to his full height, towering over her, she kept a hold of his hand, and, looking steadily into his eyes, maintained a focus with him until she felt confident that he had calmed down enough to manage on his own. His breathing was coming in slower bursts now, and he looked at the floor.

'Wow!' said Barry, who was also standing again. 'Where the bloody hell did you learn to do that?'

'Oh, I used to work in a discotheque in Manchester,' said Stephanie. 'You OK now?' she asked Oliver. He nodded shamefacedly.

'Yes thanks. Sorry.' He was angry with Andrea for putting him through this. He didn't deserve it. He could feel her waxy spirit admonishing him from every wall hanging, from every object, from every ethnic piece of furniture. Her afterglow was manifesting itself all around him; from the Malaysian rug under his feet to the Greek embroidered net curtains. It would all have to go, he realised. All of it. He would have to clear the whole house out. And, he thought with a spiteful relish, he knew exactly the right man to hire for the removal job. A man with a big van. His father, Bob Verbier of Eezy-Lay Carpets on the Harrow Road.

ELEVEN

The first thing Oliver noticed about his father was his knees. They were obviously causing him considerable pain, and the hobbling walk this forced on him had created a scoliosis which had thrown his entire posture out of alignment. The right shoulder was higher than the left and his neck sagged forward as if he was wearing a large necklace made of lead. The combination of saxophone-playing and carpet-laying for so many years had taken its toll on Bob Verbier's physique. But it was plain to Oliver's practised eye that the area of most pain was the knees, which were accustomed to thrusting forward into the spiked plunger he used to stretch a carpet up to the skirting board and hold it there while he nailed or glued it in place. There was little one could do to alleviate his father's symptoms, in Oliver's professional opinion, unless treatment was accompanied by a change in lifestyle, which included altering the regular mechanistic functions he expected his body to perform. In other words, give up carpets and the sax. So Oliver decided not to pass any comment.

Oliver's choice of removal man could not have been

more apposite, as it turned out that not only did Bob possess the van large enough to contain every piece of ethnic art and furniture in Rylance Avenue in just two loads, but he also had the perfect contact to act as 'fence' for all the gear – Julian Crechy's Arts Emporium shop under the motorway at the top end of the Portobello Road on the corner of Oxford Gardens, which was located in the old ironmonger's and had knick-knacks crammed from floor to ceiling. No doubt if they had bothered to hawk the stuff around the classier end of Westbourne Grove, or even auctioned it at Bonhams in Lots Road, it would have fetched a superior price, but Oliver was insistent that they get rid of it in one go, as a job lot.

It was a wet January morning, and the heavy rain had made loading the van somewhat unpleasant. Some of the Mexican papier-mâché figures had quickly become sodden and were ruined. Oliver was not in the mood to cover things properly in protective bubble-wrap. Oliver's toe, Bob's knees, Barry's heart condition and Stephanie's pregnancy also meant that the clearance of all traces of Andrea from Rylance Avenue had soon become a slap-stick affair. Bob had not been able to find an exploitable strong lad at such short notice, and in any case, he had not been entirely convinced, initially, that Oliver's request was genuine. It seemed peculiar to him that after a decade or more of silence, the successful man his son had so evidently become was incapable of booking a normal removal company from the Yellow Pages. That and Oliver's eagerness to accept a knock-down price for the goods had convinced Bob that there was something dodgy going on. He had done Julian Crechy several favours in the past and knew he would pay cash for the right kind of merchandise, so by two o'clock, Andrea's legacy was piled high in the back of Julian's shop – in any order – waiting to be discovered by interior designers and trendy first-time buyers keen on loft lifestyles.

Oliver derived a perverse pleasure from underselling his late partner's beloved collection. It gave him a sense of release, with a hint of new beginnings. He was also pleased to be meeting his father anew from the exalted position of employer. This little bit of status bestowed some security and ensured he would not have his time wasted again, as had happened at the Prince Albert. When they were done, he gave Bob two hundred pounds from the wedge and then returned the large roll of notes to its envelope in his inside coat pocket.

'Shall we go for a pint then?' said Bob, looking at his watch. 'I had a couple of measure-ups to do this afternoon, but I'm fucking shagged and thirsty now.'

Oliver regretted agreeing to go for a drink with his father after the first three minutes. He didn't like the area, the clientele, the atmosphere, or the drink. He was not at all comfortable with alcohol during the daytime, and now the job was done he felt a strong urge to get away from his father before he got hurt again.

'So this bird of yours, she the same one who went to Brazil to have a fibrosis removed by one of those magic surgeons who only use their bare hands?' asked Bob, as they made for a table in the smokey bowels of the Elgin.

'Yes,' said Oliver.

'Did it work?'

'No. She had to get flown back for emergency treatment at the Royal Free. How did you know about that?'

'Oh, I speak to Sandra, or she writes, once every two or three years. Keeps me informed as to the wackier details of your progress. Sounded to me like your missus was a complete fucking nutter.'

'Thanks for that.' Oliver was straining to feel any connection whatsoever with his father. 'She was a bit eccentric, I suppose.'

'You're telling me, pal. Some of that gear today was just bonkers. So why did you pick her? She was no spring chicken, from what I heard.'

'It wasn't quite like that, Bob,' said Oliver, careful not to use the word Dad.

'You know what my ideal girlfriend would be?' Bob asked, licking the Rizla on his roll-up. 'The next one!' He broke into a wheezy cackle and swivelled the spindly cigarette between his lips.

The weather had cleared. A shaft of sunlight sliced its way through the smoke in the front room of the pub. Oliver could feel the warmth of it on his shoulder. He longed to be gone. He was halfway through his beer, whilst his father had taken barely a couple of sips. 'Actually, I really ought to be going while the rain's stopped,' he said. He felt silly that having got in touch with Bob at last, all he wanted to do was leave without asking him any questions. Bob seemed not to mind either way, and blew more smoke into the sunbeam.

'That's jazz, mate. It's cool and hot. As Bing Crosby once sang,' he said.

Oliver got up, downed the rest of his beer and, promising to ring Bob again soon, strode out on to Ladbroke Grove. The winter sun was not actually that bright outside, but the sky was clear and the smell of the recent rain on the skeletal trees was almost like spring. Oliver had no idea where he was going to go, so he started up the Grove towards Notting Hill tube station. His toe was giving him a lot of discomfort, so when he got to the shops at Holland Park Avenue, he decided to buy some new shoes using some of the notes from the roll. He bought a pair of brown suede loafers one size too large, so that the wound would not rub so much at every step. 'I'll wear them now,' he said to the assistant, and then dumped his old shoes in a litter bin on Kensington Church Street. He saw a 38 bus going south and got on, riding as far as South Kensington, where he bought a cream pastry and ate it walking along the Fulham Road. He never bought cream pastries, he never ate walking along the street, and he despised those who did. He felt he could do anything, anything he liked. He even contemplated going to Tite Street to see if Carla and Eco were in, and paying them to perform for him as Barry had suggested. He found that the thought of going there, or even phoning, brought down his buoyant mood. So he banished it from his mind with ease. Maybe he'd done the right thing after all, walking out of Tite Street that night. Perhaps Eco and the sad old milksops at Mrs Baldry's Paddle Club were the ones with cause to feel ashamed. Perhaps he, Oliver Verbier, had reason to be proud. He wondered if he had ever felt so alive. At every step he could feel the envelope of money under his coat, like a protective shield over his heart.

He came down Sydney Street and into the King's Road. He felt damp and grubby in the old clothes he had put on this morning to do the removal job, so he went into Wodehouse and bought a pair of dark woollen trousers with a thin shiny belt. He was pleased to find a jacket with a long enough back and sleeves. Because of his height, Oliver was used to having little choice when it came to wardrobe. It was a beautiful jacket, made of a lightweight cloth which bounced back into place when crumpled, rather than crunching up and creasing. It was a subtle maroon colour with flecks of teal spattered through the weave. As before, he binned his old clothes and sauntered on. Looking in the window of Reason, he saw a white shirt he liked the look of. It had an Indian Nehru-style collar, and woven buttons. It was one hundred and twenty pounds and he bought it. At The Sports Shop, he bought new socks and Calvin Klein underpants. At a shop which looked more like an optical toy gallery, he bought a knee-length pale mackintosh in case there was another shower. The trappings of his old self were now scattered like murdered body parts in litter bins up and down the Royal Borough of Kensington and Chelsea. He bought a bottle of Armani For Him scent, sprayed some on and chucked away not only the expensive box, tissue and designer carrier bag it had come in, but the rest of the bottle. He wasn't sure about scent. He went into Rococo, the shop selling chocolates made from eighty per cent cocoa solids, and bought two beribboned tablets of chocolate with juniper berries, a mouthful of which is enough to keep you awake longer than a large espresso. As he rounded the wiggle in the road at World's End, he was carrying nothing – no shopping bags, no shoulder bag – but the bulge in his inside pocket did not seem to have decreased substantially.

He saw a hairdresser's called Smile, and, smiling, decided to go in for a shampoo and cut. They offered him coffee, and as he sat waiting for Leslie to become available, idly flicking through fashion magazines and listening to the Robert Palmer CD they had playing at just the right volume, it occurred to him in a moment of inspiration what he was going to do with the rest of the money. He wondered why he had not thought of it before.

With his hair looking just right – not too trendy, not too worked on – with a small amount of Kiehl's pomade in it to give it a little lift and shine, Oliver breezed out of Smile and hailed a taxi to take him to Chelsea Harbour. Only five minutes' walk away now, but there was a hint of more rain in the sky and he didn't want to test the waterproof qualities of his new mackintosh just yet.

Alighting at the Conrad Hotel, he was greeted in the concourse by a uniformed man in a gold-braided top hat. 'Afternoon, sir,' he said. Oliver returned the greeting and entered the marbled lobby of the hotel. In his new clothes he looked just right in this place. There was a model of a ship in a glass case on the large inlaid centrepiece table. The ceiling was as high as a church, but because of the massive skylight windows, the whole area was bright and even the remote corners were full of light. Enormous Turkish rugs were neatly laid out across the marble. To his left was a gift shop with a rack of international newspapers; to his right the large reception desk, behind which were two impossibly beautiful girls in dark-green uniforms. The temperature in this cavernous space was perfect, not too warm like in some lesser hotels, nor excessively refrigerated. The heating and air-conditioning bills must be enormous, he reflected.

Oliver kept walking right through the lobby, without pausing to look around, without asking anybody directions, past the lifts and up plushly carpeted steps towards he had no idea where. It was important, at least, to look as if he knew his way around. At each new hallway, uniformed staff would nod hello at him. He felt sublime. At last he saw a sign for the Gents'. The doorways here cleared the top of his head by at least a foot. For someone used to having to stoop and duck, this was pure luxury. In the cubicle, he sat and counted the money. There was four thousand eight hundred and seventy-five pounds left. He peeled off three hundred and seventy five pounds and put the notes in his trouser pocket, leaving four thousand five hundred in the envelope, which he returned to his inside coat pocket. Then, folding his coat over his arm, he swung out of the cubicle. In the washroom there was an old man in a black waistcoat and bow-tie who, without being asked, brushed the shoulders of Oliver's jacket with an old-fashioned wooden-handled clothes brush. Oliver reached into his trouser pocket and tossed a ten-pound note into the man's little wicker basket. 'Thank you, sir,' said the man, as if he received this kind of tip as a matter of course. This was fun. Looking in the mirror, Oliver realised that his glasses had missed out on the afternoon's overall make-over – they put one in mind of a trainspotter or a computer nerd – so he took them off and put them in his top pocket. Now he couldn't make out his own features in the mirror. Squinting, he took them out again. 'Allow me, sir,' said the old man and gently took the glasses from him. On his rack of cleaning equipment was a small spray bottle and a yellow dust-free cloth. With expertise, he polished Oliver's glasses, running the edge of the cloth through the hinges like dental floss. He took his time and then passed them back to Oliver, open and ready to wear, being careful not to smudge the lenses with his thumb. A first-class job. Oliver didn't tip him again, but saying, 'Thank you so much,' in as grand a tone as he could manage, he left the Gents' in search of the bar, which he found quite easily by following a waitress carrying a silver bucket containing a bottle of champagne.

In here, the uniforms were green again. It was empty apart from a small group of smart middle-aged men in suits sitting at a corner table with two overdressed and carefully coiffured women. The champagne was for them and the waitress put the bucket in a stand by their table, removing a used bucket with an upturned empty bottle in it. On the bar itself were Japanese rice snacks in little cut-glass bowls. Despite his usual avoidance of drinking during the day and his dislike of spirits in general, Oliver ordered an expensive brandy for courage, and while the barman was pouring it, he asked him casually for some help.

'I'm looking for someone who lives in the flats here and who I believe is one of your regulars. Sophie's the first name, but I'm afraid I never did get her last name. I have something for her.' In his trouser pocket he fingered the loose notes, ready to pluck one out if the barman needed encouragement. 'She's an acquaintance of Barry Fox, you know, the journalist?'

'I think I know who you mean, sir. In fact, if you'd like to take a seat, I could call her and tell her you're here. Mr . . . ?'

'Oliver Verbier. Thanks so much, Bernard,' said Oliver, reading the man's name from his laminated lapel badge. He paid for the drink with a tenner, and telling Bernard to keep the change, sat, as suavely as he could, in one of the pastel-upholstered seats by the balcony window overlooking the marina. It was dark now, the sky was overcast again, and through the immaculate double glazing, Oliver could faintly hear the squeaking of the pontoons and river cruisers in the water outside. There was low-key music playing in the bar: an anodyne orchestral arrangement of Phil Collins' 'Another Day in Paradise'. A second waitress stopped by with a little bowl of olives and cocktail sticks. Andrea would have hated this place. Oliver stretched his legs and wished he had something to read. At the bar, Bernard was on the phone.

After a few minutes, and some annoyingly loud laughter from the corner table, Bernard came over discreetly to where Oliver was sitting and told him that Sophie knew he was here, and that if he cared to wait, she would join him in a while. He asked if Oliver would care for another drink while he was waiting. Oliver ordered a coffee. He really didn't want to be drunk.

A few minutes passed rather slowly, then a very large woman of about fifty, in a patterned smock and a headscarf, came in. She had a flat leather bag with her and, flustered and out of breath, she sat at a table near Oliver's and ordered a glass of white wine and a smoked salmon sandwich, with a special request for a side order of root-vegetable chips. Thinking this must be Sophie, Oliver leaned forward in his chair expectantly, but she did not register him at all, turning instead to the contents of her document case. Around her neck was a pen on a chain with which she began to scribble notes on the stapled pages.

There was so much Andrea would have found objectionable about this place: the feeling that you were in a capsule of comfort whose exact parameters had been predetermined by a fashion designer; the overuse of plush fabrics on chairs, walls and windows, the vast vases of lilies in the vestibule; the temperature control. 'It's so eighties,' she would have said, and would have said it loudly, to Oliver's acute embarrassment.

He scanned the tall tower outside, with its impressive Canary Wharf-style roof, where Michael Caine is reputed to own an entire floor with three-hundred-and-sixty-degree views across London. Catching his own reflection in the glass, Oliver decided that he liked it here. The brandy had made him feel warm inside. He could feel the wool of his new trousers rubbing gently against his knees, the silk of his shirt cooling his armpits. It was all very pleasant. His coffee arrived and he squeezed the plunger of the cafetière down and put a rough-cut lump of raw cane sugar in his cup. He thought he would wait a while until the coffee cooled before pouring. It was there mostly to give him the appearance of having something to do.

Two of the silver-haired men at the corner table got up to leave. There were kisses goodbye and numerous 'ciao's. The two women and one remaining man poured the rest of the champagne into their glasses. The big woman was nearly finished with her sandwich and root vegetable chips, her attention never straying from the papers in her other hand. Oliver looked at his watch; it was nearly seven o'clock. He pulled the cuff of his shirt down over his wrist. He had omitted to buy a new watch, and his cheap Swatch did not fit the new image.

He recalled a time, in the early days of his relationship with Andrea, returning to a quiet Rylance Avenue with Felix, when he had told the boy, then eleven or so, to wait in the hall while he checked every room in the house in case Andrea had committed suicide while they were at the cinema, as she had threatened in a dramatic mood the night before. Other memories of the house came and went: the mess, the installation of the damp course. Evidence of Felix's experiments everywhere.

The endless washing-up. Redecorating the hall. Clearing the rubble out of the garden. Work, all of it. Hard work. He remembered the many times Andrea had been too drunk or stoned to wash before going to bed, and how he had carried her up the stairs, or tucked her in – on her side – on the sofa. He wondered momentarily whether her death had been deliberate, and dismissed the idea. Much more likely to have been a self-indulgent accident, as the coroner had decided. Her theatrics had subsided considerably since the success of the Gaia gallery. Not like her to do it without letting everyone know.

At the corner table, the remaining man helped one of the women into a fur coat. A genuine fur coat, Oliver noticed, not synthetic. Another thing to which Andrea would have objected vociferously. Not that he approved, of course, but he preferred to keep his opinions to himself in public. The lone woman now left at the table idly finishing her glass of champagne was quite something. She was black, and though she was still sitting, Oliver could see from the length of her legs that she was very tall. Poise and posture, very good. Neck long and held perfectly. Her shoulders were not rounded in any way, but relaxed and strong. Andrea would have derided her full make-up, but Oliver thought she looked fantastic.

'So, Mr Verbier? You have something for me, I believe?' she called out across the room, and gave him a

luscious smile. Afterwards, Oliver complimented himself that he hadn't revealed his surprise, hadn't done a
clownish double-take, nor stood up suddenly, knocking
over the table with his knees. He had merely smiled
back at her, and, in his own time, risen and walked
slowly over to her table. She held up her glass and raised
her eyebrows to Bernard behind the bar, who nodded
and had words with one of the green-waistcoated
waitresses, who hurried out of the room.

'A little present, perhaps?' she said, as Oliver took the
seat indicated by her.

'Actually, yes.' He reached into his jacket pocket for
the second bar of beribboned Rococo chocolate with
juniper berries. That bit had just come to him. He
hadn't planned it. He was a natural.

'Juniper, my absolute favourite. How did you know?
I'm Sophie, I've been watching you. You're all sad,
aren't you? Are you going to tell me why, darling?' She
lowered her lids and looked at him through half-closed
eyes. She had a whole armoury of techniques, and
Oliver felt flattered to be included in the game.

They shook hands, she offering him only the ends of
her fingers, not the full palm. Her nails were deep red
and long, and she had on a charm bracelet like a child's
except that the trinkets were studded with precious
stones. A fresh bucket of champagne arrived, with two
shining new glasses. Oliver was not asked if he felt like
a glass, it was assumed. Sophie waited until the waitress

had finished pouring, and then, without acknowledging or thanking the girl, raised her glass to her lips and said, 'Down the old hatch, then.' Although impressed, mesmerised even, by Sophie's appearance and charm, Oliver was still in charge of himself enough to take only the smallest of sips from his glass.

'I've come to pay you some money which I believe you are owed by Barry Fox, a friend of mine. But before I do, I want to ensure that it is used in a suitable way. I want to make sure that the flat at Phoenix Mansions is vacated so that Mr Fox can return to live there.' Sophie said nothing, so Oliver continued: 'This is not because I like Mr Fox so much and want to do him a favour, but more to get him out of my house, where he is currently staying.' He could feel his heart rate increasing slightly. Sophie still said nothing, her lack of reaction unnerved him. And suddenly, he was telling her about Eco, and about Carla's credit-card swiper.

'Oh dear,' said Sophie, smiling, when he had finished. 'We don't like that, no, we don't like that at all. I've been at Rushtons in Berkshire all over Christmas. What they get up to if you turn your back on them for a second!'

Then, getting carried away, Oliver lied. He told Sophie that he had seen the phone number of Phoenix Mansions on a prostitute's card in a phone box in Earl's Court. He figured it would be the surest way to convince Sophie to evict Eco and Carla.

'Goodness!' said Sophie. 'The dirty little scrubber.' Oliver refilled her glass as if he had been to a butler's training academy. She reached for her mobile phone, which was on the seat beside her, and pressed automatic dial with the ball of her thumb, which, because of the long nails, was the only digit capable of making contact with the tiny buttons. This is a woman who has to have everything done for her, thought Oliver, like Chinese women and their miniature bound feet. He didn't realise that the nails were fake and came off at night. After a few rings, she snapped shut her mobile and put it back on the seat. 'Answerphone,' she said, shrugging her shoulders. Feeling that the moment was right, Oliver reached into his mackintosh pocket and retrieved the envelope, which he now realised was still slightly soggy from its earlier journey in his old wet coat. Damn, he should have stopped off at Ryman's and bought a new envelope.

'This is the first bit,' he said, offering it to her. She didn't reach for it, so he left it on the table between them. 'It's four thousand five hundred. I hope that's enough for now.' He refolded his new mackintosh on the seat beside him. Sophie gave him an admonishing look, and then burst into raucous giggles, which she appeared not to be able to stop. She put her hand daintily in front of her mouth in case there was a lipstick stain on her teeth, and carried on laughing, as if from behind a fan. Then she patted her chest and swallowed.

'Oh dear! You've not done this before, have you, darling?' she said, and then the giggling started again. 'Oh my! Oh my!' When the giggling was over she reached for a cigarette from the table. Holding it close to her mouth between her first two fingers, she waited, looking at Oliver with little ripples of laughter dancing across her face. She waited some more, and with her eyes, indicated the lighter on the table beside her Marlboro Lights. He was a second too slow. 'You're supposed to light my ciggie, you gorgeous man,' she squealed, and gave a deeper, dirtier laugh. Oliver reached for the lighter, but too late. Sophie grabbed it, lit her cigarette and blew the first smoke in a long line at Oliver's face.

The big woman at the other table was paying her bill now, and packing up her leather briefcase. She walked out of the room, leaving the two of them alone. Bernard was still quietly sitting behind the bar, but the waitresses must have been called away to other duties.

'So what do you do for a living then, Mr Verbier?' Sophie asked when she had managed to subdue her mirth and taken another long slurp of champagne.

'Well, I'm an osteopath,' said Oliver, and, trying to reclaim some ground, added, 'and holistic masseur.'

'Ooooh,' said Sophie. 'How super.' She picked up the envelope and weighed it in her hand for a moment, then put it on the seat beside her. 'So, it's a deal,' she said. 'They're history. Give me till Friday. Now.

About you. What kind of a massage did you say you gave?'

Sophie's apartment was on the fourth floor of one of the blocks to the side of the hotel. It was furnished as it had been when the estate agent showed her round, like a show-home. The squared-off sofa, which ran around the corner of the open-plan living room, was biscuit-coloured. The various oatmeal cushions on it were arranged in regular diagonals and looked as if they had never been sat on. The shiny wooden floor had a plain ochre rug on it, which stretched to within a foot of the skirting. All woodwork, such as door and window frames, skirting and fitted shelf units, was painted in pale-cream silk. The coffee table, which was low-slung, was white and square, and had no magazines or books on it, only a bowl containing ceramic fruit. Side tables held black Chinese porcelain lamps with cool cream shades. A dimmer switch by the front door controlled all the lights. There were elongated empty vases in shapes which could not possibly support more than a single stem. On a pedestal painted in beige marbling was a dark-green plaster Buddha. The dining table was glass-topped and the chairs around it steel and wicker. Pure white Roman blinds hung above the main double windows, and if you stood towards the cloakroom end of these, you could see the river and the lights of Albert Bridge. No children had ever been in this flat. No students, no one elderly. Nobody had ever kipped over on the sofa, nor been sick in the kitchen sink. Oliver loved it.

He sat with his arm outstretched along the back of the sofa while Sophie went to the kitchen to fetch a fresh bottle of champagne from the fridge, which contained no food whatsoever. Oliver could feel his breathing evening out. He stole a glance at his watch. It was nearly eight o'clock. Sophie came back into the spacious room with two full glasses and an ash tray. She went over to the built-in sound system and, with one click, the room was softly filled with some unidentifiable classical music: Haydn, Handel, Bach. The volume was low enough for it not to matter. She kicked off her shoes and sat down on the sofa a few feet away from him.

'So,' she said, grinning at him, 'you can look, and you can touch. Well, obviously you can touch, that's the whole point. You have to touch. But no funny business with me. I know plenty who will be interested in funny business, if you're any good. But first, let me test-drive you.'

For an osteopath, fingertip sensitivity is an essential diagnostic tool. In osteopathic school, students are trained to be able to feel a human hair through the page of a book. Then through two pages. Then three, and so on. Oliver had come top of his class repeatedly when it came to diagnostic exams. He was good. Very good.

TWELVE

After the van was loaded, Stephanie and Barry had gone back into the house, which now seemed like a ghostly mausoleum. On the walls were pale shapes where pictures or hangings had been which resembled blank memorial stones with the words blown away like desert sand. The carpets had strange indentations, like runic signs, left by the heavier furniture. Where rugs had been, the floorboards were patterned with brighter shapes. Acoustically it had changed too; there was a brittle resonance without the bric-a-brac. Of course, not everything had gone. The Conran stools remained. One or two ordinary chairs, the beds. But the cryptic Tibetan carving had disappeared from the bedhead of the main bedroom.

Barry went to the kitchen to fetch his jar of honey. He had taken to walking around with honey and a teaspoon. He actually hadn't had a drink now for two days. There had been some shakes and sweats, but, as yet, no hallucinatory creepy-crawlies on the ceiling. He ought to have considered himself lucky. At the kitchen counter he began to roll a joint, using the last few scraps from the bag Tara had given him.

'Don't do that,' said Stephanie. 'Let's try and go for a walk. The rain'll clear in a minute. I've got to get exercise now I'm pregnant. And you ought to as well. We don't have to go very far.'

After a fruitless search for wellingtons, they left Rylance Avenue and walked on to Clapham Common. The rain had settled into a light drizzle, but there had been enough of it already to make a sloshing noise on the ground as cars drove by. The Common was sodden and their progress was slow. Barry was out of breath after the first three minutes and Stephanie was feeling bilious. But they persevered as far as the triangle – about five hundred yards away – and then took a rest on a wet bench under a plane tree.

'I'm on the way out, you know,' said Barry. 'I haven't been flavour of the month since February nineteen eighty-seven, and February's a very short month.'

'Oh don't be such a wanker,' replied Stephanie, pushing her fingers gently into her belly to see if she could feel anything yet. 'You're well out of journalism, mate. Everyone knows that the newspapers print lies. And Oliver's letting you live in that lovely place. I've got to start looking properly for somewhere today.'

'My dear girl, although he may have behaved like an absolute bastard, I can assure you that young Oliver would never dream of dumping you in the poorhouse. It's not in his nature. He's actually a big girl's blouse.

Not really his house anyway. It's mine, if truth be known. Consider yourself accommodated.'

They had another go at walking, but gave up when they got as far as the tube station, because Barry caught sight of the off-licence at the top of Clapham Park Road and Stephanie agreed it would be better to turn back rather than put him through any unnecessary torment. God smiled on their decision, and the clouds parted, making the walk home much more pleasant.

'I'm in a time of ashes,' Barry said, as they took off their wet things in the hall.

'Well, that's quite right,' said Stephanie. 'It usually takes at least a year to get over someone dying like that. I don't think Felix realises quite what's happened with regard to his mum, but he's a lot younger than you. It'll probably hit him later. He's just into his work right now. He's quite manic.'

'*Senex bis puer*,' said Barry. 'Or in your case, *bis puella*. What were you studying at university, my wise old soul?'

Stephanie told Barry about her psychology course, and how boring it had been. And also about her childhood with a schizophrenic mother, and how that had meant she had to grow up faster than her friends in Norwich. They had tea and biscuits and the last joint, of which Stephanie only took one puff. She told Barry how she was concerned that Felix, being a genius, might not be the one to reap the rewards of his own invention. FoetalWeb, an internet company in San Francisco, had expressed a great interest in Felix's software designs, and in Felix himself. It's not often – she said – that the real innovators in the world benefit from their own inspiration, because they are working in the dark, treading new paths, making surprise discoveries. It is those who follow in their footsteps who are so often able to exploit the new ideas to maximum advantage, because the path is now illuminated for them. It's not fair. Barry found himself automatically considering how he might turn this idea of hers into a thousand words and another week's rent. For a few seconds, he even gathered some possible examples in his mind: Gorbachev, Eddie Shah, Peter Cook. But then the thought dissolved, and he allowed himself to return to listening. He was sure he had never listened to someone for such a long stretch of time. It was a new and pleasurable experience.

Not that he lapsed into a humble silence. They were rummaging through the fridge for something light enough to satisfy both of their physiologically altered appetites. The trouble with not drinking – he said – and with eating properly, and taking more exercise and generally getting healthier, is that one is afraid of losing one's bite. That the dysfunctional and addictive elements within one are in fact the coals which stoke the furnace of one's genius, however limited that might be. In other words: if I cure myself, will I still be funny? Or will I turn into a tepid old bore content to live out my elongated days at room temperature?

'Who cares?' Stephanie had said, and then something about adapting to changes being a good thing. 'Happiness makes up in height what it lacks in length,' Barry had thought but not said. He had the feeling, with Stephanie, that coming up with a natty quote, even one from Robert Frost, would no longer do. They were having a genuine conversation, and to adorn it with nuggets from the encyclopaedic trash-can of his mind would have been inappropriate.

They agreed that Oliver's whole-earth, sugar-free plum jam would not satisfy, so they made cinnamon toast with a melted butter and brown sugar caramel. Stephanie only got through half of hers before feeling sick again and having to go to the macerator-toilet. When she returned, her complexion had turned a worrying greeny-white and Barry had expressed concern, which she dismissed. She lay out on a couple of cushions in the empty sitting-room area, explaining that she would be much better in about six weeks. Barry sat, propped against the wall, on the floor beside her.

He told her something he had never told anyone before, hardly even admitted to himself. When Felix was a baby – eight months old or so – and his cherubic skin was ripe and silken, his fragile scalp emitting an aroma of newness, he had on occasions spent some of the night in the marital bed with both his parents. One morning, while Andrea was bathing or sterilising bottles in the kitchen, Barry had found himself alone in the bed

264 ■ *Nigel Planer*

with the boy, naked except for a nappy, climbing over his chest and rolling in his arms. He had felt an overwhelming love for him and a joy at his son's innocent gurgles. At that moment, he felt, he completely understood that the two of them – he and Felix – were really but one manifestation of the same chemistry. And then this feeling had given him an erection. He felt ashamed and anxious. Could he not be trusted with his own child? Was he a latent paedophile? The erection had quickly subsided, of course, and the incident never recurred – he had made sure of that. He had never hugged Felix again, keeping him physically and emotionally at arm's length from then on. In retrospect, he told Stephanie, he supposed that it was merely a confusion of the body. Never having had physical contact of any sort with anyone – let alone skin to skin – other than for sexual purposes, his system had merely made an automatic assumption, like one of Pavlov's dogs. But the guilt remained to this day.

Stephanie found this story funny and her laughter brought some colour back into her cheeks. 'God, you poor thing,' she said. 'You poor old, sad old, stupid old git. What a waste. What a total waste.' Barry laughed too. She told him how her father had had to do most of her bringing-up because her mother had been in and out of mental hospitals throughout her childhood. When she was fifteen, her father had met someone else and started a new family in Spain, for which she was thankful. Happy for him that he'd had another chance, and now she had a couple of baby step-siblings.

'Well, my old man was shot down parachuting over France in nineteen forty-four, so I never really got to know him. Can't think why I turned out the way I did, really. My mother was a total pushover. I've got a very patriarchal aunt, though, if that's any help. She was an absolute sergeant-major.'

They spent the rest of the morning playing a game in which they each had to write down on one page what they considered to be their best qualities, and on another their worst bits – in stringent detail and with total honesty. Then they passed the pages to each other for perusal and amused themselves by questioning each other's choices. For instance, Stephanie wanted to know why Barry had put 'urgent impatience with the modern world' on his bad page, but 'dogged determination to see things through' on the good. This entertained them for an hour or two before Stephanie became sleepy.

In fact, Barry had become carried away when tabulating the negative aspects of his character, and this list had covered both sides of the page. As Stephanie began to drift into sleep, he started to worry that he had perhaps been too searingly honest in his appraisal of the less attractive attributes of his personality, and doubted whether he should have included 'was so pissed that I shat the bed in a five-star hotel in Torquay in 1985 and hid the soiled sheets in the swimming-pool towel trolley'. And had it really been necessary to record his unfortunate dalliances with prostitutes in the mid nineties, or the time he had lied that his mother had died to get out of doing a radio book review? When it came to Felix, his sins and omissions had warranted a whole subsection, and he wondered now, as Stephanie wavered between consciousness and slumber, whether it was such a good idea that she should possess this written testament to his awfulness. Gently, he asked her if he might have his Bad Bits back, but she laughed, telling him she owned his Bad Bits from now on. She apologised for her tiredness, and Barry left her to rest.

He pottered quietly around the kitchen for a few moments and then went upstairs looking for something to take his mind off the hunger and the emotional fretfulness which alcohol and cigarettes had staved off for two decades but failed to eradicate. On his desk in the boxroom he found a packet of nicotine chewing gum which Oliver had bought for him and placed in there. Popping three chunks in his mouth, he crossed the landing to the double bedroom where Stephanie's student rucksack and its contents were strewn across the bed. The walls and windowsills were bare. There was one cane chair still in there, and the chest of drawers which had been too heavy and cumbersome to load into Bob's van that morning. The place looked grey and sad. The little daylight there was was quickly absorbed in the dirty cream of the flattened carpet. He switched on the electric light, which was now a single bare bulb in the centre of the ceiling; Andrea's weird Spanish lace hanging shade was by now lying underneath an aboriginal rain stick in Julian Crechy's Arts Emporium. The artificial light made the room seem duller still to Barry. He switched it off again, went downstairs and, putting his wet shoes back on, tootled out of the back door. The garden was muddy from the rain, but smelt fresh and fruity. This was new for Barry, whose olfactory function had been defunct for as long as he could remember. Until last week, everything except wine and whisky had smelt of French tobacco.

He broke open the rusty padlock to the shed and found ancient carpentry tools covered in slimy cobweb dust; a side axe, a set of Stanley blades wrapped in pre-war greaseproof paper, a butterfly spokeshave, dowelling chisels with burnt umber handles. Maybe he knew these tools from years ago. He had forgotten their provenance. On the shelf were some stiff paintbrushes in an old jar, and a bottle of turpentine. Underneath were several rusting cans of paint. He levered one open. Beneath a leathery yellowing skin, Barry discovered two or three litres of bright-pink emulsion. He opened all the cans in turn, taking a mental inventory of what they had and what they lacked. It was cold in there, but the activity kept him warm.

There was half a can of indigo gloss, three unopened cans of grey primer, various quantities of white in different-sized tubs, some green deck paint, and a few good litres of primrose eggshell. He cleaned the brushes in the turps, using the last of some paint-stripper he found on the more obstinate ones. In this enclosed space, the fumes from the paint were giving him just the right kind of headache. He almost felt as if he'd had a couple of unrefined rums. He opened a can of wood glue and, holding it up to his nose, inhaled deeply. It created a thudding wooziness which would do, for the interim. People who make non-alcoholic beverages have completely the wrong idea, he thought. Aqua Libra, Ame, Purdeys. A delightful mixture of herbs and juices blended to provied a zestful and life-enhancing health drink. The creators of these drinks obviously have no understanding of the perennial appeal of alcohol, he thought. The whole point of drinking, as far as Barry was concerned, is to shake a fist at the devil, to test your mettle and risk the ruination of your mental and physical well-being. To make yourself ill and not care. He figured these herbal brewers would increase their sales exponentially if they put a dead venomous insect in the bottom of the bottle and a pounding-headache guarantee on the label, called it GutDrop, and made it hurt to swallow it. Drink that if you dare.

He put down the wood glue and carried as many of the paint cans and brushes as he could into the kitchen, where he put washing-up liquid through the brushes and left them to rinse. He walked through to where

Stephanie was still asleep, snoring now, and stood, looking at her for some moments. Her lips were bubbled out in slumber. She had rolled on to her side, with her head lying across her arm. She was quite a chubby girl, though whether this was puppy fat or the pregnancy, he could not tell. He wondered how old she was. Nineteen? Certainly no more than twenty-two, although her wisdom was indeed beyond her years. She was as beautiful as a princess, he thought. He made her a cup of sweet tea and left it on the floor beside her in case she woke, then carried the materials from the shed up to the bedroom. He dragged the bed into the middle of the room and pulled the covers over Stephanie's clobber. He was now breathless again and had to sit down for a while. He realised he was still chewing the nicotine gum. He spat it into the bin and went back downstairs to the shed to fetch the paint-spattered wooden steps he had noticed in there earlier. Where he found the energy to persevere in this endeavour was a mystery to him, but it seemed to be achievable if he kept to a slow, old man's pace, with little sit-downs every few minutes.

When the pink emulsion ran out, he began using the primrose eggshell without cleaning the brush in between, so there was an almost artful blending where one colour took over from the other. The hardest bit for Barry's heart and lungs was the ceiling, which ended up with a sort of accidental rag-roll effect in white and primrose. He had sweated and dried off three times before he got to the woodwork, which he went over roughly with floor-cleaning fluid from under the sink and was about to cover in the green deck paint when Stephanie came in, blinking and puffy from her sleep.

'What are you doing?' she asked. There were shapes like clouds across the walls, brought about by the coincidence of whatever colours the shed had yielded. Barry stood back, panting, and surveyed his work with pride.

'Decorating the nursery,' he puffed.

'Oh. OK,' she said. 'Thanks for the tea.' And she started off down the stairs again.

'You'd better not sleep in here tonight because of the fumes,' he called after her.

The doorbell rang. It was eight o'clock. More than four hours had gone by since he had started painting and Barry had not thought of booze and fags, had not thought about anything as a matter of fact. Anything that he could recall. This was a unique experience for him. He followed Stephanie downstairs to the front door.

On the doorstep was a portly man with ginger hair, dressed in a pinstripe suit and gabardine coat, carrying a flat City briefcase. He was nonplussed to find the door opened by a young and sleep-infested girl.

'Is Oliver in?' he demanded briskly of her.

'No, he's gone out with his father. He should be back

soon,' she said. Barry joined her at the door. He had droplets of different-coloured paint spattered across him, from his wild hair to his damp shoes. He looked somewhat like an aboriginal holy man.

'Oh, it's you.' A quick dart of the eyes from Barry to Stephanie and back again told them that the man had made an assumption about the two of them of which he did not approve. 'Well, tell him I called by. He is expecting us. Or should be.'

'Oh God, it's Tuesday,' said Barry, when the door was closed again. 'Oliver's masturbation class. Not like him to miss that.'

'What?' said Stephanie, smiling.

'Oh crikey, they'll all be here in a minute!'

'Who will?' she asked, following him back into the kitchen.

'The sad people. The *crambe repetita*, the reheated cabbages. Oliver has a fucking men's group here on a Tuesday. You'd better make yourself scarce or pretend to be a cabin boy or something, or they'll boil you in statistics. You don't shave your armpits, do you? Good, well that's something. Uh-oh, too late.' The doorbell rang a second time.

The worthy George was not going to let the presence of a female prevent him from conducting his men's group. They'd missed too many sessions over the Christmas period and it was time, he felt, to start a new term in their regular venue. He had arrived with John, the miserable bearded one, and, on discovering that Oliver was not there, simply assumed command of the sitting room by putting out the few remaining chairs and stools in the semblance of a circle. When he heard that Robert had already come and gone, he invited Barry and Stephanie to join the group's discussion for the evening, safe in the knowledge that Robert would have been the only one to have raised an objection to having a girl present. Claude was certainly happy with female company. Barry suggested that he and Stephanie retire to the osteopathic surgery for the duration, but a look from her reassured him that she was confident in such a situation. She really was an admirable woman as far as Barry was concerned. Michael arrived while they were setting out the chairs, bringing with him the usual excuses for the absence of Keith, the single-father minicab driver.

After congratulating Barry on his recovery, George opened the meeting with the announcement that John had finally received his decree absolute. This was something they should be celebrating, evidently.

'So tonight should in fact be a sort of Absolut party,' said Barry. 'But I'm afraid, gentlemen, that we have none of the eponymous vodka to hand, and in any case, after my recent downfall, I am not so sure it would have been appropriate.'

'Oh shut up, Barry,' said Stephanie affectionately. 'Stop being facetious.'

He shut up with grace. It seemed to him, all of a sudden, that this girl epitomised everything that has ever been right about the world. There's plenty, we know, that is wrong, he thought. But there is good, sometimes, dotted here and there, if we would only acknowledge it. And somehow this one's got it. Lots of it.

George, thought Barry, even with his counselling qualifications – whatever they might be – and his tie-less buttoned shirts and considered grey hairstyle, was still a self-serving cocky little fucker. Principally interested in showing off his own antlers and locking them in combat with other males to gain superiority over his peers, and hence conjugal rights over the does. Like all the rest, what he really wanted was to be an alpha male, but for some reason as yet ungraspable, Barry no longer felt the urge to challenge or belittle George with the sabre of his own wit.

Stephanie quickly became engaged in the debate and seemed, even, to be enjoying herself. Barry found his mind swimming in and out of focus. Particularly since John, who still looked miserable even with a decree absolute in his pocket, was sitting by the window, smoking again, and this was impossible to ignore. Stephanie was speaking: 'Well, I think history has covered up the private lives of fathers, and all the good things they've done, just as much as it has covered up the public lives of women over the centuries, and all the power they have covertly wielded.'

Sacrilege! thought Barry. 'See what happens? Let a woman into the club and first thing she starts telling you that men aren't so bad after all. Whatever next? Stephanie was aware of the cigarette smoke too. She looked across at Barry and asked if he'd mind sharing one with her since neither of them was supposed to smoke, and then, with great charm, she cadged a fag off miserable old grump-guts John. She only took a couple of puffs before passing it to Barry, and she got it back off him quite quickly and stubbed it out. Barry was damned if he could understand people who are capable of having a couple of cigarettes a day, or only smoking occasionally at parties. For him it was either the suicide black run or nothing. He watched Stephanie closely to see if he could find out how it was done. The group had moved on to a condemnation of polygamy in ancient 'harem' societies.

'Wasn't it more a question of some men doing without a wife at all so that the women could have access to the richest guy and their children would be safe?' Stephanie was saying. 'And it still does happen now, except you have to get a divorce first nowadays, which is not so honest. Presumably you still have to support your ex-wife, John, don't you?' John nodded. She was magnificent, this girl, thought Barry, totally magnificent. A goddess.

For a moment he felt a twinge of unwanted jealousy when it seemed she might be on some kind of mutually anthropological wavelength with George, who was bristling with a macho intellectualism in the wake of her remarks. But her open looks across to Barry reassured him that she did not intend to play George's game. Her social skills were in tip-top nick, thought Barry, she was making mincemeat of them.

As was his practice, George was quoting some long-interred statistic at them. 'The Beveridge welfare state model was based on full male employment and women not working at all, which actually only applies to six per cent of families.'

Barry was amazed at himself that he could not even be bothered to construct a sentence around the 'beverage/Beveridge' pun. What was happening to him? He felt most unlike himself. His blood seemed to be curdling and his vision was distorted. Was this what it was like to be normal? And then the magnificent creature got up and took his hand. Her palm was clammy and her fingernails were bitten like a child's, and she said to the assembly of men, 'I'm afraid we're going to have to leave you guys to it, because Barry's still recovering and I'm pregnant and we both need a bit of a rest. Can we get you all a cup of tea?' And she took Barry to the kitchen area and he didn't want to let go of her hand. He stood like a schoolboy waiting to be told what to do next. She smiled at him, asking if it was OK to have dragged them away from the group like that without consulting him, and he told her quietly he was completely in love with her, and she laughed and said, 'It's just that you were looking absolutely terrible,' and they made the men the tea.

It was nearly ten o'clock by the time Oliver arrived home, and the group was beginning to draw to a close. George was summing up. Barry and Stephanie had taken a short walk around the block, then retired upstairs to the bedroom, where she had helped Barry clear up the decorating things and rearrange the furniture. The smell of the paint was not too bad now, but she had agreed it would be better for her to sleep tonight on the sofa in the living room after the Tuesday group had dispersed. They went downstairs when they heard Oliver at the door.

'Wow! You look great!' Stephanie said, at the sight of Oliver in his new outfit.

'Hardly recognise you,' added Barry. 'You bring to mind a successful Maltese pimp.' It was obvious that Oliver had changed more than just sartorially. For a start, he was drunk. Not hog-whimperingly, nor stumbling, but careless, physically loosened. His eyes were glittering with an unusual playfulness, and it was evident from his surprise at seeing them that he had completely forgotten about the men from the Tuesday group. He did not seem to care what day it was.

After greeting them diffidently, he gave no excuses for his absence, saying instead: 'Oh, why don't you all just FUCK OFF and take your mealy-mouthed puritan

BILGEWATER somewhere else in future?' Barry and Stephanie retreated to the kitchen, giggling.

George looked at his watch. 'Well, it's not yet ten, Oliver. We still have a quarter of an hour to go, so . . .'

'No. Like NOW.' Oliver was insistent. He stood in the doorway waiting for them to leave. He waited through embarrassed coughs and much shuffling in seats.

'Oliver, are you all right?' asked Michael.

'I'm fine. Please. I'm asking you nicely. And can you ring Keith and tell him not to bother in future either.'

The rest of the group looked to George, who, exhaling slowly, rose to his feet. The others followed suit. As he passed Oliver, George gave him a puzzled look, a request for an explanation.

'Yeah, sorry, George. I just want you all to fuck off. I don't have to give a reason. You can work one out for yourselves at someone else's house. Should keep you busy for a year at least.'

They left. Claude offered his hand to Oliver by the front door. Oliver shook it limply, saying, 'It's nothing personal,' and closed the door. When they were gone, he turned and punched the air, giving a high-pitched whoop like an American in a game-show audience. He yanked off his pale mackintosh and chucked it on the floor, laughing.

'Barry, I did it!' he shouted triumphantly through to the kitchen. 'I've used the money from Andrea's things to pay your debts. Don't thank me, it was a pleasure.'

He came bounding through to where Stephanie and Barry were. 'You can have your flat back by the weekend. I'll help you move, if you like.'

The thought of being alone in his jolly old flat in Phoenix Mansions suddenly filled Barry with a cold fear. Instantly, he could picture what it would mean to return to his old life, but this time without even a newspaper column to be imprisoned by, just the tedious continuum of days. To have to put back on the chilly armour of sarcasm. Daily to slake the thirst of his loveless cynicism. The recycling of infinite bottles of Spanish red, Bordeaux, claret, distilled malt from Scotland. The taste of French tar and mucus on the back of his tongue. A year or two of loneliness followed by a downward spiral into bodily malfunction and death. The isolation and the alienation from kindness and shared endeavour. In that moment he saw how far he had come, and that he was a stranger now to his former self, and he became afraid. He looked to Stephanie.

'Listen, sorry about the bedroom,' she said to Oliver. 'We can easily paint it back to normal tomorrow if you want. We just had an impulse, you know, a crazy impulse.'

But Oliver was not listening. He swung open the fridge door and looked inside. Nothing in there took his fancy. He slammed it shut again with a flourish.

'Did any of those wimps bring anything to drink?' he said. 'I could murder a glass of champagne.'

THIRTEEN

In the quiet of the morning, Barry heard the letter flap clatter and got up, carrying his bowl of cereal, to amble to the front door and collect the mail. He chewed slowly as he went, and the bare floorboards creaked gently under his weight. It was an Indian summer, and dappled light entered the hall from the glass above the front door. Barry was wearing his khaki shorts, flip-flops and a shapeless baggy turquoise T-shirt whose neck-line hung down nearly to his chest. His hairy wrists were adorned with a woven leather friendship bracelet. He wore no watch. His hair had, by now, grown well past shoulder length, and he had a snowy-white beard which reached from just under his eyes to below his Adam's apple. Little drops of milk and cornflakes straggled in his moustache. He wiped his mouth with the back of his hand as he bent to pick up the one letter which lay there on the mat. Strolling back into the kitchen area, he sat back down on the now rickety Conran stool to examine the post. It contained a printed invitation card to the opening of an exhibition of the latest work of Tara Findlay-Scott, showing in the Frith Street gallery in Soho. It had the names of three sponsors along the bottom, and, in the small print, words to the effect that Tara Findlay-Scott was exclusively represented by Nicholas Vadim. As Barry rose to put his cereal spoon and bowl in the kitchen sink, he considered for a moment whether this invitation was anything which might interest him now. Whether he felt any particular loyalty to Tara or even a desire to see her again. He tossed the invitation nonchalantly in the swing-bin, and left the room to start his day.

The somewhat less auspicious exhibition which Oliver had given Tara permission to put on at Andrea's Gaia gallery eighteen months previously had, in commercial terms, been a bit of a wash-out. She had called it 'Porn Sucks' and the opening had been attended by six people in all, three of them being her stand-up comedian boyfriend, his brother and his brother's girlfriend. However, she hadn't seemed disappointed by the poor turn-out, but, rather, challenged by it. This was probably because she had managed to glean something genuinely worthwhile from it, that is, a flat with shared studio among the artists' community in Whitechapel, East London, where there are more artists per square foot than in any other area in the whole of Europe. This new accommodation came with a new boyfriend – also an artist – who had been one of the other three people to make it to Old Street to see her work. Her stand-up comedian was now an ex, and she had given up her job selling flowers on Fulham Road, and moved east.

Her powers of persuasion were such that, at the end of her three-day sojourn in the Gaia, Oliver and Barry had been the ones to help her pack away the exhibits into large cardboard boxes, which then awaited the arrival of another ex-boyfriend of Tara's who had a suitably big removal vehicle. Tara had kept the mini-video camera she had been given, and filmed the dismantling of her exhibition from strange angles. Oliver and Barry had looked like a grotesque double act from the days of silent movies as they carried the two-foot penis models to the boxes and wrapped them in old sheets and polystyrene chippings. Tara had made the penises out of painted sailcloth filled with gravel, so not only were they very heavy, but also cumbersome and bendy. The bondage photographs of herself never arrived, possibly because of some disagreement with the stand-up comedian which had presaged their subsequent break-up. But the enormous labia sculpture made of used pink bath towels had been the high point of the show, and it was a shame to de-rig it, Barry thought. He played Oliver Hardy to Oliver's Stan Laurel as they pulled apart the underwired assemblage. Tara videoed them throughout, much to Oliver's annoyance and Barry's amusement, the most embarrassing sequence to be recorded being the one where they couldn't find the candlewick clitoris.

When all was packed, labelled and waiting to be removed, they went for a cup of tea at the local works café and Tara had played them back highlights of the day's filming on the little side-viewing panel of the camera. Barry had detected a different man looking out at him from within his now saggier body. He must have lost two stone since Christmas, and his skin hung off him like a linen jacket on a coat hanger. It was then that he had decided to grow the beard. His craggier, wiser face could, he felt, sustain one, and it would save the bother of shaving.

Tara had found her new life in the East End inspirational, and the proximity of so many committed and like-minded people had generated in her, over the next few months, a spurt of creativity unlike anything she had known before. Her new lover, too, had more staying power than previous partners. He had been at the Royal College of Art, and his work was welding-based: big sculptures of tortured metal which sold well to corporations in the north. She spent February, March and April editing and re-editing all the video footage she had, until she was satisfied with the result, which was a twenty-minute film featuring Barry and Oliver. She had cut it brilliantly, from the first expression of discomfort on Oliver's face at Rylance Avenue to the last shots of them in the café on Old Street. The image of them carrying the giant sagging penises backwards and forwards was repeated and repeated from different angles, and the final cut, as well as being very funny, could truly be described as art with a capital A. The panel of judges for the Turner Prize had thought so, anyway, when it came round a year later, and Tara had received a nomination. The likelihood of her winning, or even getting on to the shortlist of six, was, she knew, very small, since she did not have the substantial body of work behind her that most of the nominees did. All the same, her dance card had been marked and she was on her way. Out of respect for Barry, she had called her piece 'The Misandrists − or the Man-Haters', and this title had contributed a little to the perception that she was now a serious artist. It was time to celebrate.

But Barry couldn't have cared less now. His acquaintance with Tara had become, like his alcoholism, a subdued chimera. He yawned and stretched in the gorgeous sunlight which was finding its way into the hall. Some of it was tinged with orange, some of it was blue from passing through the small panels of Edwardian coloured glass around the side of the front door. Outside, a blackbird was competing with a chaffinch or thrush to be the most ebullient bird on the block. It was time for Barry's walk. He checked in his shoulder bag for money and keys, and unfolded the buggy, which was stacked under the coat hooks. He started up the stairs, calling ahead of him, 'I'm going now, is she ready?' He found them in the bathroom, and scooped little Andrea off the floor, lifting her high above his head, from where she giggled down at him. He gave her a good-morning kiss, pursing his lips so his beard would not be too scratchy on her lovely fresh skin. Stephanie handed him a spare nappy and the Sudocrem in a plastic bag – 'Can you get a loaf, we ran out – and some of those chocolate croissants? – *Hasta luego*.'

On the front steps he made a mental note to cut off the dry brown fronds from the bottom of the cordyline trees when he got back. They had grown at least another six inches taller. Today he would take little Andrea to Battersea Park, which meant a short bus ride, but he had a friend in the tea shop by the lake there who let him have all sorts of odds and ends useful for his work. He had remembered to pack a couple of Tesco bags to carry home these pickings. One or two of the trees on Rylance Avenue were already yellowing, but most were still getting the last drops of moisture out of the summer, which had seen another wet August. The magnificent little Andrea loved the ducks on the lake at Battersea and would soon be mobile enough to wander off close to the water's edge. It would soon be her birthday; a little Virgo, just like her grandad – not that Barry believed in any of that stuff.

A light breeze picked up as they alighted from the bus and entered the park, making a gentle sough in the sycamore trees. Barry did up Andrea's coat as he strapped her into the buggy. Little glassy plates of tears appeared in his eyes – this happened quite often nowadays. It was just emotion, unidentifiable as happy or sad. Just a feeling. As if a long-closed psycho-physical connection in him had tentatively reopened. The traffic of thoughts and senses now flowed through a previously blocked meridian without the aid of acupuncture needles or powerful herbs. He didn't fight it, but let it pass.

He pushed the buggy along the path on the opposite side of the river from the tall houses of Chelsea embankment and took little Andrea out and held her up to show her the boats. The *Kingwood*, *Merrie Thames*, and the giant, flat orange and green *Driftwater Two*. Barry hadn't ventured north of the Thames to the Chelsea side in over thirteen months. What would be the point?

There was a new Norman Foster building shooting up fast by Albert Bridge on the south side (what would Stephanie think of that?), and the marquees for the dance festival were in place. Would Stephanie like to go? He must remember to ask her when he got back. Felix was now in San Francisco and doing well enough in his high-powered job with FoetalWeb to send the occasional maintenance cheque. He had only seen little Andrea twice before crossing the water. The seamless conversation between Barry and Stephanie had been sustained through eighteen months, and continued for Barry even when they were apart, which was only ever for hours at a time. He considered himself a lucky man. Happy not to sleep with her until his next incarnation, if that was the way it turned out – not that he believed in any of that stuff. There was tangible warmth in her eyes, and if you're very lucky, my dear little Andrea, you may turn out to be a bit like your mother in that way.

After collecting some bottle tops and ring pulls, and an interesting pile of broken coloured glass from Melanie at the tea rooms, he picked up the sliced loaf and some semi-stale croissants from the corner shop and took the bus back. Time for Andrea's nap. She had done complaining and her eyelids were beginning to droop.

The invitation card to Tara's classy exhibition had also dropped through the letter box and on to the mat at Phoenix Mansions, Tite Street, that morning, but as usual, Oliver was already out before the first post arrived. He had some clients to take on an early-morning run, and then time for a light work-out and steam in the Fitness First gym of the Conrad Hotel in Chelsea Harbour. This way he was feeling good and ready for the day before most people had downed their first coffee. After that he would usually take a couple of patients in the hotel's health and therapy salon, which left the afternoons free for visits to his personal clients, who might require anything from nutritional programmes to their own customised training regimes. It was a good idea to have regulars because results were so much more visible like that and this made the work more fulfilling. Of course, some were no-hopers − overweight aristocratic Chelsea dames with time on their hands, ageing businessmen with serious spinal deterioration − but occasionally there would be one who really made the effort, which made Oliver's job worthwhile. And, increasingly, there were the famous – movie actors, record producers, top newspaper people. He was the custodian, now, of the secrets of the stars, and prided himself on his reputation for discretion. Then there were the perks . . .

It was eighteen months since the day he had so unceremoniously terminated his involvement with the Tuesday group, sold off Andrea's effects, and paid Barry's debt. Two days later, he had received a phone call from Sophie inviting him to a soirée to be held at her friend Samantha Littlejohn's sumptuous penthouse flat off Sloane Avenue. Samantha was a society hostess, and had appeared three times already in *Hello!* magazine. Not being a keen reader of the gossip pages, Oliver was unaware of her pedigree, but he had made a swift and accurate appraisal of the kind of milieu into which he was being launched within minutes of arriving at her apartment. The door was answered by a uniformed maid, and he was shown into a room stuffed with genuinely valuable objets d'art. Immediately there was Dom Perignon, even though, as the first to arrive, he found himself alone in the antechamber for the first twenty-five minutes. The champagne continued throughout the evening and, he noticed, did not decrease in quality or quantity after the first two hours.

Of the ten or so guests that night, Oliver was one of only three men. A very camp interior designer in a spangled waistcoat seemed to be there purely for his entertainment value. The other was introduced to Oliver as Samantha Littlejohn's 'darling GP', and was a clean-shirted man of about thirty with an upper-class drawl so severe it made his conversation almost incomprehensible. Neither was any serious competition, and Oliver could not help but reach the conclusion that he was being advertised to the assembled ladies. Sophie introduced him to every woman there, commending his sensitive fingers, his good looks and his charm. He found that by smiling a lot and saying very little, his so recently acquired charm appeared to have hidden qualities which the ladies felt intrigued to unravel. The few times he did speak it was to say something flattering. It wasn't difficult to get the hang of this game.

Most of the women were in their thirties or forties, and nearly all of them were married. 'This is Mrs Natasha Codmorton-Hendon. Her husband is in property,' Sophie said. 'And he's working on a very important project in Glasgow at the moment, so he's away a lot of the time, which is sad for you, isn't it, Natasha? But it leaves her bags of time to do her charity work. She's organising a fun-run for Help a Child at the moment, which might be interesting to you, Oliver. Oliver here is a marathon runner, he's super-fit, aren't you, Oliver?' She then left him alone with the woman to chat for a few minutes before flying back in with another one. 'I know I'm being awful, Natasha, but I'm going to steal him away now, because Emily Grocklewaite will throw a tantrum unless she gets a turn.'

After some hours of this, in which Oliver had no idea how much champagne he had drunk, since the maid kept creeping up and refilling his glass, the younger and sillier of the assembled ladies decided that they would go to a club in the West End, and asked Oliver to join them. He hesitated for a moment and looked over at Sophie. He was glad he had done so because, it seemed, it would have been a poor show for him to leave without the permission of his inviter. 'Aren't you going to take me home?' she said, suggestively. 'And come in for some coffee?'

In the cab, he realised, her flirtatiousness had been merely for the purposes of asserting her superiority over the other women. Making sure they understood that Sophie had a sort of 'first refusal'. As they were driven down Sloane Street and then the King's Road, he felt certain that, although she remained familiar with him, even resting her head on his shoulder at one point and touching him several times on the arm, the coffee and indeed the invitation to come up to her flat would not materialise this time. He didn't mind. Once they were on the Lots Road, approaching Chelsea Harbour, her tone changed and she started to giggle. 'Well, Amanda's gagging for it, but her husband's a bit arsy and might get jealous. Emily and Natasha will just want whatever the other one's got, so it's up to you. Forget Yasmine and Serena. Too silly, too girly and not enough cash. Lenora is loaded, but far too ugly, poor thing, and that leaves darling Fiona. Just the right balance between cash and sexiness. I'd definitely go for Fiona, if I were you. And I happen to know she has terrible problems with her left shoulder from a riding accident, so that's a good start, isn't it?' She offered both her cheeks to him without waiting for a kiss, slid out of the taxi and waggled her fingers at him as a goodbye. It was four hours before he could get to sleep that night.

The idea that he, and not Barry, should be the one to take on the flat at Phoenix Mansions had followed shortly after this heady evening. A bachelor must have some time living alone, Sophie had said, it makes him more attractive. As for the rent, Oliver had not given any actual cash to Sophie since the initial rain-soaked envelope, eighteen months ago. There was always a favour he could do her, as indeed there were many she did for him. His job at the gym came about through her introduction, and it tickled her to have her own pet osteopath, nutritionist and 'holistic masseur'. If Samantha Littlejohn could have her personal GP in tow, then Sophie would better that.

Unlike Barry, Oliver thought he probably would go to Tara's sprauntzy exhibition at the Frith Street gallery, despite having not enjoyed being the subject of her most famous piece. He wasn't the slightest bit interested in the art, but this was an opportunity for social networking, young women, possible future clients, champagne. He would take Sophie, of course. She would be bound to know someone there already, and Oliver had discovered that having a glamorous woman on his arm meant that other glamorous women gravitated towards him. Whether this was because they felt safer or merely more competitive, he had yet to discover, but the real reason did not bother him unduly. He had quickly realised that he loved the whole scene. The expensive skimpy clothes, the body culture, the well-looked-after hair. He adored being out with Sophie, opening doors for her, shopping in Knightsbridge with her, eating at the oyster bar in Brompton Cross, going back to the Harbour for drinks afterwards. It was a society where he felt he had something to offer, where people had the time and money to take their diet and body maintenance seriously.

And of all the bodies, Sophie's was the best. Over the last year he had come to know every curve and crevice of it; its many strengths and its few weaknesses. She might have been over forty, but she had not a millimetre of excess baggage on her. She was muscular but not rigid, athletic and yet languid. Twice a week he would give her an all-over, deep-tissue therapy massage. He had done a couple of top-up courses and so now he could include reiki and shiatsu, which the clients seemed to want as well. Sophie's spine rarely needed osteopathic treatment and so he was able to use aroma oils as well, although his knowledge of these was less comprehensive.

They never had sex. It gave him a greater sense of control keeping her literally and figuratively at arm's length. It meant there was no yearning, no emotional entanglement. He was free to enjoy her, he need never experience insecurity or jealousy. And while he was sleeping with others, he could close his eyes and imagine it was Sophie, so he was safe from involvement there too. No threat of becoming a slave to his love-object, and no threat of being drawn into unwanted romance with his sex-objects. Perfect. He considered this to be a rounded, well-thought-out existence.

Most men don't realise that foreplay starts not half an hour before intercourse, not even three hours before, when he picks her up in his Mercedes to take her out for the proverbial candlelit dinner, but at nine o'clock the previous morning, when he gets into the office and calls her to say he's missing her already and can't wait to see her tomorrow night. Or three weeks before, when he chats her up at the first meeting and tells her she's beautiful, but then walks away to talk to other women. That's foreplay. 'And if you organise your diary properly, you could be starting little fires for yourself all over town. And they could all be just ready to burst into flames for you when you happen by,' said Sophie to Oliver the second time they met for a date, which was at the opening of Torso's, an exclusive new club off Berkeley Square. 'And another thing, you must double or triple your fee. It just won't do, darling. The kind of people I know want to feel they're getting the best, or at least paying for it.'

Talking with Sophie was so easy. She had the ability to be both flippant and profound at the same time. She seemed to understand what was going on inside him. What were his desires, what were his fears. And she never stopped laughing. At him, mostly, but he felt he deserved that. He recognised that it was important to have a sense of humour, and so, instinctively, he clung to Sophie's. 'The reason men are so afraid of commitment these days is that there's nothing in a modern relationship for them,' she said on one occasion. 'None of their needs get seen to, none of their rights are recognised, and they're just a laughing stock in the magazines and on telly. Poor things. Why shouldn't you sit on the toilet for three hours drooling over the 1978 owner's manual of the Ford Capri, if that's what you want to do?'

After a few months of banter with Sophie and, occasionally, casual sex with women whom he did not particularly respect or care for, Oliver had found that the secret cupboard in his mind where he had kept torrid imaginings of bottoms and thong knickers was bare. And, as the inflammation subsided, he found that he had the time and the capability to think of Andrea every now and then without spinning into a scalding rage. Once he even thought he should be grateful to her for civilising him, for giving him an interesting history when chatting up women, for dying when she did.

In fact, the one thing he should have been grateful to her for was secretly buying the lease on the small gallery space on the Upper East Side of New York. Rebecca from the Gaia had managed to sell this on most profitably, and with the proceeds they had paid Andrea's entire tax liability. 'Death tax' as Barry called it. There had even been some left over to pay the four months' salary Rebecca was owed. Rylance Avenue was safe from the clutches of the Inland Revenue and its occupants were free to make their own decisions about where and how they chose to live.

On the north side of the river, the plane trees were sporting yellows, reds and sienna browns. The sound of the hooter from a tug pulling freight barges under Albert Bridge echoed off the high buildings on Cheyne Walk. The sunlight caught on some of the windows, making them burn momentarily like a row of beacons before returning to their reflective black. Oliver turned the corner of Chelsea Bridge Road at the Lister private hospital, where he knew the consultant obstetrician. It was such a pleasant day, he had decided to walk to Sophie's along the river. He had time. He passed the Chelsea Physic Garden at Swan Walk, where the medicinal plants have been grown for centuries. On the opposite side of the Thames, beyond Cadogan Pier, the gold-painted Peace Pagoda of Battersea Park glowed in the rays of the sun, and the bright marquees for the dance festival were up. He was carrying a small bottle of ylang-ylang oil, and had his Armani jacket slung over his shoulder. He would be out late tonight.

Barry, on the other hand, now south of the river was very aware of the debt he owed to Andrea. He had turned his gratitude into a sacrament. For example, there had been no question over what to call his beautiful granddaughter. And then there was his work, of course, which was virtually a hymn to her. 'Ola. Que tal?' 'Muy bien mia guapa.' He and Stephanie had been learning Spanish since the visit, in April, of Stephanie's father and his new family, who had come to see the baby and stayed for a week. Barry and Stephanie planned to go there for Christmas, or maybe next summer. When little Andrea was old enough. Barry hoped to visit the Mesquita in Cordoba where Rennaissance, Gothic, Islamic and Baroque architecture topple over each other, struggling for ascendancy in the same building. He found the idea of this an inspiring symbol of the eclecticism of his new-found family. In such a human menagerie, he thought, even he had a place. *El viejo. El abuelo loco.* Mad old grandad.

It was a Tuesday, so Stephanie was taking little Andrea to the one o'clock club after her morning nap. Having put the baby down, Barry made his customary flask of sweet tea and, gathering up his new materials in their Tesco bags, made the short walk across the hall to work. The little shards of coloured glass made an exciting high-pitched tinkling noise as the bag swung in his left hand. Once inside what had been Oliver's surgery – and before that his own sitting room – Barry closed the door. Not so much to exclude Stephanie and little Andrea, more to close himself in. To create an alternative world of solitude where he could commune with the busy and rushing spirits who roamed restlessly through his imagination, urging him on, issuing instructions which he felt impelled to obey.

He poured the coloured glass and bottle tops into the appropriate piles on the floor. There were other piles there too: of seashells, pebbles, chipped tiles from the back yard, window lead, light bulbs, fridge and oven parts. He sifted through the pile of coloured glass like a gold prospector, occasionally picking one piece up and turning it, then putting it back with its brothers and sisters. When he was satisfied that he had thoroughly made the acquaintance of his new pieces, he poured himself the first cup of tea from the flask and began to mix his cement glue. He had found by trial and error that adding a can of Unibond universal adhesive to an ordinary plaster filler made a malleable yet permanent fixative, which was white, yet not so rubber-based that it would not take any kind of paint.

At this point his breathing would change in anticipation of the day. It became more impassioned and yet at the same time steadier, like a scuba diver achieving neutral buoyancy. He took longer, deeper breaths to clear his mind of conscious thought. One by one, he began sticking the carton tops and ring pulls into their position over the architrave, alternating them with some dark-blue slivers of glass. Although he had his old radio, Barry preferred to work in silence. As each new shape was added, he stepped back, slowly and calmly, to view its significance in the wider mosaic, unfocusing his eyes for a few seconds until an inner, deeper focus seemed possible. The meandering waves of colour which were emerging made the small of his back sweat. He was transfixed by a kind of excitement never experienced in his former life. There was a low, calm pulse in his stomach which was both passionate and relaxed. His blood seemed to course through his veins with the bass vibrato of a cello. His sense of time was altered, its demarcation points being curves and dots and light and shade, and the slow growth of the smoke-like stripes which were erupting across the wall, cornice and skirting. He had never had such a strong feeling without words.

Outsider Art has gone by many names over the last hundred years, in which the critics of the art establishment have tried to claim and hence market this essentially antisocial activity. Naive Art, Psychiatric Art, Art Brut. Its practitioners have been, typically, people in the latter part of their lives, often with some clinical history of psychological disturbance, who have, apparently from nowhere, and with no training, felt compelled to create pictures, sculptures, fantasy grottos, buildings even. The materials they use might range from the coloured pencils of Aloise Corbaz, a psychiatric patient in Switzerland at the turn of the century, to the rocks, stones and cement of Facteur Cheval, a French postman who built a cathedral city in Tersanne in the 1920s based on the images in his recurrent dreams. It is a visionary experience rather than an art form, and although some pieces are now sold around the world for high prices, generally the artists are not producing work to be exhibited, or even seen. They are individuals involved in their own quixotic derangements. Possibly its most well-known exponent is Nek Chandh, an Indian transport official who spent fourteen years from 1958 clearing the twenty-five acres of jungle where he made thousands of rock sculptures out of everyday materials. The fact that he had no official permission to use this space, and that until 1976 it was under threat from the planning department, is testimony to his lack of ambition or even concern about what the real world would make of his endeavour.

Unlike Tara's work, which, along with most proper art, was premeditated, conceived to produce an effect, what Barry was doing at Rylance Avenue was purely personal. There would be no point in an Outsider artist having his or her assistant take over the execution of the actual work, as, say, Damien Hirst has sometimes done, because there is no concept behind it to be realised. The amorphic spirit is found in the making of the work. There could be no pupils of an Outsider artist, to study the style of the master and then reproduce or propagate it, no 'school of', no forgery. Barry had found that when the alcohol had drained from his system, vivid and kinetic dreams had started to come. Wyverns and windigos, harpies and hippocampi began to possess him during his waking hours as well as at night. If ever he faltered, he had only to listen to their voices to tell him what needed doing next, which colour to favour, what shape to emphasise. It was immaterial to him whether what he was doing was good or even pleasant to the eye. The difference between failure and creating coherent images was irrelevant.

There might no longer have been words jostling around in Barry's brain, but there were plenty incorporated into the fantastical pictures on the walls of the front room. They were written in scrawls and on labels and made from old hosepipes and scrunched curtain material, or sometimes just scribbled in magic marker. Above the central bay window were the words 'The curses of contentment' made from kitchen utensils stuck on to the sash frames. And in a curly script right across the main wall, he had painted, '*La historia de mi corazon*' – the story of my heart. All around these words were garish red and blue depictions of human organs connected by an intricate network of veins made from red-wine-bottle corks. In every gap was a distorted face – some in agony, some serene – as if their creator was seeing them through a convex mirror. Where Oliver's black steel wall lights had been, Barry had attached various components from fridges and ovens and a metal chimney flue which he had found on a local skip. He had not disconnected the wiring in the room, and when the wall switch was turned on, this area lit up, illuminating the words 'Felix = *felicidad* = happiness'. Across the ceiling were many moons and many men and women in the moons performing obscene acts among shooting stars made of sugar cubes.

There had been no plan to this fragmentary universe, it followed no preconceived theme, but had arrived sequentially, as if Barry had tapped into a spirit world which was cautious about revealing its full power to him all at once. He had just started at the top right-hand corner and worked out and down from there. Despite this absence of unity in composition, the effect of the whole was exhilarating, like experiencing the beginning and the end of a roller-coaster journey in the same instant.

On the back wall, facing the window, was the largest single image of all. An enormous woman with fire spurting from every orifice straddled a giant pepper grinder. Her mad eyes were made from distressed motor-scooter tyres and her hair from torn strips of foam-backed carpet. From out of her mouth came her massive, winding tongue on which was written in ordinary biro, '*La vista desde aqui es magnifica*' – lesson four in the Spanish phrasebook they were using: 'The view from here is magnificent.'